wild ADDICTION

A *wild* NOVEL: BOOK TWO

wild ADDICTION

A *wild* NOVEL: BOOK TWO

EMMA HART

WILD ADDICTION
Book Two of the Wild series

Editing:
Mickey Reed
www.mickeyreedediting.com

Formatting:
E.M. Tippetts Book Design

Photography Copyright:
Andreas Gradin
www.shutterstock.com

For Holly, because you loved him first.

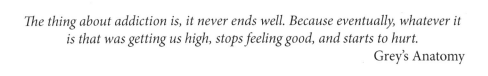

The thing about addiction is, it never ends well. Because eventually, whatever it is that was getting us high, stops feeling good, and starts to hurt.

Grey's Anatomy

Prologue

I NEVER knew true addiction until her. I never truly understood what it is to crave—mind, body, and soul—until nothing matters but fulfilling that craving. Until the only thing that matters is easing the hollow ache inside.

It's there whenever we're apart. Like a dark hole, it lingers, intensifying until my mind is full of blonde hair and blue-green eyes. Until my mind is full of easy curves, bare before me. Until my desires reflect her bending at the waist, her pert, little arse in the air, colored red by my palm, the outline of my fingers visible against her pale skin.

Every day, it's something new, something different, something I never allowed myself to think of. It's more than against the wall, more than her hands bound, more than a blindfold across her eyes. Now, I can think freely, imagine all the ways and all the places I can have her.

Because she trusts me.

And she's fucking mine.

My Liv. My bitch. My beautiful, flighty bitch.

Now, she's sitting in front of me with her eyes wide and her hands covering her mouth. She's deathly still. And quiet. So fucking quiet that every second that passes cuts deeper than anything she could ever say would.

But she hasn't moved away from me either. She's still sitting in my arms, her legs hooked over mine, staring at me like it's the last thing she ever expected me to say.

I run my eyes across her face, taking advantage of her silence to look at her. Her hair is messy, her blue-green eyes shining, her cheeks flushed. She looks freshly fucked, and she is, but more than that, she looks shocked.

"Liv?" I prompt. "Are you going to say anything?"

She drops her hands and slowly licks her lips. My gaze instantly drops to her mouth.

"I, um… I don't know what to say to that," she says slowly.

"Well, the last time I had to tell someone I fucked a student, I nearly got punched." It's one of the only times I've ever seen Aaron lose his shit.

She knocks her fist into my chest lamely. "There. Does that make you feel better?"

I stare at her. Why the hell isn't she running? Why isn't she looking at me with disgust? Why the fuck is she still *here*?

"Er, thanks?" I frown.

She sighs softly. "I think I know what you're expecting, but you're not going to get it. I'm not going to get up and demand you leave, okay?"

"You should."

"Yeah, you're probably right. But I shouldn't have slept with you a second time. Or agreed to do it on a regular basis. *Or* gone on a date with you. So I'm a fucking expert at doing things I'm not supposed to." She shrugs. "It's in the past, right? Just like you didn't push me away when I told you mine, I'm not going to do it to you."

"I still don't understand."

"You're really dumb sometimes." She taps me on the nose, her pink lips curving into a small smile. She cups the side of my head and runs her thumb across my cheek. "We said we'd try and work past all our bullshit. That's part of it. We have to accept each other's pasts and move forward. You can't change mine and I can't change yours, so there's not much point in getting all panty-twisted about it, is there?"

I cover her hand with mine and wrap my other around her neck. I pull her into me, so close that our lips touch, and hum low. I love the way she tastes. I can't put my finger on it, but it's incredible.

"You're right, baby girl," I murmur against her mouth.

"Of course I am." She rests her other hand at my waist. "I'm a woman. Sooner or later, you'll learn that I'm right even when I'm wrong."

I already know that. She was wrong to go along with anything more than just one night with me, yet nothing has ever felt more right.

Chapter ONE

"Do you think I should have asked him to leave?"

I rest my head against the back of the sofa and look across my apartment at my best friend. She pulls the wine bottle from the fridge and pauses, her fingers wrapped tightly around the neck of the bottle.

"You could have asked him why."

Yeah, probably. "I don't know, Day. I was shocked, y'know? I wasn't expecting him to say that. And now, I'm wondering if letting him stay was the right choice."

"Well, it's tough. You had just agreed to make it work no matter what, but what he did was kind of wrong."

I know that. I know, in my rational mind, that Tyler shouldn't have fucked a student. It should bother me. It's taboo. Frowned upon. Damn, it's more than frowned upon. It's fucking illegal.

I should have gotten up, asked him to go, then thought it through.

If only I were even a fraction rational around Tyler, the 'should haves' would have been 'did haves.'

"Very wrong," I correct her, taking a glass of wine with a sigh. "I don't know. It's kind of fucked up, isn't it? I mean, it's something out of a damn novel. He mocks my so-called porn on a page, but he's a living fucking book boyfriend."

Day's lips twitch. "I've never been that kind of 'forbidden romance' kind of girl. I guess it's because your dad is a teacher. Every time I tried one, I pictured him with his stripy ties as the main character."

Well, that's a visual I wasn't prepared for. Much less needed.

"Thank you for that." I sit up straight and take a long drink from my glass. "Moving on from that strange twist…"

"Yes, let's." She wrinkles her face up. "So did he just, like, come out with it? Or was there a preemptive warning?"

"There was a half-assed story but no warning. He just kind of…said it. Like, bam. Surprise!" I rest the glass against my chin. "I wasn't expecting it. Tyler is the oddest mixture of bad guy and good guy, but I never thought he'd have done that."

Day purses her lips, looking into her glass. "I don't know if you should be bothered or not. Is that bad?"

No. Because I don't think I am. I'm more pissed about the fact that I'm *not* bothered. Or that my ever-growing addiction to him makes it that way. Somehow, it takes the wrongness and reality of what he's done and twists it into something that isn't that bad at all.

That's what really bothers me. That I can disregard something so critical. Something that's made him who he is today.

But isn't that exactly what he did with me? Didn't he gloss over my teenage stupidity like it didn't impact me at all?

Yes.

Oh, sigh.

Acceptance of the past is the key to facing the future. As long as I remember that, I'll be okay. I think.

I hope.

I really, really fucking hope.

"It's not bad," I answer finally, slowly, tentatively drawing each word out. "I guess, in a fucked-up way, it's kind of similar to Aaron keeping Naomi from you. You really shouldn't have forgiven him, but you did. I really shouldn't accept Tyler's past this easily, but I have."

Dayton's lips tug up at the sides. "You know who forgives easily, don't you?"

"A person in love," I say in a cocky voice. "And again, there is a fundamental flaw in your plan, best friend."

"Yeah, you're not in love. I gotcha, Ms. In Denial."

I roll my eyes. I'm not even going to argue with her. She'll continue to tell me that I'm in denial and I'll deny being in denial. It'll be like the string cheese conversation all over again. Pointless bullshit.

"Whatever." I set my empty glass on the table next to hers and refill them. "When I fall in love, I'll be sure to send out a public service announcement so no one misses it."

"You better." She grins and her eyes sparkle. "When does Tyler come back?"

"Tomorrow sometime." Somberness overshadows my amusement. We'd barely sealed our relationship with a kiss before he was offered a shoot in Boise. He drove out first thing this morning and that's that.

I'm sitting here with an ache in my chest, waiting, just waiting, so we can actually finish our conversation. And I can maybe ask him why he slept with a student.

"And you're already missing him," Day states matter-of-factly.

"That wasn't a question. I'm not obliged to respond."

"*Are* you missing him?"

Shit. Asshole. "No."

"Fucking liar."

"Fine! Yes. I am. A little." I lean my head back against the back of the sofa. "Okay, a lot. I'm missing him a lot."

I rub my hand down my face as we both take in my admission.

"Like, shit. This isn't normal. I should not be feeling like I have to pick up the phone and call him just to hear the sound of his voice and make this fucking irritating ache inside go away. I shouldn't be feeling like I need to get in my own damn car and drive out to Boise to see him." I squeeze my eyes shut. Voicing it just makes it worse. I take a deep breath in and exhale slowly.

"Wow. You really do have it bad, don't you?"

"Excuse me, Mr. Conan Doyle? Your Sherlocks are multiplying at a sickening rate. They even come with tits and a vagina now," I mutter, opening my eyes again.

Dayton laughs loudly, digging her toes into my shin. "Shut up, Liv. Look, you're addicted to him, and you know it. It's different now because you can manage it. Just breathe and try to think about what you're feeling."

My eyes flick to hers and I hit her with a harsh glare. "I'm sorry, Dr. Black. I wasn't aware you were a fucking therapist."

She smacks a cushion over my head. "For real, shut your face." She drinks the rest of her wine and stands up. "Are you going to be okay if I leave you here?"

"Jesus Christ, I'm missing my boyfriend, not contemplating how hard my body would hit the ground if I jumped out of my window."

"Don't even joke about it." She points a finger in my direction. "Don't."

Guilt twists my stomach. "Sorry. It's bad, but if I joke about it, I can cope with it."

"You ever feel like that, then you call me so I can drag you down these flights of stairs by your hair." She slides her feet into her shoes and grabs her purse. "Oh, by the way, did you book the bachelorette party yet?"

I fight to stop my eyes from widening. "Yes," I lie. "Almost."

Dayton rolls her eyes and opens my door. "Book it, Liv. I get married in two months."

"Excuse me, Ms. Family Woman."

"Do you want me to Bridezilla your ass?"

"Honey, no one wants you to Bridezilla anything, but that doesn't seem to stop you."

She flips me the bird then follows it by blowing a kiss. "Goodbye. Love you.

Be good."

She shuts the door behind her before I can remind her that "be good" isn't a phrase I understand. Unless it involves Tyler and his sexy demands—which are decidedly not classed as "good." In fact, when I'm doing what he tells me to, I'm being both good and bad, which is quite the contradicting conundrum.

Shit. If I'm using big words, I've had far too much wine.

I glance at the bottle and decide that the remaining glass sitting in it won't hurt me. I top my glass up to the rim and overfill it. Leaning forward, I slurp up a mouthful without moving the glass.

Classy chick, I am not.

I open the laptop and type in "bachelorette party venues." Let it be noted that there's no location on the end of the search. Aaron explicitly stated that I have no monetary budget for this. My only budget is her absolute happiness. This seems to be a goal we both share.

After sifting through several sites, which aren't appealing in the slightest, I decide to tweak my search. I type in "West Coast spas" and hit enter. Dozens of websites come up, some classy, some casual, so I add "expensive" into the search bar.

Jesus. This is hard work already. Or maybe that's the wine.

I filter through the search, clicking on endless websites before finally coming up with a short list. The clock blinks at me from the bottom corner of my screen, and despite it only being nine thirty, I can feel my eyelids growing heavy.

Yep, that's definitely the wine.

I add all the 'maybe' venues into a folder on my bookmarks and shut the laptop down. Angus pads across the floor to me and stares at me woefully.

"I know, buddy. I know. The wine bottle is empty."

His look turns annoyed. As annoyed as a cat can be, at least. In fact, I don't think his expression has changed at all.

Maybe my cat just has perpetual resting bitch face.

With a sigh, I get up and put a couple handfuls of cat biscuits in his bowl. "I need to go to the store tomorrow, Lord Fussy-Ass!" I snap, dropping the box on the counter. *Damn cat.*

He sticks his tail in the air. *Fuck you too, cat.*

I lock the front door to the sound of my cell chirping on the table. I grab it. "Message? There is no—oh, shit!" I bring it to my ear. "Hello?"

A deep, rich laugh rumbles down the phone. "Hi to you, too."

Warmth spreads through me at those four tiny words, simple but strong, and I smile. "Hi."

"How much wine did you drink?"

"Not nearly as much as you think but more than we should have." I pad through to my bedroom. "You okay?"

"Better now I'm talking to my bitch," Tyler says, laughing quietly.

"I'm fine. Thanks for asking." I climb beneath my covers and snuggle down.

"Oh, I'm sorry, baby girl. How are you?"

"Cold."

"Why are you cold?"

"I might have forgotten to pay my electric bill. I have to do it tomorrow."

He laughs. "Dammit, Liv. How do you forget that stuff?"

"I just… I forgot. It's like you forgetting to pick your socks off the floor. Or put the toilet seat down."

"That's because I'm a male, not because I'm flighty. Leaving the toilet seat up is a territorial thing."

"Oh, yes. I'll make a note to ignore your territorial stake in my bathroom next time I fall down the fucking toilet."

"You do that." So much laughter is in his voice. *Bastard.*

I roll my eyes even though he can't see me. "What are you doing?"

"I'm thinking this conversation would be much more fun if I were there to shut you up."

"I'm thinking I agree. Depending on your method of shutting me up, of course."

"I can't tell you in advance. It's impulsive. You know that."

"No, I'm the impulsive one in this relationship. You're the planner one."

"I like hearing you say that."

I bite the inside of my cheek. "What? That you're a planner?"

"Don't be difficult, you awkward bitch. You know what I mean."

"Oh, yes. The relationship part. The thing that makes me your official bitch. I should get that on a badge. 'Tyler Stone's Bitch.'"

"I can arrange for one to go on your next birthday card if you'd like," he quips.

"You're about five months too late for that, honey." I grin. "Perhaps I should just get a shirt printed."

"You should. And you should wear it all the time."

"Sheesh. Honey, if you get any more territorial, you'll be pissing on my legs."

"If my cock is that close to your legs, it won't be peeing on you. It'll be between them and coming inside you. Just so that's clear." His voice takes on a husky quality that makes me shiver.

Yikes. Okay with me…

"Aren't you supposed to be all romantic now that we're in a relationship?" I ask, holding back my laughter.

"What, do you want me to send flowers and shit?"

"Flowers are nice. Handcuffs are nicer."

"Then I'll send you a bunch of flowers secured by a pair of handcuffs."

"You wouldn't."

"Try me. Goodnight, Liv."

The line goes dead. I stare at the screen dumbly.

Why do I believe he would?

Chapter TWO

I RUB the lingering sleep from my eyes as I park my car outside the bar. The new bar. Aaron's bar.

Kind of my bar.

It's an odd feeling, knowing that, in twelve days, the bar will be ready to open and I'll be the guy—er, gal—in charge. The only thing I've ever really been in charge of before is my freakin' cat, and considering his lack of canned food, he'd argue that I do a pretty crappy job.

I pause in the middle of the sidewalk and set a reminder to go to the store and get Angus some food. And food for me because my cupboards are seriously skinny right now.

Tucking my phone in the pocket of my sweater, I walk into the bar, now named Indulgence. Not much has changed since Aaron brought me here a few days ago. There's still dust everywhere despite the use of dust sheets, and I'm still given a bright yellow hard-hat before I can go more than five steps.

At least there are a million black marble tiles stacked in the corner ready to be laid on the floor.

There are no tables, no curtains, no bar, but there's flooring.

Reassuring.

I wander around for a bit, aimlessly taking in what's going on. I'm getting ready to leave when one of the builders holding a floor plan waves for my attention. I make my way through tools and various construction items toward him.

"Yes?"

"Are you Liv Warren?"

"Yes, that's me."

He visibly relaxes. "Great. Miss, we have a problem with the bar."

No, you don't. "What is it?"

He sets the floor plan out on a stack of wood that will eventually become the stairs and points to the area where it meets the edge of the bar. "Because of the poor construction in the upper level, we have to bring the stairs out by another two feet." He runs his finger down the seating opposite the bar. "This will mean that you can't have seats here and it'll thin your walkway space from the seating area to the dance floor."

I blink at the plans for a moment. "Give me a second." I walk away from him and pull out my phone to dial the number for Aaron's office.

"Hello. Aaron Stone's office?"

"Hi, Dottie. This is Liv. Is Aaron around?"

"He's just about to go to a meeting. Is it urgent?"

"It's pretty important, yeah."

"Just a sec."

I hear a rustle as she moves the phone then a low rumble of voices. Seconds later, Aaron comes on the line.

"What can I do for you, Liv?"

I explain everything the builder just said to me, but he cuts me off halfway through.

"Shit. Okay, look. I can't be late for this meeting. Just do what you think is best, even if it means overriding the plans, all right?"

"Uh"—*shit*—"sure."

The line goes dead. I close my eyes and mutter a few choice words. I did not sign up for this.

"Okay," I breathe, rejoining the builder and running my eyes over the plans. "Can you move the bar?"

"I guess… To here or here."

"Then the dance floor would be here, correct?" I circle the area at the bottom of the stairs.

He nods. "Yes. Take away a foot of floor and the stairs would come out in the seating area in front of the bar, and then you could go either way."

"And it wouldn't impact the access to the storeroom, coatroom, or restrooms?"

"No, ma'am. If you put the bar along this wall, it'll actually be easier access for staff."

"Perfect. Put the bar here"—I point to along the wall—"the main seating area here"—I circle the area in front of it—"and the dance floor here. But make sure there's a space to access the restrooms without having to go through the dance floor. And while we're here, could you put a minibar in upstairs? I believe

Mr. Stone wants it to be VIP and special occasion only, so they'll want their drinks served separately."

"We can fit a corner bar in here." He taps the paper. "It'll be big enough for one member of staff only."

"That's great. Can you start the new plan tomorrow?"

The builder confirms that they can and gets back to work. I breathe out a long sigh and look around.

Maybe I am cut out for this management malarkey after all.

Two hands grasp my hips and pull me backward. I gasp as I slam into a hard body and hot breath flutters over my ear.

"I'm disappointed in your lack of amenities. I was hoping for a Blow Job," Tyler murmurs into my ear, his fingers digging into my hips.

"I'm sorry. We're not serving yet. You'll have to try again when there's, oh, I don't know, a bar, maybe?"

He laughs low and buzzes his lips along my jaw. "Or I'll try again later today. What do you think my chances are?"

"Considerably higher if you start with saying hello."

He spins me effortlessly and clasps his hands at my lower back. I rest my own against his chest and look up at him. The bright-yellow hard hat is lopsided on his head, and his dark eyes are shining with both heat and happiness. His lips twitch twice before tugging into a smirk.

"Hello," he says simply. "You're very sexy when you go all bossy. Are you aware of this?"

"Hello. I am now." I smile as he dips his head and covers my mouth with his.

"No, I mean you're very sexy." He nudges my back with his hands. My hips push into him…and his very obvious erection.

"You've been in here five minutes and you're already ready to go? Are you a teenage boy lying to me about your age?"

"No, luckily for you. They don't have the best stamina."

"Word," I mutter. "You're back early. I wasn't expecting you to call until later."

"Couldn't say away," he replies honestly. "I was up at the fucking ass-crack of dawn to get back here."

"Why, Tyler Stone, did you miss me?"

He brings one hand up and cups my jaw, pulling my face close to his. "Missed what's inside your knickers."

I smack his chest. "Asshole."

He tries to kiss me, but I jerk my face to the side and he ends up grinning against my cheek. "Hey, fiestypants. My cock missed what's inside your knickers. *I* missed you. Just you."

"I should hope so. I'm very missable." I let him kiss me this time.

"I didn't miss your sass though."

I smack him again and step back. "Oh, romance me." I roll my eyes and set my hard hat on some planks of wood by the door.

He does the same and follows me outside. "Oh, I have." He grins and grabs my hand. His Mercedes is parked outside, and he pulls me toward it. He lets go and opens the passenger's side door then grabs something from inside it.

"Oh my fucking god."

I stare at him blankly. The roses and handcuffs thing? Yeah. He really was deadly serious.

He grins like the fucker he is. "There's actually a tie, too. I didn't know if you'd still be in a handcuff mood today."

I bite the inside of my cheek to stop myself from smiling. "You are something else, Tyler Stone."

"Will that get me a blow job?"

I cover my mouth with a hand as an old woman walks past and stares at us wide-eyed. I wait until she turns the corner of the street to look at Tyler. He's shaking with quiet laughter.

"I wasn't aware that I had a choice in the matter," I finally say, still fighting my smile.

His eyes light up and he drops the roses back into the car. "That's right," he mutters, stalking back toward me. "You don't, do you?"

"And here I was thinking you were going soft on me now that we're in this relationship situation."

"I could never go soft on my bitch." He cups the side of my head, his fingers sinking in my hair, and pulls me into him. "In fact, tonight, I plan to go very, very hard on you." He tilts my head back, his mouth by my ear, and adds, "On both your mouth and your pussy. I hope you're ready."

"That depends. Are you buying me dinner first?"

"McDonald's does not count as dinner."

"You said dinner. You didn't say you wanted a restaurant dinner, or a Chinese dinner, or a sushi dinner, so we're having a McDonald's dinner." He grins at me.

"But it's not dinnertime. It's lunch."

"It could be breakfast as long as I get a blow job." His grin widens and he leans over to speak into the mic. "Hi, can I have a large Big Mac meal with a Coke and a Quarter Pounder bacon cheeseburger but without all the gherkins and onions and a strawberry milkshake?"

My half-amused, half-annoyed stare turns shocked. "How the hell do you know what I order at McDonald's?"

"I don't. I took a lucky guess that you order exactly the same as Dayton."

She's my best friend and marrying his cousin, but it bugs me that he knows her better than me.

Is that irrational?

Fuck. It is.

I mentally slap myself. *Pull your shit together, Olivia.*

My phone rings as we drive to the next window and Nana's name blinks onscreen. Um?

"Nana? Is everything okay?"

"You said you were going to call me, and then you didn't, you wombat!"

Wombat? "Okay, one, it's only been, like, three days, and two, you told me not to call you because I'd just piss you off!"

Tyler looks at me with raised eyebrows and a half grin.

"You know what pisses me off? You not calling when you said you would," Nana replies.

"You sound like a teenage girl who fucked up her date."

"Whatever, Olivia. Did you sort your shit out?"

I smile. "Yes, Nana. I sorted my shit out."

"Good." Silence for a moment. "Did you need something? I thought I told you not to call me because you'd piss me off."

I take a deep breath. "No, Nana. I just wanted to check if you were okay."

"Good. Don't call me again, you dingbat."

"Okay. I'll remember not to call you again."

"You better. Did you make up with that boy?"

I close my eyes this time. "Yes, Nana. I made it up with Tyler."

"Good. Don't call me again. Goodbye, Olivia. Love you."

"Love you. Bye." I hang up, shaking my head, and lean it back in the seat.

Tyler hands over the money, dumps the food in my lap, and pulls away from McDonald's. "That sounded…eventful."

I laugh quietly, more to myself than anything. "My nana has early Alzheimer's. She's always been a bit on the crazy side, and the Alzheimer's exaggerates that somewhat."

"Ah. Now your side of the conversation sort of makes sense."

"Like how she forgot that she called me?" I smile wryly. "She's at the stage where she's only a little more forgetful than any other old person, so I dunno. It's kind of funny sometimes. When I went to my parents' place, she told me, like, five times that she was staying in my room." I roll my eyes.

"It must be hard."

I shrug a shoulder. "She's still 'there.' She's still her, just with extra bounce, I guess. When she starts forgetting her way home or who we are, then we can worry. If we worried now, she'd just claim we were doing it deliberately to piss her off."

"Sounds exactly like my sister," he replies with a dry tone. "She's sure my anger at her knobhead of an ex-husband is because I'm trying to piss her off."

"Eh, I can see where she'd get the idea." I dig my hand into the bag and shove a few fries in my mouth.

Tyler shoots me a glare. "What the fuck does that mean?"

"You are kind of annoying sometimes. And persistent. And 'Me man. Me always right.'"

"What does *that* mean?"

I roll my eyes and feed him a handful of fries. Mostly so he can't argue while I talk. "It means your sister is a big girl and doesn't need her *little* brother"—a noise that sounds like a growl leaves Tyler—"bugging her ass and looking after her."

He chews quicker. "She's smaller than me."

"And if she has half your no-shit attitude, I'm sure she'll be just fine." I raise my eyebrows and get out of the car.

"She actually has *your* no-shit attitude, but that isn't the point," he argues, walking around to me. "How did this conversation even get to this from McDonald's?"

I shrug and hold the food out to him. He looks at it then back at me.

"You don't expect me to carry this, do you? That's what boyfriends do."

Tyler's lips pull up on one side, and the next thing I know, he's wrapping one arm around my back and sweeping the other behind my knees. I scream when he lifts me and holds me snug against his body.

"No," he laughs into my ear. "*This* is what boyfriends do. Wrap your arm around my neck."

"This is ridiculous. You've clearly watched too many Disney movies." I rest my arm around his shoulders, both the drinks and the food in my lap.

"Enough to know there's always a happy ending."

I open my mouth and close it again. I don't want to think about endings. I want to think about beginnings.

"And the fact that there's nearly always a sequel, so if you fuck it up the first time, you get a second try."

I dig my fingers into the hollow of his collarbone. "Where is your faith?"

He pushes the button on the elevator. Somehow. "This from the woman who argued the toss with me until giving in to me in a post-orgasm haze."

I purse my lips. "Well, this is kind of fucked up."

"We're the best kind of fucked up, baby girl. You know why? We know it and we don't give a shit." He winks and steps into the elevator.

I kick my legs softly. "The elevator? That's not very boyfriend-like."

"If you think I'm lugging your ass up those stairs, you can think again."

"Are you calling me fat?"

"No. I'm calling myself lazy."

I purse my lips again. *Good answer, dick. Good answer.* I shake my head as the elevator shudders to a stop on the third floor.

"You have to put me down. I need to get my key out."

"Where is it?"

"My ass pocket. I'm pretty sure there's a key-shaped imprint on my butt cheek from sitting in your car."

"Never mind. I'll put my hand imprint there later." He eases me to standing, and I shiver at his words.

He dips his hand into my back pocket, gives my ass a hard squeeze, then pulls out the key. I give him a dirty look, but I'm certain it's spoiled by the half grin on my face.

Tyler smirks and unlocks my door. Then freezes. "Shit, Liv. And you say my apartment is messy."

Oops. I did kind of forget to tidy up. "Um."

He glances back at me, the smirk still in place, and shakes his head. "Put The Big Bang Theory on and I might just forgive the fact your bra is hanging over the back of the chair and making me hard as hell."

"Really?" I raise my eyebrows, dump the food on the coffee table, and turn to the DVD player. "From a bra?"

"Yes." His eyes darken. "Because I can imagine chucking your bra over the chair then bending you over that table."

I swallow, ignoring the ache in my clit. "Honey, you need to get laid."

"That's the plan."

I grab the DVD controller off the table, ignoring him, and sit back on the sofa. He swipes the food from the table and drops next to me. I hold my hand out expectantly for my food. He stares at my hand for a moment.

Then he pulls his fries from the bag and pushes play on the controller.

I cough, waving my hand. He eats some fries and moves my hand down.

"Can't see the telly," he mumbles through his food.

"Gross." I make a swipe for the bag, but he holds it to the side. "Tyler! You're such a fucking child!" I jab him in the bicep.

He winces, dropping his arm, and I take the chance to grab the bag.

With a laugh, I say, "Ha! Who has the food now?" I get up and run around the table, digging in for my burger. I unwrap it and tear a bite off in a very unladylike way.

Hey, if the guy can fuck me on a regular basis, he can deal with my eating habits.

"Liv," he says slowly, standing, his eyes dead on mine. "Give me my burger."

I shake my head.

"Liv." An undercurrent of a threat is in his voice, and despite the small thrill it sends through my body, I take another bite of my burger.

"Yes?"

"The burger."

I shake my head for a second time. "Nope. You take my food, I take yours."

"You took it back." He cocks an eyebrow, taking slow steps toward me.

I back up until I hit the counter. "And I'm keeping it."

He sighs, letting his shoulders sag. "I didn't want to do this, but..."

Quicker than I can move, he darts around the table toward me. He flattens his hands on the counter on either side of my body and rests his hips against mine.

Dipping his head, he runs his nose along my jaw. "Are you going to give me the food?"

"Are you trying to seduce me into giving you it?" I gasp at the feel of his tongue flicking against the tender spot below my ear.

"I'm not *trying* to seduce you, Liv. I am seducing you. I don't try." His lips brush along my neck, just below my jawline.

My eyes flutter shut, and he settles one of his hands on my hip. His fingers edge beneath my sweater and my shirt, tantalizingly rubbing against my skin, and I tilt my head back. He continues his exploration of my neck with his mouth, humming against my skin, whispering into my neck, pushing his hardening cock into my thigh…

"Thanks," he says, grabbing the bag and stepping away.

Oh holy hell fucking no!

"Going somewhere?" I snap out, discarding my burger to the side and grabbing his sweater. I tug, spinning him.

Amusement and desire battle in his eyes. "To the sofa. To eat."

"Oh, no, you're not. You're going to come over here and finish what you just started, Tyler Stone."

He sets the bag on the kitchen table and studies me. "Am I adding demanding to my list of adjectives for you?"

"Go ahead."

A smirk teases his lips. "Okay, my demanding bitch." He comes back to me and stands in front of me without touching me. "What exactly am I supposed to be finishing?"

I look up at him. "Don't play dumb with me. You can't come over here, turn me the fuck on, then walk away like my panties aren't soaked."

"They're soaked, hmm? Just from that?" He traps me with his hands again. His breath fans across my mouth, and I lick my lips.

"Why don't you find out?" I challenge, his eyes sparking immediately.

"In that case…" He hooks his fingers in the waistband of my jeans and tugs them down over my ass.

I gasp as he wraps his hands around the backs of my thighs and lifts me up onto the counter. Perching on the edge, I watch as he pulls the jeans from my legs and dumps them on the floor. He runs his hands back up my legs, spreading his fingers wide when he reaches my thighs, and pauses just before his thumbs touch my thong.

"I think I will."

Tyler nudges the material of my thong to the side in one jerky movement. His thumb brushes along my pussy, circling my clit quickly. I gasp and he groans.

"Good girl." His voice rumbles through me as he lifts his hands and eases my sweater over my head.

My shirt quickly follows, and as he steps closer, he cups both of my breasts. He kisses along the cup line of my bra and up. Deftly, he undoes my bra and it falls down my arms.

"I can't decide if I want to tie your hands or have them in my hair," he whispers in my ear, rolling my nipples between his thumbs and fingers.

I wrap my legs around his waist and tug on his sweater and shirt. He releases my breasts long enough to pull them over his head then pulls my body against his. The movement is hard, and my lips part at the exact time he touches his own lips to them.

Tyler's tongue sweeps through my mouth in familiar, easy movements, desperate movements, needing movements. His fingers slide up my thighs, probing, squeezing, and they leave me only long enough to undo his belt and shove his jeans down.

He grabs my wrists and flattens my hands behind me so I'm leaning back and slowly rubs the end of his cock against my wetness.

"Please," I whisper.

It's been two days. Two long, seemingly torturous days since I've had him inside me, and I've never been so desperate for him. For that fleeting feeling of completeness and rightness.

In one swift movement, he's inside me and gripping my hips. His teasing movements of earlier are gone as he drives himself relentlessly into me. It's raw and unbridled.

It's perfect.

He sucks hard on one of my nipples, making me cry out in both pain and pleasure. He does the same to the other then slides a hand up my back, fists my hair, and pulls my mouth down to his. His kiss is as rough as his fucking, every thrust of his tongue matching that of his hips.

It doesn't take long for that sweet heat of an impending orgasm to overwhelm me. I reach forward and tangle my fingers in his hair the way his are tangled in mine. I break the kiss and rest my forehead against his, breathing heavily, moaning with almost every exhale.

"Liv. Fucking hell, Liv," he groans, moving even faster. "God, I need this. I need you."

His words are my undoing. They scare me and thrill me and consume me. I clench around him, my world utterly silent except for the rush of blood in my ears and those three final words spinning inside my mind.

"I need you."

I come back down with a crash. His arms are tight around me, and both my arms and legs are still wrapped around his body, holding us together.

But they're not really holding us. The thing that's holding us is the strength of our addictions. It's gluing us to the other, all while we're trying to make something potentially beautiful from something incredibly ugly.

"Oh, look at that. We went straight to dessert."

Tyler's words make me laugh, and I pull back. His eyes are bright, much brighter than before. If that doesn't tell me the intensity of his addiction to sex, I don't know what will.

I'm sure my eyes are just as bright.

"Come here." He nudges my nose with his and slides me off the counter.

Without letting me go, he carries me through to my room. Just when I'm smiling at his act of romance, he pulls out of me and dumps me unceremoniously on my bed.

I shriek and grab my sheet to stop myself from falling onto the floor. "You dick!" I yell as he disappears into the bathroom.

Of course, he laughs. He never takes me seriously when I yell insults at him, and that's half the fun.

"Hey, bitch." He throws a towel on top of me and then jumps over me. His knees are on either side of my thighs, his forearms by my head, and his grinning face is hovering just inches above mine.

"What?" I ask, awkwardly reaching between us and wiping. Somehow, I ease my panties down and throw them on the floor.

His smile widens. "You never gave me my blow job."

My own lips move to mirror his, and I tap his nose. "That's what you get for teasing me and fucking me on my kitchen counter. Now, if you don't mind, I'd like to clean the counter while you call and order me a replacement dinner."

I scoot up the bed and swing my legs over the side. Then I grab a pair of cotton shorts from my drawer and pull them on.

"You forgot your underwear."

I pause at the door and glance over my shoulder. "A woman never forgets her underwear. What she puts on—or doesn't—is entirely deliberate and always serves a purpose. You should remember that."

Chapter THREE

I RUB my temple as the receptionist on the other end of the phone babbles on about…well, I don't know. Nothing informative.

"Yeah, okay," I cut in. "But can you give me prices? Packages? Or do I physically have to come to California to get this information?"

She pauses. "I can email it to you."

"That would be great."

"Okay. Can you give me your preferred dates so I can check availability… for how many people?"

"Uh…four or five." Despite the wedding, I know that Day doesn't want a huge friggin' bachelorette party.

"For a bachelorette party?"

"You know, there's another spa two blocks away from you that was very accommodating when I called earlier today."

"Just a second, ma'am."

I can't help it. I smirk.

"We have availability for you, but not for our complete package."

"No good," I say immediately. "All or nothing."

"We don't have time slots for five of you that day, ma'am."

"Okay. Thanks." I hang up and drop the phone.

Three spas. Two no-gos. One possibility.

Fan-fucking-tastic.

I drop my phone on the coffee table and stand up. Immediately, Angus starts mewling at me and runs over to his food bowl. I check the time. *Shit.* I have to get ready for work.

I dump a can of food into his bowl—much to his Lordship's delight—and dart into my room. I pull some skinny jeans and a black shirt from my drawers and quickly slink into them. As quickly as you can slink into skinny jeans, that is. And, let's be honest, there's no graceful way to do it.

I hop into the bathroom, still tugging them up my thighs, and fall into the doorframe. *Yup, definitely not graceful.* That bitch will bruise in the morning. I shove toothpaste on my toothbrush then the brush into my mouth, holding it still with pursed lips as I button the jeans. Success!

Brushing my teeth with one hand, I run my hairbrush through my hair with the other. And look in the mirror. Fuck a duck, have I been wandering around with panda eyes all day?

So nice of Tyler to tell me when he left a few hours ago.

I spit out my toothpaste and wipe the makeup from my face simultaneously. I hope my best friend appreciates the late and frantic efforts I'm putting into this bachelorette party business. I was kind of hoping that I could forgo the planning shit and just turn up somewhere… Alas, no.

I have a list in my messages. A real fucking list. A to-do list.

Until this morning, there was only one thing on my to-do list: Tyler Stone. Now, there are around fifty million things she wants me to do.

Book the party. Invite Tessa. Email details to everyone. Find a hotel to stay at. Organize a restaurant and book a table for dinner and drinks. Find evening entertainment.

Yeah. I'm not even going to think about the effing bridal shower.

I grab my phone and keys from the side and run down the stairs. It's raining outside—of course it is—and I forgot my coat. Fantastic. This isn't how Wednesdays go. It's how Mondays go.

Or is Wednesday the new Monday?

I tuck my phone into my bra and ready the key fob between my fingers. I press the button as soon as I open the door and run to my car. I yank the door open and slide in.

Pushing my hair from my face, I tear out of the parking lot.

I can just tell that this shift is going to be complete shit.

"Did Tyler tell you that Tessa is staying with him for a month?"

I pause and look at Dayton. "No."

"Oh." She sucks in her bottom lip. "Then this is awkward. I thought you knew."

"No. I wonder why he didn't say anything."

"He fucked you before he told you his name. And you're surprised he hasn't told you that his sister is staying with him?"

"I… No." I take my cup of coffee from the counter and sit down. She takes the seat opposite me and I continue. "When she is coming?"

"Three days from now. Said she needs to get away while her divorce is going through."

"Great. So, essentially, seven days after officially starting to date, I'm meeting the family."

I don't like families. Not that I have anything against them, per se. In fact, I'm sure his sister is lovely. I just don't like them. Families are…serious. When you meet them, you get all…well, serious.

Sure, I'm thinking about beginnings with Tyler, but I'm not thinking about serious beginnings. Because, really, how serious can a relationship between a sex addict and a love addict be?

"Liv…" Day says slowly. "You can breathe, you know, sweetie."

I shake my head. "Nope, nope, and nope."

"No, you're not going to meet his sister yet?" Day raises her eyebrows with an amused twist of her lips.

"Nope. I'm not going to. I'm going to hide for the next three weeks, because then it'll be, like, a month and a totally acceptable duration of a relationship for that stuff."

"Liv, snap the hell out of it!" Her words are short and sharp.

I blink harshly.

"Honestly, I can't decide if you're addicted to love or a commitment-phobe."

"Both. Definitely both."

"Don't tell me you're seriously thinking that being with Tyler is a bad idea."

I lean back in the chair. "I've never not thought that. He's a very, very bad idea."

"You really piss me off sometimes."

"Good. At least the feeling is mutual." I grin and she returns it.

"Seriously, meeting his sister isn't a big deal. You don't even have to meet her with him. We'll go for drinks or something." She shrugs. "Aaron's working late, so I'm basically sitting around like a dick every night, doing nothing."

"Mmph," I grunt.

I know there's absolutely no way I'm going to get out of this. I'm going to have to meet Tessa and accept that this relationship is heading to pretty serious pretty damn fast.

The hilarious thing is that the way we feel, is about as serious as it's gonna get.

I stare into my coffee with this thought. Strip away the sex and the jokes and you get the reality of us. Of LivandTyler. We are addiction, alone and together, and we're intense and obsessive and probably a little destructive.

We're unhealthy. It would be naïve to convince myself otherwise. But that doesn't mean we can't be healthy eventually.

I hope.

Dayton sighs and glances at her watch. "I have to go to a shoot. Want to come with me?"

I raise my eyebrows. "Because Tyler will like that."

"It's you," she replies, standing up and shrugging her jacket on. "He likes anything to do with you."

I try not to roll my eyes. "Fine. I'll come."

"God, Liv, I can feel your excitement from here."

"I know. I'm about to burst with it. Can't you tell?" I follow her outside to the sound of her laughter. "I'll follow you there."

She nods and gets into her car. I do the same, checking my phone before starting the engine. Day pulls out of the parking lot and I drive after her.

I'm not sure how I feel about watching Tyler work. Since I've managed my addiction through avoidance for six years, putting myself in a situation that could make it worse doesn't seem like a good idea.

Shit, I know it isn't. But I'm still driving, because right now, my need to see Tyler is more than my need to run away from watching him take pictures of another girl.

If that's what he's doing. I don't know. I should have asked. I shouldn't have agreed to come. I should turn around and go home and have a staring competition with my cat.

I nibble on my nails at the intersection. Since they're fake, the motion does nothing but comfort me. My jaw moves in tiny little tics, clenching when I have to pull away.

This is dumb. This whole thing.

My heartbeat is steadily growing faster with both fear and anticipation. And jealousy of something that might not be. Jealousy because I don't want him to look at another girl, although it's his job. Jealously because I wish I could lock him away and be the model.

I drive into a parking lot behind Dayton. My palms are sweating against the steering wheel, and I take a minute to take a deep breath while she gathers her stuff from her car.

I should still turn around and go.

I don't.

I grab my purse and get out.

"Are you okay?" My best friend pauses by my car.

"Fine. Where are we?"

"Tyler's new studio. Well, I say studio. It's just a room and a kitchen right now."

He has a studio? "Oh." I swallow back annoyance of another little thing she knows that I don't.

Fuck. This is my best friend!

Next time I come across a frying pan, I'm smacking myself over the fucking head with it. With any luck, I'll knock some sense into myself. With a lot of luck, I'll knock myself out so it won't even matter.

Day leads me into the building. And she's right—it's not decorated or even particularly organized. Oddly enough, the lack of organization doesn't surprise me. Tyler Stone is as organized as a freakin' junkyard.

"Cooey!" Dayton chimes, setting her things on a desk in the corner.

With a mug in his hand, Tyler appears from what I'm guessing is the kitchen. "You're late."

"You're happy."

"You're late and our model is a diva with wandering hands. I'm fucking ecstatic."

"Then you should probably tell her what to do with those wandering hands before your girlfriend cuts them off." I smile sweetly from the door, my words conveying only a fraction of my annoyance.

Doesn't this just get better?

Tyler's eyes shoot to me and his eyebrows go up. "What are you doing here?"

I find his eyes, and this time, I don't bother to hide how pissed off I am. "Right now? I'm thinking I should probably leave."

His eyebrows rise even farther. "I didn't mean it like that. I'm just surprised to see you."

"Evidently," I reply dryly, sitting at the desk. I dump my purse on the floor. "Or you probably wouldn't have spoken about wandering hands so easily."

"Day? Can you go and see if our model is ready?" Tyler asks her.

She nods, shooting out of the door.

Tyler puts his mug down on the desk and slowly moves around the wooden furniture. I tilt my head back as he gets closer to me. He grips both arms of the cushy leather chair I'm sitting in and lowers his face toward mine.

"Cut it out," he says softly yet sharply, his contradicting words setting off an equally contradicting mix of soothing and riling feelings inside me. "I have a job to do, Liv, and if you're going to have a problem with me doing it, then my studio isn't the place for you."

My jaw drops. "Are you kicking me out?"

"No. But I am reminding you the door is to your left if you need to use it."

I narrow my eyes at him. "Don't worry. There's no need to flick your dickhead switch to 'on.' I'm totally aware of where the door is."

A terse moment passes between us until it's broken by Dayton's voice. A high-pitched giggle follows it, and Tyler straightens.

"We're ready," Day says, her eyes flicking to me.

I shrug my shoulder the tiniest bit and she seems to get it, because she turns her attention back to her job.

The model stares at me with an affected look before she turns to Tyler. A flirtatious smile stretches across her face and she flicks her hair.

Oh, please. Is this fucking high school?

"Let's get started," Ty says casually.

You wouldn't believe that, just seconds ago, he was leaning over me, half threatening me.

He casually picks up his camera and directs the model where to stand. I hook one of my ankles over the other. Resolve is building inside me. I will stick this shoot out.

I'll sit here, jealousy and anger and possibly a little hatred building inside me, and I'll watch the whole damn thing.

Just to make a point.

I rest my elbow on the desk and put my chin in my palm. I'm not sure who this model is or what she's doing, but she has a really annoying laugh. All high pitched and almost squeaky. The ones you cringe at.

I tap my nails against my leg, watching the shoot play out before me. I know how this works. I know how shoots go.

And this model wants Tyler to shoot more than just his camera.

But it's cool. I mean, this happens all the time. He's hot. She's crushing on him. I can cope with that.

Model Girl looks seductively at Tyler. Not the camera. Him. And laughs.

Jesus, it's like nails on a chalkboard.

My foot takes up a steady rhythm tapping against the floor. Onetwothree. Onetwothree. Onetwothree. Like a motherfucking waltz. Tap, tap, tap. Over and over, silent against the carpet.

What isn't silent is the way both Ty's and Day's cameras click. Tyler's quiet orders. Model Girl's breathing. Hell, I can hear the fluttering of her fucking fake eyelashes. I can hear the swishing of her hair.

Shit, she's flirting so hard that I can practically hear her gushing into those designer panties.

It goes on and on. Her eyelash-fluttering, her smiling, her giggling, her hair-flicking… Every fucking thing she does makes me wonder if she's here for the job or for Tyler. And it pisses me off.

It twists my stomach and tightens my chest with an intricate knot of jealously. I hate sitting here, watching him watch her, when she's so obvious.

And I can't.

My resolve wavers until it shatters. With my stomach coiling with nausea and hot tears stinging the backs of my eyes, I grab my purse. I slip my hand inside, set my phone vibrating, and answer my fake call quietly.

I slip out of the room with it attached to my ear. I can't stay. I was dumb to think I could.

It's been days and I'm already done.

This is bad. So, so fucking bad.

I push open the door and step outside. Rain is falling lightly as I make my way to my car, and I hear the door open quietly behind me.

"It's a good thing you're a better model than you are actress," Day says softly. "Your trick isn't fooling me."

"You created the trick, dumbass. It wasn't to fool you." I yank my car door open. "I'm going. If I stay there much longer, I'm going to strangle her with her own fucking extensions." I throw my purse across the car into the passenger's seat.

"What do you want me to tell Tyler?"

I look at her. "Tell him whatever the hell he wants to hear."

With that, I get into my car, slam the door, and rev the shit out of my engine. I tear out of the parking lot before she can respond and tell myself that the emotion in her eyes wasn't real.

There wasn't an abundance of fear and worry in them. They were simply concerned.

I have to believe that. Perhaps wrongly, but I have to. Sometimes, believing the wrong thing is the right thing to do. Sometimes, believing the wrong thing will keep you sane.

So I drive through the city, telling myself that what I'm feeling is totally natural. That any girlfriend feels the same way.

I park outside my apartment block and lock my car with way too much vigor. I take the elevator in the same way, jabbing the buttons way too hard. My key fits in my keyhole after three forced attempts, and the way I slam my front door surely shakes the whole building.

I throw my purse across my apartment. It lands with a thud on my floor, waking Angus and making him screech. The high-pitched sound goes right through me and I respond with one of my own.

I scream into my hands, bending over onto the kitchen table. All my frustration, all my jealousy, all the ramifications of my need for that infuriating fucking man are tangible and audible in my cry.

Only I don't know who I'm madder at. Model Girl for making me feel this way or myself for allowing me to. I don't know if I'm madder at Tyler for reminding me where the door is or myself for using it.

In the end, it all comes down to me. I let myself feel things and do things that are sometimes irrational.

But you can't always help it, I remind myself. I can't control the addiction. The addiction controls me.

But is that only true because I let it?

Is it only my controller, the truly dominant thing in my life, because I allow it to be?

No. I tell myself no because I don't want to believe that my addiction is causing this. Through it all, through my fears, I don't want my addiction to be the reason I walked out of that studio. I want my stupid fucking heart to be the reason.

I want to believe that there's more to us and our fucked-up fairytale.

I want to believe that there are feelings, real feelings, that tie us even deeper than the bonds of our addictions.

And maybe that's the problem.

Maybe my addiction is ruling because I'm not allowing reality through.

Maybe I am falling in love.

Maybe I am falling in love with his crisp accent, his dirty words, his burning touch. Maybe I'm falling in love with the snark and the cockiness and that stupid love for snuggles.

Maybe I'm falling in love with the way he makes me feel.

Maybe I'm falling in love with more than just love.

Maybe… Maybe, in a cruel twist in Fate's Big Fuck-Up, I'm falling in love with Tyler Stone.

Chapter FOUR

I PUSH off from the table and yank open the cupboard that holds my alcohol. I drag out the bottle of vodka and pour some in a short glass. I throw it back without thinking. The hot burn of the spirit sliding down my throat is better than the burn of my realization.

The burn of alcohol will always be better than the burn of a maybe-love.

Alcohol doesn't hurt half as much as love. And the pounding head alcohol will give you is fixed with a glass of water and a couple of Tylenols.

If only Tylenol worked on the heart, too. They'd make a mint.

The glass clanks on the counter as I put it down. The vodka settles into a warm ball in my lower stomach. *Shit, shit, shit. Fucking shit!*

I kick the cupboard shut and look at the clock for the first time since leaving the studio. At least I lasted most of the shoot. That's better than running at the first glance.

Ha. Running. I'm good at running. So much so that I should live in my fucking sneakers.

I pour another drink and drink it as quickly as the last. Shit. What if I am falling in love? What kind of fucked-up bullshit would that make our relationship? It certainly wouldn't be a fairytale.

It would be nothing close to a fairytale. Not even good ol' Walt could spin it into a Disney-esque happy ending.

Another clank of the glass against the side and I storm into the bathroom.

I turn the shower on—full heat and full power—and strip off. I step beneath the burning flow of water and let it wash over me as it almost scalds my skin.

Like it can wash away what I feel inside, on the outside.

Like the red-hot sting can seep into my skin and burn through the clusterfuck of emotion I don't want to feel.

Because, god fuckin' dammit, I don't want to fall in love with him. I don't want to feel the way I do because of real emotion. Unmanageable feelings.

But I do. I want this sickening feeling in my stomach to be because I'm falling for my twat, as he calls himself. I want it to be because my heart and soul are in agreement and there's nothing they want more than him.

Just him.

Mostly, I wish I didn't feel a thing.

Love or addiction, it doesn't matter. It still fucking hurts.

I kill the water without washing my hair or soaping my body and wrap myself in a towel. Feeling no calmer than before, I walk into my room and pull on some underwear and some shorts. Then I roughly tug a tank over my head.

My temples are throbbing. Pounding. It's almost painful, and I rub the towel across it. I grab my brush and yank it through my hair. Every movement shows the unending conflict and pain inside me.

I throw the towel to the floor and walk out into the front room. Angus is whining at the door, so I open it and let him out. He'll just jump out the open window in the lobby.

The door slams too harshly, but no sooner have I closed it than it opens again.

I spin at the same time that I'm grabbed and slammed into the door. Lips cover mine harshly, the feel of fingers digging into my biceps painful and sweet at the same time.

The material of Tyler's shirt curls beneath my hands as I fist it. I pull him closer. His tongue sweeps through my mouth, battling against mine. His teeth nip my bottom lip and he gently sucks after each bite, soothing the sting, but right now, I don't care.

I want the sting. I want the physical to overpower the mental. I want him to tear off my clothes, pin me against this wall, and fuck me so hard that I can't feel anything but him moving inside me.

He dives his hand into my hair and tugs. Hard. I whimper into his mouth as the jolt of pain registers through my nerves. And despite what my body is screaming for, my mind is yelling that this is the worst thing I should be doing.

I shouldn't be surrendering to him this way. I should be fighting him.

I should be pushing him away from me because sex won't solve it.

With one final deep kiss, I release his shirt, flatten my hands against his shoulders, and shove hard. He steps back, letting me go. I shake my head and move around him. Away from him.

"What the fucking hell was that, Liv?" he says between clenched teeth.

I run my fingers through my wet hair to untangle it. "I used the door. Just like you told me to, remember?"

"I didn't mean use it halfway through the bloody shoot and fuck me up for the rest of it!"

"Oh, well, I'm sorry if needing to get the hell out of there before I murdered your model was a burden to you!" My voice echoes around my apartment.

He takes a deep breath. His nostrils flare, his chest heaves, and his eyes pin mine with an intensity I feel rushing through every single one of my veins.

"Explain. Now." Not a question. A demand. A harsh, final demand.

I storm past him and stop in the middle of the room. "That. Her. I couldn't watch it! The way she was throwing herself at you. She wasn't even playing the camera. She was playing you!" My gut wrenches with the thought.

"Don't be stupid."

"I'm a model. I know how it works. She wasn't interested in anything except what's in your fucking pants!" I wrap my arms around me like a safety net, turning. "I couldn't fucking watch her sitting there drooling over you and shoving what are probably fake tits toward you, knowing you were looking at her. Knowing you were watching her every goddamn move!"

"I'm not interested in her!" He steps forward. "Fuck. All I see is you, Liv. Every time, it's you!"

"That doesn't matter!" Tears really do burn my eyes now. "You were watching her. *Her…*" My voice trails off on the last word.

Tyler walks toward me, and I back up until I hit the wall. With nowhere for me to run, he lays a hand on either side of my face. Leaning in, breathing harshly, each one seemingly pained, he consumes me.

"Stop," he whispers. "Please, baby girl. Stop. Stop these stupid, irrational thoughts."

"I'm not irrational. My addiction is irrational. My need for you, my crazy, overwhelming need for you, is irrational. But I am not."

"You don't think I feel the same? You don't think I don't bloody well need you either?" He wipes his thumbs beneath my eyes.

I look at him. Shake my head. How can he need me the way I need him?

"I do." He steps closer, his body flat against mine. "It took everything I had to not follow you out that damn door. To stay and take pictures of that woman."

"I would have gone," I whisper. "If it were the other way around, I wouldn't have been able to stay."

"I stayed because I was made to." He finishes his words with a firm kiss. The warmth from his mouth seeps through me from my lips to my toes. Every part of my body feels it.

"You don't get it, do you?" I look up, my eyes wet. I can feel the sting every time I blink.

"Yes, I do. I get it."

I wrap my arms around his wrists and pull them down. "No, you don't. What if I get like this every time you shoot another woman? That happens, what, four times a week, at least? It's been five days and I'm already falling apart over it. This isn't normal."

"And when you go for the Balfour shoot in two weeks? Then what, Liv? I know the guy shooting it. How do you think I'll feel knowing you, my bitch, my girlfriend, *my* Liv, is on a beach in front of some other knobhead while he takes her picture?"

"I'm not shooting in two weeks."

His lips curl up. "Yes, you are. Sheila just didn't call you yet. You got the campaign. And while you're on a beach in fucking Mexico in a fucking bikini in front of some fucking knob, I'm stuck here, waiting for you to get back."

I can't even be happy. I can't be thrilled about getting the campaign. All I can hear is the thickness in his voice. The one he's trying to hide.

"You are mine, Liv. Don't ever doubt that. Every part of you is mine. And I'm yours. Every part of me is yours. Don't doubt that either."

I bury my face into his chest. He's right. We belong to each other, even if it is in the most fucked-up way. In a way that makes no sense at all.

"I don't doubt it," I whisper into him. "I never doubt it. Not when I feel this way. I can't. It's impossible, Ty. I can't not believe it."

"Then listen to it. Please, baby girl. Please just fucking listen to it when I make you crazy."

"You don't make me crazy. Other people make me crazy."

He laughs softly. His chest rumbles and vibrates beneath my cheek, and I find myself smiling a little. *I love the sound of his laugh.*

"I take offense at that. Don't you know I wake up every morning and figure out a thousand ways to make you go crazy?" he asks, kissing the top of my head.

I squeeze his waist. "I can believe *that.* I have a question."

"Have you calmed down now? Can we have a conversation without shouting?"

I nod. "I just needed to get the crazy out."

Tyler pulls back and runs his hands up my body until they reach my face. "What is it?"

I swipe under my eyes, wiping away the remaining wetness, and look at him. "Why didn't you tell me your sister was staying with you?"

A smirk tugs at his lips. "I didn't want you to freak the hell out. Like you did when Day told you."

I bite the inside of my lip. "It was a surprise."

He laughs and releases me, heading toward my kitchen. "No shit. She wants to get away from London. I told her she could stay at my place for a few weeks. She'll stay, go home for a couple weeks, then come back for the wedding."

The wedding?

Oh, Aaron and Dayton's. Right. *Phew.*

Little mind-jump there.

I follow him and sit at the table, bringing my feet up onto the chair and hugging my knees. "Do I have to meet her?"

"If you think you can avoid her, I'll give you a medal." He opens my cupboards one by one.

"Okay. I guess I'm resigning myself to the seriousness of our five-day-old relationship."

His brown eyes shine with amusement. "I love how you think this just started."

"It only just officially started. I'm going with official."

"The day you walked into that damn shoot and didn't fight me, you were mine. It's been way longer than five measly fucking days." He shuts the fridge and sighs, turning. "Do you have anything to cook in this place?"

My gaze flicks from side to side before finally finding his. "Um." I chew the inside of my cheek and shrug in a way I hope is cute.

He fights his smile, shakes his head, and pulls out his phone. Muttering the word, "Dominos," he holds the phone to his ear and grins at me.

And as he reels off an order, it doesn't escape my notice that, despite my breakdown, we didn't really sort anything out at all.

I open my legs and arch my back. And hit a solid wall of muscle.

The solid wall of muscle groans, and I roll onto my side at the same time that it—Tyler—makes a grab for me. Unfortunately for me—or fortunately, depending on how you look at it—he's quicker. He loops an arm over my body and physically yanks me back into him.

I squeak as my back hits his chest.

"Morning," he mumbles into my shoulder, leaving a line of kisses along my skin.

"Go away," I reply, shuffling away. "I need the toilet."

"Sexiest thing I've heard in a while." He laughs, releasing me, and blood rushes to my cheeks.

Shit. Note to self: replace brain-to-mouth filter.

With my cheeks still flaming, I climb out of bed and run into my bathroom. I flatten my palms against my cheeks while I…take care of business. Then I slowly walk back into my room.

Tyler's leaning against the headboard and has turned the TV on. "Be a love and get me a cup of tea."

"That has to be the most British sentence I've ever heard," I reply, whipping the covers away from him. "And the answer is a big fat no."

I jump into the bed next to him. The controller hits the ground with a thunk and Tyler's hands grab my waist. He tugs me down the bed until I'm flat on my back and leans over me.

"I wasn't asking you, babe. I was telling you."

His voice hums over my chest, making my pulse thrum in my neck.

"Unless you're telling me to get on my knees and suck your cock, I'm not good with being told what to do."

His lips twitch up. "Oh, believe me. I know." He trails a finger across my bare stomach, up to my breastbone. He teases it between my breasts until it climbs my neck, ghosts the curve of my jaw, and rests on my bottom lip. "And being told what to do it isn't all you're good at."

"Honey, you're telling me things I already know. This conversation is completely pointless." I kiss his fingertip then bat his hand away.

"Had much experience with it?" His eyes spark with heat.

I roll out from under him, get up, and slide my panties down my legs. I grab some clean underwear from the drawer and proceed to get dressed. All the while, his eyes are roving over my body like he's been starved of me.

Finally, I turn, glancing at him over my shoulder. "Experience means shit. I know I could give you the best damn blow job of your life."

"Is that so?"

"I challenge you to find out."

"Accepted. My place. Seven p.m." He swings his legs out of bed and grabs the navy lingerie he bought me. "Wear this. Or else."

"Or else what?"

"Or else I'll smack your arse so hard you'll feel my hand there for a week."

"Tempting." I catch the thong and tuck it into my palm. "I happen to be fond of your spankings… And your hands."

I laugh and run out of my room. Tyler's own quiet laugh follows me, and I flick the kettle to boiling. *Brits and their fucking tea.*

He wraps his arms around me from behind and buzzes his lips down my neck. "You're a dirty, rotten tease, bitch."

"And you're awfully demanding." I smile and throw a teabag into a mug for him. I spoon coffee into the second.

"It's hard not to be when you give in to every single one… Especially if handcuffs are involved."

"Or ties. Or scarfs. Or maybe chains," I tease.

"Chains, hmm?"

"Are you getting ideas now?"

He reaches out and grabs his tea. He curls his fingers around the mug handle. "Liv," he breathes close to my mouth. "All you have to do is exist and I get ideas. About you over my sofa. In the bath…. My balcony railings."

A shiver runs through me from head to toe. "Balcony?"

"Where everyone could see you. I'll give you three guesses where you'll find yourself tonight." He steps away as another shiver grasps my body.

I turn and watch him as he walks to my sofa. His steps are so steady, so smooth. Yet me? I don't dare take a step because I know my legs are trembling.

The balcony? Over the railings? On the chair? On the table? Against the wall?

The possibilities are endless, and each idea scoots through my mind with a blinding flash. And I ache everywhere, already desperate for his touch.

The man is destroying me. And I'm relishing every second.

Tyler props his feet on my coffee table and looks over at me. His dark eyes glint knowingly, and the mug he raises to his mouth covers his smirk. "Aren't you joining me?"

"Now or later?" I quip back.

"There's no question about later, Liv. There never is. We both know you'll be there."

"So sure?" I cock an eyebrow.

He shows me his smirk now. His full, shit-eating, smug-ass smirk. "Positive. You're forgetting one tiny detail."

"And what's that?"

"Our previous agreement still stands. When I call, you come running."

"I'm your girlfriend. Not your fuck buddy."

"So the only thing that's changed is I get to buy you dinner before I fuck you how I want to." He shrugs his shoulder. I bite my tongue. Damn him!

I bite my tongue. *Damn him!* "You're hard work, you know that, Tyler Stone?"

He grins, showing his dimple. "Is hard the operative word in that sentence?"

I run my tongue across my teeth, fighting my smile. "I'm going to get ready for work before you decide you need yet another cold shower." I set the mug on the counter and turn away.

"Liv? Don't forget the underwear."

My eyes cut to him and I snatch it from the table. "I never do."

Chapter FIVE

THE bar is slowly starting to take shape. And when I say slowly, I mean slowly. The issue with the stairs from last time means it'll take an extra three days to finish.

Which is something that isn't going down well with Aaron right now—no matter how glad he is that it got him out of a third and final round of cake-tasting.

"I'm sorry, Will. I don't have the time or the schedule for you to finish three days after agreed. You'll have to bring some extra men in." Aaron drops the blueprint onto the table and adjusts his tie.

"I have no extra men. They're all booked."

"Then I have to let your team go and bring in my standby builders."

Standby builders?

Will, the guy in charge, bristles. "There's no need for that, Mr. Stone. I'll call the office and see if we can bring another team in."

"There's no seeing about it, Will. If you wish to keep this job, you will bring them in. You knew the schedule when you took the job on." Aaron turns away from him, effectively ending the conversation, and waves me after him.

"Well, I'm glad you were here to have that conversation."

His lips twitch. "Get used to it, Liv. Managing people means keeping asses in check by whatever means possible."

"And I'm watching and learning from you." I laugh. "Do you think they'll have another team in here?"

"Absolutely. I paid them twice their fee for the short notice and rush job. They won't want to lose the money or contract with me."

"Power makes you kind of arrogant. Have you noticed that?"

"I believe Dayton once told me something similar, and I'll say to you exactly what I did to her: It's not arrogance when it's the truth. With power and money comes ruthlessness. You don't do what I want, then we're done."

I raise my eyebrows. "No, that's not a power thing. That's a Stone thing."

He holds the door open for me with a smile. "On second thought, you could be correct there."

"There's no could be. I am correct."

"See? You have the 'don't argue with me' mentality already."

"I have that because I'm a woman, not because I'm the manager of this place. I've had it since I was freakin' two years old."

Aaron laughs at the same time that my phone buzzes in my purse. I dig it out and look at the screen.

"Dayton," he reads over my shoulder. "If she asks, I'm still busy with the builders."

I purse my lips and answer. "Hi, Bridezilla."

"Fuck yourself," she responds without a beat. "Is Aaron there?"

"He's right beside me. Would you like to talk to him?" I smile sweetly at the man glaring at me.

"Yes. Now."

Uh oh.

I hand the phone over to him. "Your fiancée would like to talk to you."

He shakes his head and steps away to talk to her. I grin, leaning against my car. I watch as he obviously tries to calm her down for whatever bridal kick she's on today.

I am so never getting married.

Ever.

After a few minutes, Aaron brings my phone back to me and rubs his temples. "She wants you to meet at her Starbucks. I asked her which, and she snapped, and I quote, 'She knows which fucking Starbucks I mean. We've used the same place for five fucking-ass years.'"

I hide my smile and take my phone. "Seriously. Is she pregnant?"

He shakes his head. "After the last few days, thank god she isn't. The day she does get pregnant, I'm going on a nine-month-long vacation. Now, before she marches over here and strings my balls from the pier, go to fucking Starbucks. I'm going to get Tylenol and a nap."

I get in my car, laughing loudly, and wave to him. I think I want to feel sorry for him, but he can be just as bad.

When I arrive at Starbucks, and she gets in my car before I can even cut the engine.

"Drive. Now. To your apartment," she demands, clicking her belt into place.

"I thought—"

"I need a tequila shot and a bottle of wine—something Starbucks can't provide me. Foot down, Liv."

She's lucky I always have tequila and wine in my apartment.

"What's wrong with you? Aaron said you weren't pregnant, and if it weren't for the demand of alcohol, I'd say he was lying." I cut her a glance.

She clicks her tongue loudly. "I got my implant out and went on the pill. It's fucking with my hormones. I'm like a walking ball of PMS."

Ah. Wait… "You got your implant out?"

"Yes."

"I thought you weren't going to." I pull up in the parking lot and we get out of the car.

"I wasn't. But I thought about it and thought, 'Hey, I'm not ready now, but who's to say I won't want a baby in a month? Or even two weeks?' So I got the damn thing out and switched to the pill. It's seriously messing me up."

"Does Aaron know?"

"No." She jabs the button for the third floor. "Hell no. If that man knew I was on the pill, he'd throw the fuckers in the bin and have my dress around my waist quicker than you could say, 'fuck me!'"

I snort and let us into my apartment. Now that I can believe.

She heads straight for my liquor cabinet and pours a shot of tequila. She throws it back, winces, then slams the glass on the counter.

"You know, that's probably something you should keep an eye on," I tease her.

She glares at me then sighs. "Is this the right thing? Taking the implant out?"

"I don't know. Ask your ovaries." I kick off my shoes and drop onto the sofa.

"Ha, ha, fucking ha." She mocks, flopping down next to me. "Seriously."

"I don't know. How are we ever supposed to know what's right until we've done it?"

She ponders this for a moment, her beautiful face marring with a slight frown. "But what if we do it and decide it's not so right after all?"

"Then we're pretty damn fucked." I shrug. "I don't know, Day. Stop overthinking it. You've done it now."

"You're so reassuring." She sighs again. "How do you know you and Tyler is the right thing?"

"How did you know leaving Monique and forgiving Aaron was?"

Another tongue click. "Touché, asshole."

I smile. Really, how do any of us know what's right? It's not as if life is like math—where one plus one will always equal two. Life is random and crazy. Sometimes in life, you can add one and one together and end up with thirty-two.

I look at my best friend. She's chewing her thumbnail, staring at the wall. Her eyes are a little glossy, and in them, I see a slither of fear.

"Day? Are you getting cold feet?"

She drops her hand. "Yes. No. I don't know."

I tuck my feet beneath me.

"It all seemed easy, you know? Leaving Monique and my life behind. Giving him everything, moving in, saying yes. Now, the wedding is in like, seven weeks and I'm crapping myself. Seriously, I need a diaper on hand at all times." She runs her hand through her hair. "I love him so much, but I guess it's dawning on me that, when I walk down the aisle and say, 'I do,' that's it. Forever. Done. And that's scary."

"You know weddings are bullshit, right?" I say after a moment. "You know they're just a shitty little scrap of paper that tells the state of Washington that you're in it for life? That they don't really mean anything."

She turns her face toward me.

"You weren't afraid until now. You always knew you'd spend your life with him, even when you didn't. The wedding is just the official crap." I rest my hand on her shoulder. "I'm the runner. I'm the freaker-outter and the commitment-phobe. Buck up, sweetie, because there ain't enough room in this friendship for two of us!"

Her lips crack into a smile, and she laughs. "Too true. Yet here you are, in one of those scary relationship things."

"I'm all for trying new things." I shrug nonchalantly. "If I can be in one of these crazy commitment situations, you sure as hell can. Besides, that dress is way too pretty to freak out."

Her eyes brighten at the mention of her dress. "Yes. I suppose. I don't know—I was just having a moment. See what I mean about the hormones? They're like evil little douchebags."

"They've been that way since you were thirteen. I don't know why you're so surprised."

She rolls her eyes. "Did you plan the bachelorette party yet?"

I smile wryly. "And we're back to normal."

She smacks me in the face with a pillow, and I grab the phone to call the spa I spoke to the other day.

I pull the navy thong up my legs with an odd sense of calm. In the week since our relationship became real, this is the first time it's felt like us. It's the first time his expectations have been truly hanging over me.

I prefer this. This controlled interaction, where I know exactly what he wants and exactly what I have to give. It's clear-cut. I can breathe this way, with his desires and demands laid out in front of me.

My phone buzzes on the counter and I pick it up. Before I can answer, Tyler says, "Wear a dress."

"I'm sorry?"

"Wear a dress," he repeats. "Something easy to lift."

That husky undertone I love is prevalent in his voice, and I find myself nodding. I set the call to speaker and lay my phone back on the counter, crossing to my closet. I pull out a black dress with a plunging neckline and tug it over my head.

"And stockings. Black ones."

I swallow and open the drawer. My words are caught in my throat, but I get the feeling that he doesn't want me to talk. He just wants me to do.

The bed creaks as I perch on the end of it and roll the silky stockings up my legs.

"Good girl. Leave your hair down. You have two minutes to get some shoes on and meet me outside."

The line cuts out with those words, and my eyes widen. *Two minutes?*

"Way to give a girl some warning, asshole," I mutter, simultaneously brushing my hair and sliding my feet into some heels.

I run another layer of pink gloss across my lips, and after double-checking that my MIA cat has food in his bowl, I lock the apartment. Damn cat has been out somewhere for three days, probably humping a bunch of lady-cats in a desperate attempt for baby Anguses. Unfortunately for him, his balls are as MIA as he is right now.

Tyler's Mercedes is out in front of the building, the engine purring quietly in the waning light. He leans over and opens the door for me. As I slide onto the passenger's seat, he shoots me a panty-wetting smile.

Oh yeah. He means business tonight.

He reaches over and runs his hand up the inside of my thigh. His fingers tease the material of my dress until it's at my hip and the string of my thong is visible.

"Right on time and dressed perfectly." He runs his thumb along the skin between my hips. My breath catches when he dips it down between my legs and presses it against my clit.

The simple action sends a jolt through my body, and I grab his wrist. Tyler covers my hand with his own, pries my fingers from him, and links our fingers. He brings our clasped hands to the side of my neck and leans toward me, pulling me to him at the same time, and closes the distance between us.

He nibbles my bottom lip, nipping and sucking alternatively, each gentle motion making me ache beneath his hand still firmly wedged between my legs.

At my neck, he curls his fingers around me, drawing me closer. At my pussy, he rubs my clit in tiny, gentle circles, contributing to the light throb there. My stomach muscles tighten and I gasp, pulling away.

"Tyler, we can't—"

With a forceful shove, he pulls my face to his and silences me. He pushes harder at my clit, and with the steadiness of his grip on the back of my head, I'm trapped. I'm encased in his hold, unable to do anything but surrender to what he's doing to me on the side of the street.

Anyone could look into his car and know exactly what he's doing. If the jerking of his arm as he rubs me wouldn't give it away, the fact that my dress is up would. But as a wave of heat overcomes me, I realize I don't care.

I'm about to fall apart in downtown Seattle, where anyone could see us, but all I can do is grab Tyler and grind my hips against his hand.

It's quick and intense, the peak of the orgasm coming with a long, drawn-out moan from me.

"Shit. I love that sound," he murmurs against me. He dips his thumb beneath my panties and coats it in my wetness. Bringing his hand up, he rubs it along my lips.

I open my eyes and, in one quick motion, suck his thumb into my mouth, tasting myself on him.

His pupils dilate, his eyes flaring with lust, and his fingers grip me. "Liv, if you know what's good for you, you'll let my thumb go."

I suck hard.

"I can fuck you here. I don't particularly care, but I think it would be rather obvious."

"And that just wasn't?" I ask, releasing his thumb so I can talk.

He trails it down my neck and settles it between my breasts. "If you think that was obvious, you haven't had nearly enough sex in public."

He puts his foot down on the accelerator, finally driving away, and I settle back into my chair.

"It sounds like you have plenty of experience." There's that irrational jealously streak again. Damn. Can't someone tell her that she isn't welcome?

He settles his hand on my thigh again. "I, too, haven't had nearly enough sex in public. I'm not exactly an exhibitionist."

"Right. So the florist wasn't public?"

He smirks at me. "Semipublic."

"Or the boat in Paris?"

"Neither of them was actually sex—like this. But that's beside the point. I don't plan to do these things to you. I just can't help myself."

"That's the excuse a toddler gives when they've raided the cookie jar." I roll my eyes. "Besides, I thought it was dinner before orgasm?"

"It is." He looks at me at the intersection, deadly serious. "That was your starter."

He eyes me across the table. Dark and brooding, his gaze roams over my face, touching every part of it, until it drops and rests against my chest for a long minute. Heat flushes up my body with the intensity of his stare. It's almost as if he's stripping me bare in his mind, and the twitch in his fingers makes me think he's imagining every way he could touch me.

"You're blushing," he whispers, leaning forward.

His words break the spell, and the conversations from the tables around us filter back into my world.

"No, I'm not." I cut into my salmon.

"Yes, you are." He curls his fingers around the stem of his wine glass, the long, flexing motion drawing my eyes there.

"It must be the lighting." I lift the fork to my mouth and seal my mouth around the fish.

His eyes drop to my mouth, and he stills as I slowly withdraw the fork from between my lips.

"The lighting," he muses, his eyes never moving, "seems fine to me."

"It's all perception." I set my cutlery down and pat my mouth with my napkin. Tyler's eyes travel up my face to find mine again. "Don't you think?"

"Perception. It's a funny thing, that." He sits back in his chair. "But I agree. After all, I'm sure we both have different perceptions of how public my balcony is."

I'm still aching from both my earlier orgasm and the promise of more, and his words do nothing to help that anticipation.

"I've never been on it. I can't say."

"Something you'll remedy tonight. I'm sure you'll be happy to offer me your opinion then."

This over-polite conversation is driving me crazy, but at the same time, I can't get enough. Every sentence is flirty without being obvious, every word building a tight tension that coils in my stomach.

"I'd be more than happy to." I take a sip from my wine. "Do your neighbors have balconies?"

"I'm the only one on my floor. It's…convenient." His lips curl at the corners.

"Very much so." Another sip. "And you have quite the uninterrupted view over Elliot Bay. Another convenience?"

"I enjoy waking up to nature on a morning. It's very pleasurable." The inflection on the last word reaches out and grabs hold of me.

"I'd imagine it is."

I sit back while the waiter removes our plates and offers us the dessert menu. Tyler politely declines, instead requesting the bill.

"Tell me." I lean onto the table. "What else do you find pleasurable?"

His jaw ticks, and he reaches out to cup mine. "Beautiful blond women who wear lacy, navy lingerie and do as they're told."

"How convenient," I murmur, turning into his hand. I kiss him palm softly. "Your night seems to be full of conveniences and pleasures, Tyler Stone."

"There's nothing convenient about you, Liv Warren. Pleasurable, yes. Convenient? No. You are far more than a convenience." He hands his card to the waiter without looking at the bill. "However, the way you're about to follow me to my car and allow me to take you home to my balcony is very convenient indeed."

He takes his card, slots it into his wallet, and stands. Then he nods to the waiter and holds out his hand. I lay mine in his and he tugs me up, releasing me immediately to rest his arm around my waist.

I let him lead me from the restaurant without another word. Then he stops, turns me into him, and rests his mouth against my earlobe.

"I despise being that polite to you," he breathes.

"Is that so?"

He taps my ass. "You know it, babe. Fuck the conveniences. You know I'd much rather tell you how I'm going to tie your wrists to the railings on my balcony then bend you over and fuck you from behind."

I swallow, my heart thudding, and run my hands down his stomach. My fingers ghost over his belt until they find his hard cock straining against the confines of his pants. I cup him, squeezing lightly.

"Is that a promise?"

"You bet it is." His voice is tight, needing. "Now move yourself and your pretty little ass inside my car before I bend you over that instead."

Chapter SIX

I GIVE his erection another light squeeze and release him. He follows me to the car. His eyes are burning a hole in my back, and I can feel the heat in his stare. I can feel his promises in the way he slowly rounds the car and sits inside, in the way he takes my hand as he drives away.

I can feel everything he wants and needs tonight.

He wants to make me lose control, to take me into a blacked-out oblivion where nothing matters but us. He wants to work my body and make me lose myself the only way he knows how to.

But every time he does, I crave a little more. Of him. Of his touch. To the point where not touching him for an hour is driving me insane.

Not having his hand around mine or his lips at my neck is unsettling.

I'm already losing control. He doesn't need to fuck me into next week to propel me into oblivion. The guy just needs to exist. Pure and fucking simple.

And I can feel it. Everything slipping away. Control over my addiction. The control I've exercised for so long is now truly disintegrating right beneath my fingers.

"What's your favorite fruit?"

"What?" Tyler glances at me.

I ask again.

"Peaches."

"Vegetable?"

"Uh, I've never thought about it, but I guess it's a carrot?"

"Are you asking me or telling me?"

"Telling you."

I nod once. "Okay. Good."

He doesn't say anything else as we drive, and neither do I. I didn't mean to ask those two questions. They just slipped out. With the thoughts of loss of control come the actions to prove it.

When Tyler kills the engine, I take my hand from his. I get out of the car before he does and walk into the elevator. Then I press the button for his floor and stare at his confused face as the doors shut.

"Liv?"

I lean back against the elevator wall and close my eyes. Back and forth, back and forth, constantly. Never-ending indecision. Never-ending fighting. Never-ending fucking battling the little bitch inside my head who tells me that it's all or nothing.

I wish I could be Tyler.

I wish I could accept and live with my addiction. He doesn't fight at all. He embraces it wholeheartedly. He just gets the hell on with it in a way I can only dream of.

His addiction ignites mine. It sets mine alight with barely a flicker of a flame and stokes it until it's a consuming roar, until every second is about fulfilling the tempting crave that flows through my veins.

Every word, every touch, every kiss. Every single thing he does is bad. But I'm addicted to the bad. I want the bad. I need the bad. I fucking crave the bad.

I fight. He doesn't.

By not fighting, every time he touches me, he destroys me a little.

But I'm far too weak to walk away.

The elevator doors open and he's standing there in front of me, his shirt half untucked, his eyes dark, his chest heaving. He reaches forward and grabs my wrist. He tugs me from the elevator, the sound of his labored breathing filling the lobby.

The buzz from his fingers wrapped at my wrist spreads up my arm. Goose bumps follow it, coating my skin as he pulls me into his apartment. Then he releases me, leaving me cold and alone in the hallway.

My eyes follow him as he walk into the kitchen. They follow him as he reaches into two cupboards and pulls out a glass and a bottle of whisky. I watch as he pours two fingers of the amber liquid into the glass and tips it back in one go.

I hide my flinch as the glass hits the countertop in a deafening crash.

"You drive me crazy. And not always in a good way." Tyler's voice carries through his apartment, echoing through the silence. "A relationship. We said we'd make it work. I'm trying, Liv. I'm trying so fucking hard, but you keep changing your mind. One minute, you're hot. Then you're cold."

I draw in a deep breath because he's right. It's true. I'm all over him one minute then nowhere near him the next. But if he could see inside my head, remember what I do, fear what I do, then maybe it would make sense.

Maybe it would make sense if I could put my weaknesses into words.

"What is it, Liv? What the hell do you want? Because you better start making your fucking mind up before I make it for you." He turns and his eyes bore into mine, the city lights seeping in through the windows, reflecting off the shadows of his gaze. "What do you want?"

I drop my purse and slowly walk to him. My heels click against the marble kitchen floor, each clack strengthening my resolve.

I stop an inch away from him and look up at him. The shadows play across his face, making the intensity of his expression scary and alluring at the same time.

Slowly, I reach down to the hemline of my dress, and crossing my arms, I pull it up and over my head.

His eyes never leave mine. Through every one of my movements, they are fixated wholly on my gaze.

I reach forward and undo the buttons of his shirt one by one. I tease the material until it's completely free from his pants and step back, bringing him with me.

"You," I answer, opening the balcony doors with one hand. "I want you, Ty. Every second of every day. If you knew how much, if you could see into the insanity inside my mind, you might have a chance at understanding."

"Then let me see," he whispers, reaching his hand toward my face.

I block him. "But I have to have you on your terms. That's the problem. You're giving me everything, but you're not letting me take what I need."

"I don't understand."

The chill of the night air ghosts across my bare skin. I drop my hands to his pants and undo his belt then the button. I push him back a step then yank the material down. It pools at his ankles.

"Sometimes, I need you on my terms." I ease my fingers beneath the waistband of his pants and slowly push them down, bending as I guide them over his legs. "And sometimes, you have to let me have you that way."

He's still hard, and his cock jerks when I wrap my hand around him.

"Liv." He hisses my name from between his teeth.

I ignore him and press my lips to the head of his dick. I flick my tongue out, tasting a small drop of come, before I take him in my mouth fully. I glide my lips across his smooth skin and run my tongue over the vein throbbing at the side of his shaft. My movements are slow and deep, my fingers firmly wrapped around the base of him, my tongue drawing swirling movements across his hardness.

He dives his hands into my hair, tangling my loose locks hard around his fingers. The sting radiates across my scalp and makes my eyes water, but I welcome it.

I welcome the physical pain to block out the emotional.

My free hand finds his hip and my fingers dig into his hot skin as I grip him tight. His hips jerk, his cock hitting the back of throat. I fight my gag at the sudden intrusion and open my mouth wider, move faster, take him deeper.

I suck him harder, working the base of his cock with my hand, making sure no part of his erection is untouched by me.

My name is falling from his lips in pleasured yet tortured groans. The repetitive sounds are crawling over my skin, warming me, almost fueling my movements.

Because right now it isn't about him.

This is about me.

This is about me giving him something but not really letting him take anything from it.

Because I need him to lose control. I need *him* to find that blissful, fucking blinding oblivion. I need him to lose himself, forget his own name.

I need him to surrender to me.

"Liv. Shit, Liv!" He swells in my mouth and tries to pull me away.

I dig my nails into his hip, suck hard, and make my message clear. It's as if a switch flips in his mind and his hips take a pace and rhythm of their own.

He fucks my mouth hard. My teeth graze his skin. He groans my name. My eyes burn.

He pushes my head forward at the exact moment that his hot, salty come spurts into my mouth. I seal my lips around him and swallow it, wincing at the vile taste. *Shit.*

When he stills, I release his cock and kiss his thigh. His hip. His lower stomach.

He runs his fingers through my hair and pulls me up, flattening me against his body. His hands run across my back and down to my ass. His fingers brush my pussy, and I shake my head.

"No," I whisper.

He stills for the second time in as many minutes. "No?"

"No," I repeat, my voice still quiet.

His chest rises forcefully with his deep breath. It lowers slowly after a moment, and I expect him to push it. I expect him to try and tease me into letting him do what he wants, but he doesn't.

"Okay," he replies just as quietly and slides his shoes off with his feet. He steps out of his pants and underwear. "Bedtime." He kisses the spot beneath my ear and grabs my thighs, lifting me up.

I wrap my legs around his waist and my arms around his neck. I bury my face against him, a slither of control sneaking through my veins.

I feel guilty—for forcing him to my will then denying him his.

But I also feel stronger.

And very, very fucked up.

Tyler literally drops us onto the bed and I shriek.

"Fuck! That was my ear, you bitch!" He jolts away, clapping his hand over his ear.

I laugh. "Oops."

He stares at me for a moment like he can't decide if he's done telling me off or if he's going to laugh at me. He does neither. In the end, he grins, lies next to me, and yanks me to him.

I rest my head against his chest, feeling the steady beat of his heart beneath my cheek. "You didn't take your socks off."

"You didn't take your knickers off. I say it's fair." He kisses my forehead and sighs deeply.

Okay. I'm not going to reply. I'm going to lie here, fall asleep, and pretend I didn't just give him a blow job for entirely selfish reasons.

"Tyler Stone, one of these days, I'm going to bloody well kill your useless arse!"

My eyes widen.

"Shit!" Tyler snaps, slapping his hand over his face. He yawns and heaves himself out of bed. "Shit. Sorry!" he yells. "Hang on!"

"Um." I push myself up to sitting.

"That would be my sister." He pulls some jeans on, totally forgetting his underwear, and rubs his eyes.

"I thought she wasn't supposed to be here for another three days?" I whisper angrily.

"Shit. Me too." He opens his bedroom door and slips out. "Tessa! You're not supposed to be here."

"Thursday, dickhead!" a very British accent replies.

"You told me Sunday!"

"Where the bloody hell did you get Sunday from? Honestly, Tyler. You're like a child. Sun-hun-day," she says, enunciating each sound. "I had to call Aaron to get him to get me collected from the airport because you weren't there and you wouldn't answer your phone."

"I guess he gave you his spare key," Tyler groans.

"No, I'm an expert lock picker. Of course he did." The door slamming follows her words. "What are you doing anyway? Why didn't you answer your phone?"

"I'm not alone," he says flatly.

"You're not—oh! Oh, bollocks!"

Oh, bollocks indeed. I'm apparently about to meet Tyler's sister and the only clean item of clothing I have is panties.

Fanfuckingtastic.

"Mm," Tyler says. "Give me a minute." He walks back through the door and closes it behind him. He leans against it and covers his eyes with his hand. "Shit.

I am so sorry. I swear she said Sunday."

"It's okay," I squeak out.

No. It's not. It's not fucking okay. Not at all. I am not ready to meet any of his family I don't already know.

Shit. No. No. No.

Can I climb out of the window? Scale down the wall a la Spiderman?

"Then why do you look like you just saw a ghost?"

"I'm thinking how lovely it is that I get to meet her?" I offer lamely.

He walks to the bed and bends in front of me. His palms are soft as he lays them on either side of my cheeks. "I know you're not ready for this yet. I don't expect you go out there and be best mates with her. I can take her for breakfast so you can leave."

"Who said I'm not ready?"

The lead weight in my stomach, perhaps? The erratic beat of my heart, maybe?

The panic written all over my motherfucking face?

"I can see it in your eyes, baby girl. You look like you're about to shit a brick."

My lips twitch in a mirror of his. "Okay. I'm a little freaked out. A lot freaked out."

He raises his eyebrows.

"Freaking the fucking hell out," I admit. "Like, look." I lift my hand so he can see the tremble there. "This is…big. Like. Yeah. Um."

"I'll take her for breakfast." He kisses me softly.

I shake my head. "That's so rude, Tyler! I have to meet her. It's not that I don't want to. I'm just a little afraid."

"She won't bite, I promise. I got that trait." He stands and winks with a wolfish grin spreading across his face. "There's no need to be afraid."

Maybe not for him. Maybe meeting the family isn't a big freaking deal for Mr. Addicted To Sex. For me? It's huge. Massive.

"Liv? What is it?"

"Aside from the fact that I have no clean clothes?"

He holds up a finger, opens a drawer, then throws a pair of jeans and a shirt at me. I raise my eyebrows and he shrugs.

"Don't ask. Now what is it?"

I look down, fiddling with the tag on the pants, and say softly, "I'm afraid to meet her because it's another part of you I could love."

"Hey." He bends over and tilts my face back up. "No worries. I'm way more lovable than Tessa."

I take a deep breath and smile at him. "You're such a twat."

His lips curve into a grin. "What can I say? You bring it out in me. Now stop fussing and get dressed woman."

I raise my eyebrows.

"And you better believe that's the only time you'll ever hear me say those bloody words to you."

I laugh into my hand and take my clean panties from him. I note that they're not the ones I left before. What the hell has he been up to? And why did I not know that there are brand-new clothes in his apartment that happen to fit me perfectly?

Why are they here?

I close my eyes briefly, shove those thoughts to the back of my mind, and swing my legs out of bed. I'm half dressed when I hear, "Tyler! Why are your trousers on your balcony?"

Blood rushes to my cheeks. *Holy fuck!*

Tyler bursts into laughter. There isn't a trace of embarrassment on his face, but mine is flaming.

"I gave the old bird in the opposite block a striptease last night!" he yells, winking at me.

Holy nononono*no*!

"I've changed my mind," I breathe. "You can take her for breakfast!"

He looks at me, still laughing. He moves quickly, tugging me toward him, and presses his lips against mine. His teeth graze across my bottom lip as he pulls away.

"C'mon. Time to face the music, little exhibitionist."

"It was your idea," I murmur, trotting behind him. I hope I'm not still blushing.

"Yeah, well," his sister says, "they're soaking wet because it rained last night."

"So you can dry them. You're not staying here for free."

"I'm not picking up your shit. I'm your *older* sister, not your slave, you messy git."

I hide my laughter behind my hand, and Tyler looks at me. I shrug. "You are messy."

He clicks his tongue. "I can see the next three weeks are going to be fun," he says dryly. "Tessa, this is Liv. Liv, my sister."

"And who is Liv?" Tessa asks, grinning.

"Tess."

"Ty."

I chew the inside of my lip.

"Tessa, this is my girlfriend."

She smiles widely and bounds forward to hug me. *Oh, wow. Okay.* Apparently these two are huggers.

"I'm so glad to finally meet you!" She squeezes me then pulls back, holding me at arm's length. "You're gorgeous! Gosh, Ty. She is gorgeous."

Now I'm definitely blushing.

"Tessa. Shut up. Not everyone has word vomit like you." Tyler knocks her arms down.

"Oh, shit. I'm so sorry. I kind of did the same thing to Dayton last year. She looked at me like I had two heads," Tessa muses. "I thought we were supposed to be the reserved ones, hmm? You guys are all shy and stuff."

"Um," I say. *Way to make an impression, Liv. Good job, you fucking star.*

I sigh internally.

Seriously though. How am I supposed to respond to that? '*Thank you?*' I'm not even sure who she's calling gorgeous.

She's fucking stunning.

She's the spitting image of Tyler, just oh so feminine. Her nose is tinier, her lips plumper, her eyes wider, her hair curlier.

The Stone family is so unfairly blessed with good genes.

I kind of hate them all.

"I'm sorry. I am kind of overwhelming sometimes." Tessa smiles apologetically. "And I'm really sorry for barging in here like this. I didn't realize Tyler wasn't alone. In fact, I didn't realize he was here at all." She shoots him a glare.

I can tell by his sigh that he's rolling his eyes.

"Jesus, Tessa. I thought you said Sunday. Ever heard of calling ahead to confirm?"

"In my defense, bro, you don't usually have company the next morning."

Tyler stops, rests a hand against the countertop, and rubs his forehead.

Tessa snaps her head toward me with wide eyes. "No offense. Crap. I think I'm jet-lagged. I'm sorry."

"No worries," I offer.

"Okay." Tyler turns and hands her a cup of tea. "You drink this, replace your brain-to-mouth filter, then for the love of my sanity, and go to fucking bed. The spare room is made up for you. I'll take you out for dinner tonight."

"Okay." Tessa meekly takes the tea. "Really, I'm sorry."

"It's okay, honestly." I give her a genuine smile. She's so fucking adorable.

"Sure. Right. Okay. Going now." She waves goofily and turns off to the left.

"To the right. Third door!" Tyler yells, shaking his head.

"Fuck you very much!" she shouts back, making an about-turn in the hall.

I watch the mini exchange with a smile slowly spreading across my face. These two are like bread and butter and chalk and cheese. It's incredible to see. So alike but so different.

I also get why he's so protective her. She looks so innocent, so freakin' *cute,* but her personality totally makes up for it.

I mean…*wow.*

Tyler runs his tongue across his teeth with a grin. "I need some ibuprofen already."

I laugh and wrap my arms around his waist. An uncontrollable urge to just hold him is coming over me. A scary, enticing urge I simultaneously want to fulfill and fight.

His arms circle me tightly and he breathes me in deeply. "See? That wasn't so bad."

"Yet. I think I'm already kind of in love with her," I tease.

"Oi!" He nuzzles my cheek. "You don't get to fall in love with her first. I'll have to withhold all spankings if that happens."

"That's quite the threat."

"Mhmm. In fact, I'm pretty sure you're not allowed to love anyone other than me. Ever."

"I never said I did love you." Wow, this is awkward.

"Does it matter? You're still not allowed."

"What if I never love you?"

"Then you best hope Angus lives another fifty years, 'cause you're totally fucked, babe."

I smack his ass. "Bastard."

He pulls back and grins. "Breakfast?"

"If you're paying."

He lets me go, sighs dramatically, then passes me my heels. *At least they match the shirt.*

"If it's not my mouth, it's my food. If it's not my food, it's my money."

My lips curve and I rest my hand on his chest. "And if it's not your money, it's your cock. I guess that's what you get for being so goddamn irresistible, Tyler Stone."

He runs a hand through his hair and closes the door behind us. "I try, baby girl. I try."

Unnecessarily, I want to add.

The guy would be irresistible wearing an Olaf costume.

Chapter SEVEN

I SLIDE two pints across the bar and take the offered ten-dollar bill. I ring the order up on the register then hand the guy back his change with a smile. He nods in response and grabs his drinks.

Old Dill waves his glass from the end of the bar. I make my way down to his end and grab his glass.

"It isn't gonna be the same around here without you, Liv," he says, watching as I pull his pint.

"Don't be silly. I've only been here a few months. Give it a few weeks and you'll forget all about me." I wink and set the full glass down in front of him.

He hands me a twenty, and I raise my eyebrows.

"What's this? Spoiling me by paying cash on my last day?" I tease.

He laughs. "Don't tell Donny. He'll expect it every fuckin' day."

I laugh and ring it up. I set his change on the bar next to his glass and lean against it. "I might actually miss this place, you know."

"Of course you will. What's the name of the place you're managing?"

"Crimson Lounge."

"Sounds fancy."

"Aaron Stone is the owner. What do you expect?"

Dill whistles low. "In there with the big boys."

I laugh. "Perks of having a best friend who fucks the guy in charge." I wink and move to serve a couple halfway down the bar.

I regretfully tell them that we don't serve food when they ask and get them two glasses of Pinot and two bags of chips instead. Hey, they must really need a drink.

"So how fancy is this fancy bar?" Dill asks when I return to him.

I open the glass dishwasher and wave the steam away. "Cocktail-shaking men," I answer. "VIP area. Dress code. Opening night is invite-only."

He whistles again. "And you're going to manage that?"

"Right?" I raise my eyebrows. "I can't even paint my friggin' nails without them looking like a toddler tried it. Now, I'm going to manage a place like that. Moving up in the world." I wink.

"How about that there modeling? Seems like you were busy a couple weeks back."

I inwardly wince. Despite Tyler's proclamation that I got the Balfour campaign, I still haven't spoken to Sheila about it. In fact, we haven't spoken for a week—and it's not like I can call her.

Can you imagine? "Hey, Sheila. I heard I got the Balfour campaign from the photographer I'm fucking. Thanks for reintroducing us on that Victoria's Secret shoot that totally failed, by the way. Mind? Blown."

Yeah.

No.

"Waiting to hear back on a couple of things," I tell Dill evasively. Hey, it's not a lie. Technically, I am.

"Well, I hope they see sense and get your pretty face up on them boards." He tilts his pint toward me.

"Hitting on my woman, Dill?" Tyler slides onto the stool next to him.

I can't help my smile. It's automatic at the sight of him. Much like the butterflies in my tummy whenever I hear his voice.

"Wouldn't dream of it, son!" Dill laughs and slaps the bar. "Tried it more than once and she put me right in my place. Didn't ya, Liv?"

"If only I were thirty years older." I wink.

"Hey now." Tyler holds his hands up. "Don't let me interrupt."

I laugh. "Shut up. Aren't you supposed to be taking your sister for dinner?"

"Yeah," Tessa says over his shoulder. She sits next to him. "Do you know his idea of dinner is Mc-fucking-Donald's?"

I chew the inside of my cheek and nod. "Um, yes."

"Hey, y'all want me to buy you dinner all the time, you gotta take the cheap stuff."

I stare at Tyler flatly. "Honey, we aren't in Texas. Tuck your *y'alls* away and don't bring them out again until you dress up as Woody from Toy Story for Halloween, okay?"

Dill laughs loudly. "Hell, I'm gonna miss you, girl."

"Is this a Liv Love Fest? I want in!" Rosie cries, squeezing me tight.

"Holy…crap!" I squeak. "I'm only moving to a bar two blocks away. Y'all are acting like I'm moving to Australia."

"Why the hell can you say y'all and I can't?" Tyler demands.

"I'm American." I shrug. "You're British. Don't be thinking you can come over here and start talking like one of us." I grin.

The look in his eyes says that I'm going to pay for that.

I'm pretty sure the look in mine says that I'm going to enjoy every damn second of it.

The clock ticks to seven p.m., signaling the end of my final shift at the Stag, and I hug Rosie tight. We go through a round of, "I'll miss you. I'll miss you, too. Come see me, okay? Don't forget me. We'll meet for a drink."

I'm almost certain we'll never see each other again or get that drink. That's the thing with moving on—you take almost nothing with you when you go. The only things you do take are the things that really matter. And more often than not, that doesn't include people.

Tyler takes my hand and leads me from the bar with Tessa on my heels. We walk for a block in silence before coming to a small wine bar. Tyler's phone rings just before we enter, and he waves for us to go in.

"What do you drink?" Tessa asks, leaning against the bar. Almost every guy in the place stares at her, but she's oblivious.

"If it's wine, I'll drink it," I answer honestly.

She beams and turns to the barman.

I wonder if she's jaded by her husband cheating on her. I wonder if it's destroyed her in any way… If she's sworn off love or relationships. She doesn't seem like it. She seems perfectly happy, like it wasn't just weeks ago that she was calling Tyler to tell her what she'd seen.

What if I were her? What if it were Tyler cheating on me?

Oh, god.

I feel sick.

That wouldn't happen. I know it wouldn't.

I hope it wouldn't.

Holy shit.

I'm actually going to vomit.

"Liv? Are you okay?" Tessa's sharp accent brings me back to now.

I grab a glass and take a big mouthful of wine. "I am now."

Note to self: never imagine that again.

I follow her to a table by the window. My heart pangs as I remember how Day and I used to do this all the time—once or twice a week at least. I almost feel like I'm cheating on her by sitting here with Tessa.

Holy heck. Fuck the glass. I need the bottle of wine.

"Are you okay?" Tessa asks.

"Fine." I smile. "Fine. I guess I was wondering… Shit, this is awkward."

Tessa laughs.

"You seem happier than I'd thought you'd be," I blurt out.

Well, that's one way to put it.

She laughs again. "Oh." She shrugs a shoulder. "I can't change my situation. I don't want to be getting divorced less than a year since I walked down the aisle, but equally, I respect myself far too much to be in a marriage where I'm treated like I'm not worth the mat he wipes his shitty hunting boots on."

"I get that. I just didn't expect you to be so…bubbly."

"Do you want the truth, Liv?" She twists her glass. "I don't know if I ever loved him. Maybe I only thought I did. I'm certainly not heartbroken, and I'm not numb. I just feel…indifferent. And sorry for the poor bitch he was fucking on my sofa."

Well, that's one way to put it.

"Either way," she continues, "I'm taking his sorry, cheating ass to the dry cleaners and I'm going to wring it out until he's got friction burns on his dick."

I clap my hand over my mouth to prevent myself from spitting out my wine. Yep. The British are definitely not reserved. In the slightest.

Tyler enters the bar and takes the seat next to me. He rests his hand on my lower back and splays his fingers. His pinkie finger creeps beneath the hem of my lower shirt to my bare skin, and I fight a shiver.

"Okay?" Tessa asks him.

"Yep." He nods once and grabs my wine glass.

I raise my eyebrows. He grins in response and tilts the glass for another mouthful.

"I suppose I should be polite and ask how the business is," Tyler says.

Tessa snorts. "That's dinner conversation."

"And since you spent dinner bitching at me, I'm asking now."

"McDonald's isn't dinner," she says, repeating her words from earlier. "Never mind…" She launches into a description of how their parents' restaurants and hotels are running in the UK.

I tune out after a few minutes. They continue their conversation regardless, both of them fully versed in something I know nothing about. I can pour a pint and mix a margarita like a pro, but I couldn't tell you how to run a huge business.

Instead of listening to their words, I listen to them. I observe the way they are together, how they talk, their body language. It's a conscious move. I know I'm doing it as much as I know I shouldn't be.

Adding Tessa into the mix is dangerous. She brings out a protective side of Tyler that I haven't truly experienced yet. He's turned toward her as she talks, but his eyes flick over her shoulders now and then, warning off any man who so much as breathes in her direction. She only has part of his attention as he strives to keep her from anyone who could put her through pain.

And it's endearing. They bitch like cat and dog, but they care about each other so obviously. I can see how much he loves her—she's an extension of him, almost literally.

I'm also jealous.

It's stupid. But I see the way his lips curve as they talk, the way his eyes smile when she makes him laugh, and I want it.

I want him to smile whenever he looks at me and I want his eyes to laugh when I'm an idiot and I want to feel the strength of the love he has for her directed at me.

Do I want him to love me?

It burns. That question burns so harshly in my mind. Mostly because I already know the answer.

Yes.

I want Tyler Stone to fall in love with me. I want him to fall so far that there'll be no chance of him ever getting back up.

More than that, I need him to. I crave the idea of him loving me. I want to know that his skin buzzes at my touch. That my kiss ignites a fire inside him. That my voice is a soother to him. That being without me for even twenty-four hours is a completely inconceivable idea.

Because I'm there. I'm teetering on the edge of the fall.

"Liv?" Tyler says softly.

I look at him. "Hm?"

"Are you okay? You've been staring at your empty glass for the last five minutes."

Oops. "Yeah. I'm just tired." I offer a small smile, and right on cue, I yawn.

"Do you want to leave?" He turns in his chair and runs his fingers through my hair.

"I think I should head home, yeah." I catch his hand and kiss his wrist. Savor the sensation of his pulse pounding beneath my lips. Imagine that it's beating wholly for me.

"Want me to come with you?" He leans in, his mouth hovering just in front of mine.

I never want you to leave. I want you to stay always.

I take a deep breath. "It's okay. You stay with your sister."

"Are you sure?" He pulls back, questions in his eyes.

Yeah. It wasn't exactly what I planned to say either, but somehow, I know this is right. I need to be alone tonight.

"Yes." I rest my hand against his cheek. The slight stubble lining his jaw scratches against my wrist, and shit. I want to rub my fingertips along it the way my cat rubs against my sofa.

"Okay." He sounds put out. Is it because he wants to come? Because he was hoping I'd say yes?

I pull his face toward mine and press our lips together. The sauvignon lingers on his lips, dry and fruity, and I flick my tongue against his bottom lip to taste it more. To taste him. So that, when I lick my lips before bed, he'll still be there.

"I'll walk to you to your car," he whispers.

"It's okay."

"No. I'm walking you to your car." He gets off the chair and takes me with him. His tone and gaze both tell me that he's not arguing.

I guess he's walking me to my car.

He explains to Tessa where we're going and she nods from the bar, waving goodbye to me. I barely have time to lift my hand in response before Tyler pulls me outside. His fingers slide between mine in a grip that may as well be made of iron. Hard. Sturdy. Unrelenting.

The sounds of the city waft around us, neither of us talking. It's an odd kind of silence zinging between us—it's comfortably awkward. Like we both know what needs to be said but neither of us is willing to say it.

Is he thinking the same thing I am?

Is he thinking that maybe he's falling in love?

Is he just as afraid? Just as apprehensive?

We stop next to my car. Tyler pauses for a moment, his eyes colliding with mine, then pulls me into him. I can barely comprehend his movements right now. Our lips fuse together in a desperate crash full of begs and pleas, full of promises.

If only I knew what we were promising.

Because every touch makes it harder than before.

I wind his hair around my fingers and hold him close. Hold him completely to me, so tight that you'd have to pry my clenched limbs away from him.

With every brush of his lips, I know that this kiss is different. This kiss isn't sexual or teasing. It's full of emotion, full of pureness.

Of needing.

Of craving.

Of addiction.

"Sleep tight," he whispers, ghosting his lips across mine one last time.

"I'll try," I whisper back.

Who am I kidding? I won't sleep tonight. I'll toss and turn all night long, my skin cold without his touch and my body begging for his oblivion.

I watch him for a moment as he walks down the sidewalk, back to the bar. "Ty?"

He stops, turns, shoves his hands in his pocket. "Baby girl?"

My throat constricts. "Why do you have clothes that fit me? With the tags on? In your apartment?"

His lips twitch, and slowly, they curve at the corners. "Because I live in hope."

"Of what?"

"That, one day, you and I will be able to be honest with ourselves…and each other."

Without another word, he spins again and carries on walking.

"Are you telling me in an ass-fucked way that you love me?" I whisper entirely to myself, watching him as he goes.

His words are heavy. Lead weights, they settle low in my stomach, making me want to be sick.

No.

He can't love me.

Chapter EIGHT

I OPEN the front door and stare at the tabby cat that strolls past my feet like he's only been gone for an hour.

"Well, hello, you dirty little tramp. Where have you been?"

Angus looks at me for a moment before deciding that his empty food bowl is far more worthy of his attention. He meanders to it and sits right in front of it, looking at it forlornly. When I don't immediately fill it, he turns big, brown eyes on me and stares at me.

"What? You think you can disappear on me for a few days then come back in here one morning demanding food like you own the place?"

He blinks.

"You are such a male. I knew I should have gotten a female kitty." I huff, stomp across the kitchen, and grab a can of food. I dump it carelessly in the bowl and leave the empty can on the counter.

My phone rings loudly from the sofa and I leap across the apartment to grab it. "Hello?"

"Liv?" My agent's voice comes through the line.

"Hi."

"Hi. I have great news! You got the Balfour campaign! You have to be in Mexico in two weeks!"

Holyshititwasn'tajoke.

"Holy shit!" I clap my hand over my mouth. "Sorry. Shit. Oh, shit!"

Sheila laughs. "I'm getting final details now. I will call you when I have them. Then you can come down to the office to look at everything. Okay, I have to go. It's crazy here. Just wanted to let you know. Bye, honey!"

The line goes dead and I stare at my phone.

I have no idea what I'm supposed to do now. So I do what I'm not supposed to do and grab my car keys.

As I run down the stairs and jump into my car, I question my decision to go to Tyler before my best friend. Not that it makes the slightest bit of difference because I'm already driving to his apartment. My body is controlling in place of my mind.

I park outside his apartment block and take the elevator up. My heart is pounding, but I can't decipher between the thump of excitement and the thump from Tyler.

I think they are one and the same.

I knock on his door three times, but when it opens, it isn't him.

"Oh, Liv! Hi!" Tessa chirps. "If you're looking for Ty, he's on an early shoot. Said he'll be back around ten. I'm going to get breakfast since he's left me absolutely nothing. Did you want to come?"

Wow. Word vomit indeed.

"Oh, it's okay. I'll just wait here. I already ate," I add as an explanation.

"Are you sure?"

"Yeah, I'll be fine. Thanks for the offer though." I smile, which she returns as she bounces past me.

I walk into his apartment and close the door behind me.

I've never actually been here alone, I quickly realize. He's always been with me. And right now, with his words about hope and honesty whispering in the back of my mind, my feet guide me toward his room.

It's not snooping if you know it's there.

Right?

I move to the dresser he pulled my clothes from yesterday and open the drawers. There are a couple of sets of underwear in the top drawer. Nice underwear, I notice. Expensive underwear. More-than-my-monthly-paycheck kind of underwear.

I chew the inside of my lip. So much for not spending his money. Opening the second drawer, I see a couple of pairs of jeans. The tags are still on these, too, and he sure as hell didn't buy these from Forever 21.

My eyes flick to one of the prices. *Hell.* Definitely not a Forever 21 item.

I'm almost afraid to look at the next drawer, but curiosity gets the better of me and I pull it open. A few shirts, sweaters, all tagged and priced still.

I do note that there are no pajamas. Of course there wouldn't be.

I close the drawer, feeling a little sick from the cost of those items. I'm still wondering what he's hoping for, really. That, one day, I'll turn up naked and need the clothes to go home?

I laugh to myself. How ridiculous.

But I wonder…

I pull open the closet door and look inside. On one side, there are sweaters and shirts hanging. There are smart dinner jackets, perfectly pressed, and smart pants without a crease in sight. I raise my eyebrows. *Tyler Stone, I am impressed.*

Shoes are neatly lined up on the shelf that runs above the clothes rail. Sneakers, dress shoes, sandals, flip-flops. Everything. And not all as cheap as he said before, I think, noticing some Armani jeans.

Levi's over Armani my left ass cheek.

On the other side, there are a handful of dresses. All my size. All tagged. All brand freaking new. I'm almost afraid to look up, but I do. Shoes to match them—and the underwear in the drawer.

I draw in a long, shaky breath and slowly walk backward.

I won't lie. It's thrilling. There are little happy jolts bursting through my veins.

If he has things here, he wants me here. He could be falling for me. He could actually want to love me. He could really, really need me.

It's scary. Thrilling and scary and exciting. That there could be someone who has the ability to love me as much as I could them, to be as addicted as I am… It's the best and the worst thing in my world.

All I really want is someone who is as addicted and consumed by me as I am by them.

All I really want is Tyler to crave me like I crave him.

And this helps. Despite the red flags, the panic boiling in my stomach, I fucking love looking in this closet and those drawers and seeing things for me.

I sit on his bed and run my hands along the softness of his sheets. He's out right now working—taking photos of someone who is probably a hotshot, gorgeous model with teeth whiter than the Ice Queen's and curves that would make Madonna cry. But he has things for me in his apartment.

Me.

I cover my face with my hands. *Deep breaths, Liv.* My fingers are twitching with the need to explore more. I need to pull open all the drawers and know more, see more, feel more about this man.

I spy the nightstand. I've looked in the drawers before. *It's not snooping if you know what's there,* I tell myself again. *It's just…remembering. Right?*

I slowly pull open the middle drawer. Three kinds of lube. Condoms. The bullet… My body flushes. Holy hell, that bullet. That delightful little bullet.

I shut the drawer and open the bottom one. Last time, he surprised me with handcuffs, and *is that a fucking vibrator?*

My eyebrows shoot up. A laugh bubbles inside me and I clap my hand over my mouth. Fucking hell. I reach in and grab it. I run my finger down the bright-purple, rubbery…shaft. Can you call it a shaft if it's fake and battery operated?

I flick the little finger designed for the clit. And purse my lips, fighting a smile. I lose my fight, and I'm soon giggling.

Oh, bottom nightstand drawer, I dub thee the Drawer of Sexual Surprises.

I'm almost afraid to look in here ever again. Ever. Again.

A glint of silver catches my eye and I pick up the… Oh, well, apparently, he took my joke about chains seriously. I hold up the short chain, just thick enough to restrain my wrists, and stare at it.

My eyes flick to the vibrator and I look at that, too.

My gaze jolts between them. Chains. Vibrator.

I look to his bed.

And close my eyes so I can't see anymore. But that fucks up, too, because now all I can see are images of him chaining my wrists together and sliding the vibrator inside me.

I clench my legs together as the front door opens. And my eyes shoot open. Keys clatter against the side, and Tyler walks into his room before I can shove the things back into his drawer.

We stare at each other for a long moment. His lips twitch, his eyes darkening with a sexy kind of amusement.

"Well, that's a nice sight," he finally says. "Exploring?"

Nice choice of a word. "Um, discovering, too, apparently." I hold the chains out to him. "More fantasies, Tyler Stone?"

He grins and takes them from me. "Not fantasies, Liv. Plans."

Consider me turned. The. Fuck. On.

He sets them on the nightstand and approaches me. Laying his hands on either side of me on the bed, he leans in, smirking. "You keep spoiling my surprises," he murmurs, dropping his lips to my jaw.

"I'm sorry?" I breathe in. I actually am. That's the sad thing.

"How sorry?" His mouth travels along my jawline to my ear.

"Probably not as sorry as you want me to be."

"Good answer." He nudges me back until I'm lying flat on the bed and leans over me. "I'm mad at you, you know."

"What did I do now?"

He flicks his tongue against my neck and it moves downwards in tiny, spiraling circles. "While I appreciate the best blow job of my life and never plan to turn you down ever again, I'm pissed you didn't let me return the favor."

He slides his hand beneath my shirt and pinches my nipple through my bra. I gasp at the rough sensation.

"You weren't supposed to return it," I breathe as he finds the button to my jeans.

"I gathered. Now, though, I'm going to, and I'm going to return it good." He kisses my stomach hotly and tugs my jeans hard. He stands, pulls off my boots and jeans, and gets back onto his knees.

I look down, adrenaline thrumming through my veins as his dark eyes meet mine.

"Spread these legs, beauty," he murmurs, his words vibrating against my skin. He slides his hands up my thighs and parts them slowly. "I'm going to lick your gorgeous pussy until your taste is branded onto my fucking tongue."

And he slips two fingers beneath my panties, moves them to the side, and runs his tongue along me in a long, hard sweep. I gasp. He pins my hips to the bed, his tongue working every bit of my aching core.

His movements are rough and harsh yet so tender at the same time, every nibble followed by a soft lick. Every pressured rub of my clit is followed by a gentle suck, the contradictory feelings and sensations building and climbing…

…and climbing…

…and climbing…

…until they hit their peak and his tongue presses against me and heat floods my body and pleasure stings my eyes and I cry out.

His mouth covers me, his tongue massaging my opening until I'm silent, trembling, gasping.

He replaces my underwear and slides up my body. With a smirk, he closes his lips over mine. I can taste myself on him, but I'm too spent to move, to turn away. So I let him kiss me. Let him spread my own wetness over my lips. Let him kiss me and tease me until I'm aching with the promise of a new orgasm.

Tyler's hands curve beneath my ass and cup it, his fingers curling around it, squeezing. He shifts me up the bed and hooks my legs over his hips. His erection pushes against me, hard and ready. The pressure it's putting on the zipper of his jeans is central to my core and rubs my clit as he leans into me.

I curl my fingers in the soft material of his shirt, ready to lift it up his torso and over his head, and then—

"Ty? Are you here? Liv?"

Tyler drops his forehead against mine and growls. "Fucking hell."

I swallow my giggle. "You invited her to stay with you."

"I'm a stupid twat," he mutters, kissing me hard. "Put your clothes on," he says, getting up.

"Second time in two days? I'm unimpressed, I admit."

He yanks me to standing and shoves my jeans at me. "What can I say? My sister is a giant cock-block."

I smile and perch back on the bed to get dressed. I'm just buttoning my jeans when I hear Tyler say, "I'm moving in with Liv."

"I'm sorry, what?!" I shriek, running out of his room in my socks.

Tessa is staring at us both, her eyes wide. "Wow. That escalated quickly."

"Yeah. No fucking kidding." I'm sure my eyes are as wide as hers.

"Jesus, you're like a pair of bloody Bambis." He shakes his head. "Liv, I'm staying at yours until my sister leaves."

"Um, since when?"

"Since it's clear she's going to interrupt us."

"Tyler!" I gasp.

"Oookay," Tessa laughs out. "Really, Ty, I can stay somewhere else. It's not a big deal. Day offered me her house if I want it."

"No. You're my sister and you'll stay in my apartment. I'll stay with Liv."

She looks at him flatly. "Just so you can get regular sex? Really?"

"Regular, uninterrupted sex," he corrects, boiling the kettle. "I'm not fifteen anymore. It's not like a wank while looking through the pages of Playboy will get me off now."

"I am not having this conversation with you!" She holds up her hands and glances at me. "Okay, I'm going to go to my room and let you two talk because your poor girlfriend looks like she's been hit with a fucking lorry."

She leaves us both in the kitchen. Tyler continues to make his tea, apparently completely oblivious to my staring a hole in the back of his head.

Move in with me?

"Just while she's here," he says. Apparently, I said that out loud.

"I'm not… I'm not sure how I feel about that." I swallow.

No. I know. I don't like it. At all. His things in my apartment?

"You look like you're shitting out a watermelon."

"You're not reassuring me at all, in case you were wondering." I walk into the living room and sit on the sofa. I pull my knees to my chest and wrap my arms around my legs.

Tyler sits next to me and puts his legs on the table in front of us. He takes a sip of his tea before he speaks. "I was actually kidding."

"No, you weren't."

"Okay. I wasn't." He shrugs and puts the mug down. "I just didn't think you'd freak out quite that much. Sex on tap. Can't be that bad."

How am I supposed to say out loud that it's not the sex thing that bothers me, but the fact that he'll be there all the time? In my bathroom. In my shower. On my sofa. At my kitchen table. In my bed. In my parking slot, probably.

Every second of every day. He'll be there. Always.

"Fucking hell," he groans. "By the look on your face, you'd think you didn't want me to be anywhere near you."

I dive my hands into my hair. Where are my words? *Hello, brain-to-mouth filter? Now would be a great time to fuck off.*

"And now I'm thinking I could be right."

"No!" I finally blurt. I look up at him and hate what I see in his eyes. There's a vulnerability there. Hurt. Something that shouldn't be there. "That's not the problem. The problem is that I do want you there. All the time. But that isn't a good idea."

He drops his head back. "One step forward, two steps back."

"Jeez, Ty!" I stand and walk to the window. "We've been dating for, like, ten days."

"And fucking for weeks."

I close my eyes briefly. "Apparently fucking and dating are one and the same for you."

"They are where you're concerned."

Because our relationship is primarily sex, I want to say. *Because it follows your addiction with barely any regard for my own.*

"I'm not having this conversation. I'm not going to argue about this. It's ridiculous." I walk into his room and stuff my feet into my boots. I grab my purse and head toward the door.

"What is it with you and running away?"

"I'm not running away. I'm walking away from a situation I'm not prepared to deal with right now. Like an adult." I put my hand on the door.

"No, you're running. Every time I talk about us, you turn around and you run away from me. Ten minutes ago, you were moaning my fucking name."

"This is me!" I yell. "Okay? This. Is. Me. If you stopped for two seconds and really thought about it, you'd see it. You think I don't want to be around you or be in a serious relationship with you, but you couldn't be further from the truth."

I press my fingers to my temples and fight the sting of tears.

"I want to be around you, Tyler. All the fucking time, I want you next to me because I am so goddamn addicted to you that it hurts when you're not there!"

"Then let me be there!"

"It isn't that simple! I wish it were, but shit, it isn't. Just like your addiction is about you, mine is about me, okay? If I want to keep any semblance of myself, I need time away from you. Otherwise, you will consume me and I won't even be the person you wanted at the start."

Nothing. No words. No reply. No fight back.

I turn the door handle and pull it open.

"There isn't a single day I can think of where I won't want you. Even when you're walking away from me, I want you. And not to fuck you. Not for your body. I want *you.* Because I hurt when you're not there, too. I want you always. I'm as addicted as you are." His words fill the silence.

"You're not allowed to be addicted to me," I whisper as he steps up to me and envelopes me in his arms.

He pushes the door shut with his fingertips. "I've never been very good at doing what I'm told," he says softly into my hair. "Because tell me not to do something and you bet your hot arse I'm going to do it."

"Why do I believe you?" A smile twitches my lips despite the tears rolling down my cheeks.

He smiles against my temple. "Getting addicted to you was never a choice. It was always inevitable. I couldn't resist you if I tried, baby girl. You're my kryptonite."

I drop my purse and wrap my arms around his waist tighter than I ever have. Because the escape his touch gives me anchors me at the same time. It's contradictory, hot and cold, ice and fire, chalk and cheese. Everything about my growing addiction to this gorgeous man is a big fucking ping-pong game.

"What are you doing later?"

"Nothing. Why?" I answer.

"I have another shoot. Want to come with me?"

I pull back and look at him. “After last time? Really?”

A heart-thumping smile stretches across his face. “It’s not that kind of shoot. I promise. You won’t want to leave.”

Chapter NINE

I DON'T want to leave.

Ever.

There are little girls dancing around in front of me in the most beautiful frilly dresses. They're accompanied by the cutest little boys in suits, who are holding flowers and teddy bears and lollipops for their "dates."

They're giggling at each other. The girls are blushing. The little boys are bowing. They're all jumping around and smiling the most adorable smiles… And laughing at the funny man behind the camera.

He's holding my attention as much as the cuties he's taking photos of. He's making funny faces and singing silly songs—I have no doubt that he knows that he looks like a total idiot.

"Stefanie!" Tyler calls the name of a little blond girl. "Why aren't you singing?"

"Because you're silly and my mommy said not to talk to silly men." She pokes her tongue out and laughs.

He gasps. "I'm not silly!"

"Are too!" the kids all cry. Some of them echo after, keen to be included in the chorus. They all break into giggles, and almost instantly, Tyler clicks on his camera.

I'm not even sure what this shoot is for. Party dresses and bridesmaid dresses, I think… But all I'm thinking right now is how amazing this man is with these kids. He's so patient, so tender. It's a whole other side to him I haven't seen.

A side I'm quickly coming to adore.

It's like he's finally found an outlet for that childish, playful side of himself he keeps hidden so often. Like when we were in Santa Monica and he tapped my hand until he finally took it.

I wish he'd let that side out more often. Because it's a side that invokes more than base attraction. It's a side that tugs on real emotion. It's a side that shows more than the addiction.

It shows me the man beneath it all. The handsome, soft, gentle man beneath the rough addiction and the ugliness of our everyday reality.

It's a little slice of something that shows me how it could be. The kind of man he truly is. The kind of father he could be one day.

I wrap my arms around my stomach and watch him as he continues to tease the children and make them feel completely at ease with him. You'd think he was ten years old the way he's laughing with them. My lips curve upward as I study them all. I could sit here and watch him make these kids laugh all day.

The sound of his own laugh, louder and deeper and richer than theirs, wouldn't get old either.

Too quickly, the shoot comes to an end. The children are swept away to change out of their expensive frocks, and Tyler packs his camera away with a solid promise to email the best photos over once he's edited them.

He zips up his camera bag and walks over to me. After a quick look around to make sure the studio is kid-free, he touches his lips to mine.

"See? I told you you'd love it."

I smile and link my fingers through his. "I did. So freakin' adorable."

"I try." He winks, laughing when I raise an eyebrow. "I'm kidding. I don't need to try."

I smack his chest with the backs of my fingers. "You're such an idiot."

"It's why I'm so endearing. I mean, who wouldn't want a complete and utter idiot who makes kids laugh by singing Humpty Dumpy out of tune?" He carefully puts his things in the trunk of the car.

Warmth spreads through my stomach and I smile, leaning against his car, my eyes following him as he walks around it. "Oh, yes. A guy who can make kids laugh is the most undesirable thing ever. How dare you be so cute?" I roll my eyes and sit in the car.

"Cute? Did you just call me fucking cute?"

I look over at him. Well, he looks kind of offended. "Honey, you have dimples. *Dimples.* You are, by default, totally damn cute."

"I am not cute."

"You are."

"Am not."

"Are too."

"Am not!"

"That. Do that again." I turn in my seat gleefully.

"Am not?" He glances at me at the intersection. I nod. "No. Fuck off," he laughs. "I'm not cute," he says while grinning.

Right. I reach out and poke my finger into the dent of his dimple.

"You so are." I rest my head against the back of my seat and drop my hand to his thigh. "And you don't know it because you don't need to try, remember?"

He clicks his tongue. "All right. You win. Smartarse."

I grin and squeeze his thigh. His eyes shoot to me but he says nothing. I do it again and he shifts in his seat. My lips twitch and I squeeze his leg a third time. Again, he fidgets.

"Will you stop that?" he mutters, pulling up outside my apartment block.

"Are you ticklish, honey?"

"No. I'm not five."

I open my door and swing my legs out with a giant grin on my face. "If you say so."

I could swear that he mutters, "I do," but I'm not entirely sure.

He heads to the trunk while I enter the lobby without waiting for him. He's not five, after all. He can find my apartment without an escort.

He shoves his hand between the elevator doors and I jab frantically at the 'open doors' button.

"You dick!" I cry, tugging him into the elevator with me.

He laughs. "Don't worry, feistypants. They have sensors. I wouldn't have lost my hand."

"Feistypants. I hate that."

"Stop being so feisty then."

"And let you get away with all sorts of shit? Never." I reach down and squeeze his thigh.

"Fuck off!" he shouts, laughing.

"Tickle tickle." I grin, grabbing both of his legs and squeezing several times very quickly.

The elevator doors ping open and I back out, laughing. Tyler walks toward me with a playful yet predatory glint in his eyes that makes me tingle all over. I walk backward until I hit my door, laughing, and he pins me.

"I warned you."

"Technically, you didn't," I retort, flattening against the door like it'll get me farther away from him.

"My bad." He grins and grabs my sides.

His fingers dig into my sensitive spots and I scream a laugh. My knees buckle, my head throws back, and I grab his arms so I don't drop to the floor. He tickles me intensely, my shrieking laugh mixing with his rich, deep one.

"Ty! Stop!" I beg through my laughter.

"Say I'm not cute," he bargains.

"Never!"

"No stopping then."

I somehow manage to dig my key from my pocket and shove it into the door. I push it open forcefully and fall through the open space. I regain my footing and dump my purse on the floor, still laughing, my sides aching and hurting from both my laughter and his tickling.

"Say it," he demands, slamming the door shut and advancing toward me.

I shake my head, still walking, still backward.

"One last chance, Liv."

"Or what?" I challenge. "What will you do if I don't?"

He slaps his hands against the wall on either side of my head. "I'm not sure you want to find out."

"Fantasies?" I look directly into those intoxicating, dark eyes.

"Plans," he murmurs.

"I like plans," I breathe.

"No, you don't. You're impulsive and indecisive and spur-of-the-moment." He runs his nose up my neck. His breath coats my skin in a swath of heat that sends tingles through me. "It's what I love about you. I love it when you don't think."

"Because when I do, I overthink to hell."

"Precisely." He smiles against my skin. "So stop thinking."

"Even if I think you're cute?"

"Especially that." He laughs, his hands settling against my waist.

I expect them to slide down, to cup my ass and pull me toward him. They don't. They flatten against the small of my back and linger there. The heat from his hold seeps through the material of my sweater.

The tension zings. It bounces off him and me, colliding in the tiny space between us and igniting like fireworks on the Fourth of July.

My chest heaves with anticipation. I want his touch. Despite my earlier thoughts about the sex overriding the rest of our relationship, when we're here, like this, so close, I can't help but need him inside me. I can't help but want to be so connected to him.

"There's more to us." The words leave me, barely audible, unintentional.

"What do you mean?" he whispers into my ear.

"Than our addiction. There's more, isn't there? It's stronger than our addiction. More intense, yet just as dangerous. It's lingering under the blanket of our addictions."

Tyler eases one hand around my front and up my body until he's cupping the back of my head. "Yeah. Yeah, there's so much more than our addiction."

I press my face into his chest as Nana's words come back to me. "*When you're in love, you'll know it.*"

"We are so fucked," I whisper into his shirt. "So fucking fucked."

He laughs quietly. Sadly. "You think that's what this is? Fucked?"

"Feels like it."

He cups my face. His palms are hot against my cheeks, burning into my skin as his gaze sears into mine. "Liv, when you see you and me as something other than 'fucked,' we can come back to this."

He releases me and heads for my door.

Panic constricts my lungs. I can't breathe. He's going. Why? Why is he going? He can't go.

"Where are you going?" I almost shout, pressing my fists into my stomach.

"Somewhere other than here so you can think about what you and I really are."

Going? No. No—he's not walking away when I've finally told him that there's more than just sex. It was a totally roundabout way, but I told him. And I don't need to think.

I know what we are. We're crazy and painful and consuming. We're the rainbow through the storm and the rain on a hot summer's day. We're the light and dark, everything bad and everything good.

"Don't go." The words tumble from me. Desperately, my voice cracks and I beg. "Ty. Don't. *Please.*"

He stops in the doorway and turns. I can only just see his eyes meet mine. My eyes are blurred from the tears filling them.

He can't go. Shit. This is fucked because I make it so. Every time. Me. Always me.

"Please," I whisper, looking down. "Please."

"Fuck." He kicks the door shut with a resounding bang and pulls me into his arms. "I'm not going anywhere."

I grab his shirt and collapse into him. "Don't. Don't go."

"I'm not." His words are shuddery, and he soothingly runs a hand through my hair. He holds me tighter.

"Good," I whisper, fisting his shirt tighter. "I'm sorry. I just…" I squeeze my eyes shut.

"What, Liv? You just what?"

"I'm so afraid of loving you."

"Don't fear that, baby girl. Anything but that." He drags me toward my room and onto my bed. My head rests against his chest. His heart is pounding beneath my ear, his fingers gripping me tight, his breath hard and fast against the top of my head.

"I am. Do you know how close I am? Do you know why I fight you? Why I fight us?" I pull up and pinch my finger and thumb, leaving a tiny space between them. "This close, Ty. This fucking close. And it scares the ever-loving shit out of me."

He grabs my face and makes me look at him. He physically forces my eyes to look into his.

"Don't fear it. Let it happen. I don't give a shit how long it takes or how uncontrollable it is. I need you to love me."

"I need you to love me." "Need you." "Love me." "I need you." "To love me."

"I need you to love me."

"What?" When he doesn't reply, I push his hands away and grab his face through my tears. "What?"

"I need you to feel the way I do." He pulls me into him. "I need you to know that. Think whatever the hell you want about our relationship as long as you know that, below the addiction, there's a whole bunch of fucking emotion, all right?"

I inhale sharply, holding the breath until it fucking burns me.

"No."

"Yes," he says sharply. "Yes. I won't say it because you can't deal with it right now, but it's there. Ever since you told me never to touch you and threw my money back at me. It's been there. Growing."

"No," I repeat, feeling smaller and smaller.

"Come here." Tyler pulls me down and wraps me into his body so hard that I can't escape.

I'm trapped. I'm tied in yet another way by this man, unable to free myself from his unrelenting binds.

"Don't say it," I beg, pushing my face into him. "Please. Just...don't say it."

A shudder racks his whole body. "I promise I won't. Not until you want me to."

You get me, I think. I don't know how it's possible, but he fucking gets me. Gets that I need to know it but not hear it.

I need to know that he feels the way I do.

In this second, it doesn't matter that the length of us is undefined. It doesn't matter about the demons we fight or the bumps ahead.

It just matters that, in the space of seconds—mere, seemingly inconsequential seconds—I've both admitted to myself and accepted that Tyler and I are falling in love.

Very, very quickly.

Chapter TEN

I OPEN my eyes and stare straight at a mug of coffee with a backdrop of abs. *Well, that's one way to start a day.*

I stare longingly, undecided if it's the abs or the coffee making me sigh happily, and drag my gaze upward to smirking lips. My eyes find the dark-brown ones of my dirty British boy, and this time, my sigh is definitely for him.

"Good morning." Amusement filters through his words.

"Morning." I smile lazily and sit up. "Is that for me?"

"The abs or the coffee?"

"Hilarious." I reach out and grab the mug.

He laughs and perches on the edge of the bed. "What are you doing today?"

"I'm meeting Day at the new bar. We're coming up with the final cocktail menu so I can order everything from the supplier this afternoon." I sip my coffee. "The fridges and stuff were installed yesterday, and since it opens in, like, two weeks, we really need to get moving."

"You could have told Aaron he's expecting too much, you realize?"

I stop my lips from twitching. "One of the builders tried that. It didn't go well."

"Good point." Tyler leans back and gazes up at me. "Interviewing any hot cocktail-shaker guys yet?"

"Not yet," I say nonchalantly into my mug. "I was going to set up interviews this weekend. Do you know I required pictures with the applications?"

"Liv," he says firmly but through hidden laughter. "Hiring someone on looks is shallow."

I put the mug down and give him my best unimpressed face. "I'm sorry. Remind me what it is you do for a living again?"

He laughs and pulls me over with him. "I take photos of children in pretty dresses, sunsets over Elliott Bay, and loved-up couples who put a ring on it."

"And half-dressed women." I tap his nose and look down at him.

"But the only half-dressed woman I particularly like taking photos of is you." He grins and bats my hair from his face. "In fact, I more than like it. I bloody love it."

"I was about to be offended, but I think you saved yourself." I drop a kiss onto his lips and get up. "I need to get ready. If I'm late, I'm likely to get a Louboutin up my ass."

Tyler's laugh follows me through to the bathroom—probably because he knows I'm not exaggerating.

I jump into the shower, wash off, and walk out into Tyler's arms. He wraps a towel around my body, grinning, and kisses my forehead.

"Towels. So overrated."

I laugh and step back, tucking the end of the towel in at the top so it stays in place. I grab the second from him and wrap my hair up. "Overrated but necessary," I respond, shoving my toothbrush in my mouth.

"Depends on your definition of the word necessary." He grabs a second toothbrush from the holder.

I pause, stare at it, then point my own brush at it. "What is that?" I ask through a mouthful of froth.

"It's a toothbrush, baby girl. What else would it be?"

"Cocky prick." I spit out the stuff in my mouth. "Why is it here?"

"So I can brush my teeth."

"You are all for stating the obvious today, aren't you?" I give my teeth another quick once-over and rinse. "I pretty much figured that out for myself, if I'm honest."

He laughs. "I'm not kicking my sister out of my apartment," he calls as I walk into my room. "Which means I'm going to have to fuck you here, and since you wear me out with your sexual demands, I'm going to need to stay over, which means I'm going to need a few things."

"*I* wear *you* out with *my* sexual demands?" I shriek, my shoulders shaking with silent laughter. "Mr. Owner of The Drawer of Sexual Surprises?"

"You named the drawer?" Now, he really does laugh.

"What?" I gaze at him innocently, my eyes wide, and pick some panties from the drawer. "It's like Pandora's fucking box in that thing!"

He takes the underwear from my hand and switches it with a bright-pink pair. I roll my eyes and ditch the towel so I can slide them up my legs. He watches me, his eyes following the path of the skimpy material until his gaze hovers over my now-covered core.

I cough, and he lifts his eyes to my bare chest. *Shit.* Note to self: put on a bra before trying to drag your boyfriend's gaze away from your vagina.

I grab an equally bright-pink bra from the drawer and put it on, obstructing his view. Thankfully, because my nipples are now hard and achy from the way he was staring.

"Tyler!" I snap. "My eyes are up here."

"And they are very, very beautiful," he replies automatically, finally meeting them.

I shake my head and get dressed before he decides he's going to make me late, because the bulge in his pants is telling me that that's exactly what he's considering. I braid my wet hair to one side and apply my makeup, Tyler watching me the whole time.

Angus meows loudly from the kitchen, no doubt unimpressed that his food bowl is empty. I stroll past Tyler and into the room where my grumpy kitty is mewling like he's never been fed.

"Untwist your tail, Angus. I'm here." I grab a can, open it, and tip it into his bowl. My cat rubs against my ankle in an affectionate—and very rare—thank-you and dives into the meat.

Someone got kitty sex last night if there's ankle-rubbing happening.

I locate my phone on the counter and throw it into my purse, which is sitting on the table. "Ty?"

"Mhmm?" He comes into the kitchen, now wearing a shirt, and his hair is done.

"Can you give me a ride?"

"I'll give you several if you're asking me that nicely."

I slap his chest as he pulls me into him. I open my mouth to respond, but he silences me with a long, deep kiss that curls my toes.

"Shut up," I mutter.

"I'll drive you to the bar. Why can't you take yourself?"

I shrug. "I can't be bothered to drive this morning."

Now he's the one rolling his eyes and shaking his head. "Come on, my little lazy bitch. Let's go."

I grin and grab my purse before following him out. He wraps his arm around my shoulder in the elevator and lowers his mouth to nibble at my ear.

"Did you say you were making a cocktail menu?"

"Yep." I jerk my head to stop his nibbling. That shit tickles.

"Put a Blow Job on the menu. You know how I like them." His breath crawls across my neck, and his suggestive tone warms every spot in my body.

"They can go right under my personal favorite, Sex on the Beach," I reply, pressing a kiss to his jaw just before the doors open.

"If I didn't know better, I'd say that was a challenge."

I spin from his hold and grab the car door handle. "Good thing you don't know better then, isn't it?"

He looks at me through heavy eyelids and places a hand against the car.

"You should be careful what you challenge me to do. You know how I like to win."

"I'm counting on you winning."

He unlocks the car with a beep. "Get in the car."

"Someone's eager," I tease. "I have somewhere to be, honey. You'll have to beach-fuck me another time."

"Liv." He pushes off the car and walks around it. "I'm not going to fuck you somewhere right after you challenge me to. I have plans, remember?"

"What am I, penciled in for nine p.m. tonight or something?" I sit next to him in the car.

"Do you want to be?" He glances at me as we pull out of the parking lot.

"Do you have time to fit me in? I mean, I'd hate to mess up your sex plan with a flippant comment."

"I can squeeze you in, babe. I've left a few slots in my diary."

"Oh, that's so kind of you. As long as it won't affect your plan."

He shrugs. "Plans can be changed."

I smirk. "So the beach thing?"

"Plans can be changed, but they're more fun when they're surprises." He laughs.

"Which translates to?"

"I'll fuck you on a beach when I want to, not when you ask me to."

"You could have just said that in the first place, you know?" I poke his thigh. "Instead of all the plan shit that was a waste of my breath."

Tyler laughs, stopping outside the bar. He shifts in his seat to face me and reaches a hand out. He curls his hand around the back of my neck and pulls me into him. "Hey, feisty bitch, you're more than penciled in. You're written in in fucking permanent marker. Every night."

"Yeah? How long for?"

"Only 'til the end of the year. My diary doesn't go past that yet." He grins and pulls me in for a kiss. He hums against my mouth, the gentle sound vibrating his lips against mine. "Now go make up a menu. I expect a Blow Job as soon as possible."

I drop my hand to his pants and brush my thumb over the material covering his half-erect cock. "And I expect a Screaming Orgasm. Pencil *that* in."

I leave the car after one final kiss. He laughs yet again, a sound I'm certain I'll never tire of, and I wave just before stepping inside the bar.

Now, the bar is a totally different place than it was the last time I was here. Downstairs is painted, the bar is completely erected, and all the necessary furniture is on the dance floor, still covered in plastic. The bar is covered with a plastic sheet, too, and I guess that's to protect it from the final building work going on up in the VIP section.

At least I don't have to wear one of those fucking hard hats any more.

"Is upstairs almost done?" I grab Will on my way to the bar, where my best friend is sitting.

He nods. "Yes, ma'am. They're just building the bar and laying the final tiles on the floor. Then we'll be able to get it decorated and the lights fixed up. That's what we're doing right now."

"Great!" I smile and head for the bar.

"You're late," Dayton says, teasing.

"Blame your future cousin-in-law. He started with Blow Jobs, so naturally I had to respond with a Screaming Orgasm."

She stares at me for a moment. "Cocktail innuendos. I would have loved to be a fly on the wall for that conversation."

I can't help but grin as I sit down on the plastic-covered stool and put my purse on the plastic-covered bar. "It's like a warehouse in here," I mutter, grabbing a pen from the bar and clicking it.

Day opens a notebook and hands it to me. "Lights and restrooms today. Then they'll start with furniture and getting all the little things out of the way."

"I guess they got a few too many extra men in." I laugh.

"Probably. So, aside from a Screaming Orgasm and a Blow Job, what are you thinking?" she grins devilishly. "Slippery Nipple? Silk Panty Martini? Climax?" Her eyes glitter with laughter.

"This is a high-end establishment." I sit up straight. "But I really, really want to put them on just for giggles."

Day snatches the pen and writes them all on the paper. "Do menu sections. These can be in the section titled 'Final Night of Freedom.'"

Oh my god. "Put All Night Long in there, too."

She scribbles it down. "Classics?"

"Mojito, margarita, Bloody Mary, daiquiri, martini—all versions—whisky sour, cosmopolitan, mimosa, and Bucks Fizz."

She blinks at me. "Wow. Why are we writing a menu again, Ms. I Know My Cocktails?"

"So everyone else knows them, too. Duh." I take the pen from her. "Do you have another notebook? I need to write down the ingredients so I don't get swamped later."

She hands me another notebook and I flip to the first page. Using the other list, I write down all the ingredients so I can put the order through. We shoot more cocktail ideas and section titles around as I write, switching between the two lists. When we have a great basic menu, I add all the beers, lagers, and wines to the order sheet.

When it's done, I call the supplier Aaron wants to use and place the order. Dayton hands me a card with his name on it and I pass the details over the phone.

"New card," she explains once I've hung up. "Especially for this place. This is yours, so every time you need to get something for the bar, you can use this. There's a new accountant and he has a link to the account to do the books every week. As long as you keep your own notes so we can match it up, she's yours." She hands me the card.

I stare at it for a moment. This managing thing is more responsibility than I realized. Keeping books? I can just about keep my 'porn on a page' tidy on my shelf, never mind actual numbers books.

Oh well. I guess I have a hot date with Google and Bookkeeping 101 tonight.

"Okay," I reply, tucking it into my purse. "At least that's done. Are the menus going to the designer now?"

Dayton nods and pulls her laptop open on the bar. "I'll type it up now and send it all to her. She'll work on them tonight so you can look it over and send it to the printer tomorrow. I'll CC you into the email."

I blink at her as she types furiously at the keyboard. "Are you a trainee photographer or working for your fiancé?"

She laughs. "Bit of both. Apart from my day at college, the photographer thing is pretty much random. I don't go on all Tyler's shoots with him, so I have a lot of free time. I can't deal with nothing to do, so I do the little things that bug him—like sending emails like this."

"I see."

"And I prefer working *with* him, not for him." She winks. "Okay. Done. Now talk."

"About what exactly?"

"Have you met Tessa yet?"

I see where this is going. "Yes, I met Tessa. It was…awkward."

Day clicks her pen. "Awkward because you were naked or because you freaked?"

"Ohhhh," I groan, dropping my forehead to the bar. "Both. Both."

I explain the day she walked through the door when I was basically naked—both times—and about Tyler's bold proclamation that led to my freak-out. I'm getting irate as I talk about it. I can feel my chest tightening, and I might slam my fist against the bar a couple of times. Might.

"And then, there's a fucking toothbrush in my bathroom this morning," I finish and take a deep breath. I am so not over that toothbrush thing. At all.

"So what? Is he moving in one little object at a time? A toothbrush here, a dirty sock there?"

If I find a single dirty man-sock in my apartment, I will strangle him with it. I tell her as much.

"Well…" She pauses.

"Go on."

"Uh, no. Never mind."

"Dayton Black, talk right the hell now."

She flips me the bird then sighs. "Look, maybe this is how it's supposed to be. Maybe you guys are supposed to move fast because a whirlwind luuuhhh—*relationship*," she corrects herself, "is the only way either of you will accept more than one night."

Her words ring true. Too true. I meet her eyes for a second before looking away again.

Fuck. Give Ms. Love Cynic a ring on her finger and she really does turn into Seattle's resident love guru. *Give me a break.*

"You'll be pleased to know that I finally booked your bachelorette weekend," I say, knowing it'll get her off the topic of my relationship.

"No shit?"

I grin. "Next weekend. You, me, Tessa, right?"

She nods. "Monique has to manage the girls and Aunt Leigh is on vacation with her new boyfriend. I can't believe you actually booked it. For next weekend like I wanted?"

I examine my nails. "I may have dropped Aaron's name into one or two phone calls." I glance up and smirk.

"Of course you did." She smiles and stands, grabbing her purse. "I'm going to go and get the last of the stuff we need to make the wedding favors this weekend."

Oh God, no.

"Remind me why you aren't hiring someone to do this for you?"

"Because," she answers, opening the door to the bar, "I thought it would be a really good idea until I realized how much fucking work it would be, and now, it's too late to hire someone."

"So buy some ready-mades off of eBay."

"No. His Royal Highness likes the idea of Bridezilla making the wedding favors. Apparently, the annoyance I'll feel after a few hours of it will give me an idea as to how he feels when I'm in planning mode." She slams the door behind me. "He's a sweetheart, isn't he?"

"How he feels? Most of the planning has been dumped on me!"

She snaps her head around.

"And I couldn't be happier about it! I love you. Please don't hurt me." I put my hands together in front of my body in a praying action and smile sweetly.

"I'll call you tomorrow. Aaron is going to New York with Tyler, so you and Tessa can stay with me. Okay?" She hugs me briefly then heads for her car. "Bye!"

I wave her off, and it's not until she drives away that I remember that I had Tyler drive me here.

Goddammit.

Chapter ELEVEN

"WHAT are you doing?"

I turn my face toward the door. "I'm watching TV. What does it look like?"

Tyler raises an eyebrow and kicks the door shut behind him. "With one leg hooked over the back of the sofa?"

Seriously? Why does everyone have a problem with the way I watch TV?

"Am I supposed to have my legs closed all the time because I'm a woman? I can slouch as well as any man, thank you very much." I wriggle slightly.

"Believe me, babe. I have no problem with you having your legs wide open."

"Then stop complaining."

"I do, however, have a problem with the fact you're not naked."

"Oh, I'm sorry. Be sure to text me next time you're dressed so I can be naked and ready for you." I roll my eyes and swing my leg down so I can sit up.

Ty nods, a smirk teasing his lips. "That's more like it."

He walks into the kitchen and dumps a bag on the table next to Angus. Angus opens his eyes and stares at his disturber before closing them again and returning to his nap. Tyler chuckles quietly to himself.

"Still doesn't like me, huh?"

"Angus doesn't like anyone unless he's just had pussy. Literally." I get up and lean against the kitchen table.

"He sounds exactly like me. Maybe we need some guy time." Ty tugs on my hair.

I bat his hand away. "By all means, take him home with you. You do know cats pee to mark their territory?"

He pauses. "On second thought, I'll pass." He dives his hand into the grocery bag in front of him and unpacks.

I watch as he pulls out various ingredients—ground beef, kidney beans, tomatoes, pepper, onion…

"What are you doing?" I ask, grabbing the pack of tortilla chips.

"I'm cooking you dinner."

"Why?" I open the bag and grab a few chips.

Tyler frowns and snatches it off me. "I'm away all weekend. Tonight is for you."

"Oh, a whole night. I'm honored. Is it just dinner or are we on a schedule?" I reach for the bag again.

He drops it on the chair behind him and grabs my wrist, pulling me into him. "We're on a schedule," he murmurs, sucking gently on my bottom lip. "Because I need enough time to tie those pretty little wrists up and fuck you until you scream."

I inhale sharply. "Promises, promises."

"Never promises. Always certainties."

"Then you should start cooking dinner, shouldn't you?" I grin, kiss him quickly, and then swipe the bag of chips off the chair behind him.

He sighs, but it's spoiled by his laugh. I deliberately take a huge bite of three chips in one go. They make a loud crunch as I do, and my grin widens when he glances over his shoulder at me. His shoulders tremble with the laughter he's failing to hide.

It's shining in his eyes. A sparkling, warm glint that makes my heart thump, it's a beacon of his amusement.

I perch on the chair and dump the bag on the table. Resting my cheek on one of my hands, I scratch Angus's head with the other. He purrs loudly beneath my fingertips, but most of my attention is on Tyler.

He navigates my kitchen with ease, and I wonder if he's as…*curious*...as I am—if he's stolen a minute of searching my apartment here and there like I have his. I've sure as shit never shown him where I keep my saucepans!

He deposits the meat into a pan and heats it. Sizzling fills the air as it cooks, the sound interrupted whenever he stirs it. He chops the onions and peppers like a pro, slicing them up small, and I could swear he sets a second pan of water boiling and stirs the meat at the same time.

"How was your day?" he asks, opening the can of kidney beans.

"That's a cozy question," I reply. "I did everything I needed to and managed not to anger Bridezilla in the process. So all in all, it was a success."

"Did she ask about the hen party?"

"Yes, she asked about her *bachelorette* party. I thought she was going to die of shock when I told her I finally booked it." I grin, remembering the way her eyes widened. "She couldn't believe I booked in ten days before she wanted it."

"How *did* you manage that?"

"I might have booked a hotel that Aaron manages the advertising for. I might have name-dropped, and they might have conveniently had a cancellation while we were on the phone."

Tyler laughs loudly. "And did you get that from my sister?"

"Actually, no. I used this thing called a brain. You might have heard of them."

"Oh, you mean you have one, too? I thought that peculiar phenomenon only existed at the end of my cock."

I bite the inside of my cheek. "Dick."

"How apt."

"You're such a twat."

He looks over his shoulder and winks. "I love it when you call me that. It's kind of hot."

"Twat? Really? That's hot?"

"Oh, no, wait. That's just me."

I cover my mouth with my hand to stop my laughter escaping and hold my phone to my ear. "Hello, 911? We have a serious cause of Overgrown Ego-Itis that needs immediate attention."

Tyler leans across the table and grabs the phone off me, laughing to himself. "You'd be missing out if I wasn't so cocky. Shit, Liv. Could you imagine how bad I'd be in bed?"

"What the hell does that have to do with your ego?"

"Clearly it has everything to do with it. If I weren't so confident in my abilities to fuck you into next week, I wouldn't be able to tell you all the filthy things I want to do you."

"Oh yeah?" I raise my eyebrows. "Like what?"

"Like how I want you to get your arse into your room and get some stockings on purely so I can rip one off later to tie your hands."

"And?"

"Let me finish, woman." He tuts. "To tie your hands to your headstand so I can fuck you from behind and spank your arse."

"That's a total waste of my time."

He looks offended.

"The stockings. Not the sex," I say quickly. Definitely not the sex. Never the sex. "Why don't you just get one out of the drawer?"

"Because it'll be far more fun to peel it down your leg while my tongue fucks your clit." He shrugs like his words haven't just sent a lightning bolt of desire straight to my clit.

"Fair point," I squeak out.

He turns and his gaze collides with mine. His hot, demanding, dominant gaze. "Now get in your fucking room and get changed."

I swallow, my pussy clenching, and get off the stool. I run into my room and step out of my jeans. I roll a pair of stockings up my legs and pause in front of the mirror, fingering the hem of my sweater before pulling that and my shirt over my head. I dump them in the corner of my room and free my hair from its braid.

It's soft and silky as I run my fingers through it while walking back into the kitchen. *I'll give you get changed, Tyler Stone. How's stripping off for you?*

"Turned on, Liv?"

"I'd challenge you to find out, but you're cooking, and I wouldn't want to distract you." I sweep past him and reach into the cupboard to get a can of food for Angus. I hook my finger through the pull-ring and pull the top off.

Tyler's hand slides over my ass cheek as I bend to dump the food in the bowl.

"No," he says huskily. "Wouldn't want to distract me at fucking all."

His hand connects with me in one sharp slap. The sting radiates across my skin, the tingling sensation as pleasurable as it is painful.

He leans forward, his lips brushing the curve of my ear. "I'll soothe that when you soothe my dick." His finger hooks inside the top of my panties and pings it. "Because you are giving me so many fucking ideas wandering around in your underwear."

"You told me to get changed."

He squeezes my hip. "You're a tease, you bitch."

"Yeah? What are you going to do about it?"

"I hope you can eat fast because you have ten minutes until you find out." He releases me and kills the flames on the cooker.

I think I just lost my appetite.

"Sit," he demands, pointing a wooden spoon at my chair.

I lower myself onto it. I know that low, husky tone he's talking in. I know the way it vibrates through my body and across my skin. I know the promises and threats it contains. I know the inevitable pleasure that will be borne of the intensity of the dirty words it accompanies.

I know the anticipation, the struggle, the release.

He slides a plate of chili in front of me. "Eat."

He sits opposite me and stares me down as he grabs his fork. His eyes are burning into mine. His gaze is hot and lustful, and the power it holds makes me shiver. It never wavers as he eats slowly. Never leaves mine. Never falters.

My throat is dry. Swallowing is like sandpaper, like rubbing silk against a rugged cliff edge. Because with every beat of my heart, my control slips away.

But this is a control I can lose. This is pure sex. It's desire and lust. There's no deep emotion except what lies on the surface.

This is safety.

Tyler's commands, his control, his total dominance over my body whenever he demands it.

What was once my danger is now my safe place.

What once was my temptation is now my addiction.

"Not eating?" His voice is low, and I can only imagine what he's thinking.

"I'm not hungry," I breathe, my chest tightening.

Slowly, he puts his fork down and studies me. From the flushing of my cheeks to the parting of my lips and the obvious rise and fall of my chest, he doesn't miss a thing.

He never does. He knows my body the way a piano player knows the keys. He plays it the same way—with ease and finesse—pleasure falling from his fingers the way music falls from the pianist's.

And the way he stands and stalks toward me resembles that. He grabs my wrists roughly and pulls me up. My skin burns beneath his touch, and I whimper as he crushes his lips against mine.

It's heaven and hell, saint and sinner, all in one desperate touch.

His tongue flicks against my lips, his teeth nip the tender flesh, his lips caress. He pulls me back toward my room and, once inside, flips me around against the door.

My back flattens against the surface, and Tyler holds my wrists at my sides. His mouth travels along my jaw, down my neck, across my shoulder… My chest heaves as blood rushes through my body in a heated pulse of desire.

He kisses his way down my stomach until his mouth is hovering above my clit. His breath crawls over the sensitive skin, gentle yet hot, and he releases my wrists. He grabs my thighs and kisses me through the lace of the panties. Then he flicks his tongue out, the roughness burning my clit.

He does it again, and again, and again. Short, fleeting movements that feel so intense. So intense that I feel nothing but that until he stops and stands. And turns me, grabs my wrists, and ties the soft material of my stocking around them.

He ties the knot firmly and steps forward toward me. He trails his fingertips up my spine and entwines my hair around them. Then, with one tight tug, he pulls my head back.

"There," he whispers in my ear. "Perfect."

His breath fans across my skin hotly as he pushes me toward the bed. His movements are so controlled and precise, an absolute contradiction to mine. I'm shaking, trembling, quivering.

Tyler eases me to kneeling by the side of the bed, and resting my hands on top of it, he sets his mouth by my ear. "You still owe me a fuck over the bed," he rasps. "And I'm taking it now."

His blunt words do crazy shit to me. I draw in a breath, my heart pounds, and my pussy throbs all at the same time. If it weren't before, my body is on high alert, ready to take him and all he has to give.

He bends down behind me and pulls my panties over the curve of my ass and down my legs teasingly. The gentle brush of his fingertips across my skin with his movements is the worst kind of torture. And he knows it. He knows what he's doing and what he's doing to me.

And I know he's loving every fucking second of it.

Bastard.

I jerk when his thumb eases between my legs and he runs it along my—

"I love how wet you are," he murmurs against my shoulder, pushing his thumb inside me. "How easily your cunt gets ready for me."

That.

I gasp when he withdraws his thumb and replaces it with the tip of his cock. His hands leave my hips and hold my wrists in place on the bed, and he whispers in my ear again.

"Keep your hands there. I plan to fuck you hard and you'll need something to hold on to."

He buries himself inside me on his last word with a brutal thrust. I cry out at the motion, the roughness expected but surprising, but the sting of pain with the stretch of my muscles soon soothes with his rhythmic thrusting.

It's rough and it's primal. His fingertips dig so hard into my skin that they burn. Our skin slaps together as he moves my body against his. Heavy breaths and those sweet slaps fill the air until he pauses briefly and another slapping sound fills the air and another sensation assaults my skin.

I moan, and he leans forward, his cock fully inside me, and whispers, "Mine."

A word so small, so simple, and my eyes burn with tears from more than just the pressure of his movements.

"Mine for this," he says, pulling back, his words breaking the haze of tears. His thrusts are slower yet somehow harsher and deeper. Somehow more meaningful that before.

His hands palm my ass, light slaps alternating with caresses, and I don't know where to feel. I don't know what to feel. Until…

"Mine for this." He reaches beneath me and grabs my jaw, turning my head forcefully until our lips meet. He rocks his hips against me and I moan into his kisses, my wrists bound and tied, my body irrevocably held to this man's.

He's gone—his mouth, his hands, his cock. And I'm flipped onto the bed and he's over me, grabbing my legs, hooking them over his hips, gripping my jaw, forcing me to look into his eyes.

"Mine for this," he says a third time, entering me again.

My hands are stretched above my head and there isn't a thing I can do but lie here and let him take the control over me I deny him elsewhere.

Because that's what it's really about for both of us. A fleeting moment in time where we truly have what we desire.

Freedom.

"You look at me as you come." His words come as my pussy tightens around him and I hook my ankles behind his waist. "Do you hear that, Liv? You look in my fucking eyes as you come."

I nod. I can't look away if I wanted to. I'm mesmerized by this moment, a moment where I'm so afraid to yet so ready to relinquish control.

"Mine," he repeats again, like he needs to tell himself it, like he can see the fear in my eyes. He grips my jaw tighter until I clench it.

Warmth.

Heat.

Pleasure.

Throbbing.

Clenching.

Tyler.

"*Mine.*"

It seeps through the heaviness in my mind, the swirling craziness of my release. It enriches it. The possessive, definitive word sends me on another tailspin, and I flip my arms up and forward to around his neck. His hair slinks between my fingers. His cock swells inside me. His mouth descends on mine…

He joins me in craziness, the whole time whispering the word 'mine.'

Chapter TWELVE

THE bed is empty and cold when I wake. Brief memories of lips ghosting mine and a whispered goodbye come to me, and I roll over onto Tyler's side.

The pillow smells like him, and despite my previous thought, I swear the duvet is still warm where he was lying. I snuggle beneath it, pulling it right up to my face, and breathe him in.

I can count on one hand the amount of hours he's been out of Seattle and my heart is already aching.

It aches so much that it hurts—and that's the brutal reality of my addiction. Take the item of my craving away and I'm no different to anyone else experiencing withdrawals. I'm snappy, shaky, antsy. I'm irrational and constantly looking for the thing to sate the insatiable.

And I hurt. Everywhere. Bone-deep pain.

I close my eyes and take another deep breath. I know that being here, surrounded by something that's so him, even if it is just his smell, isn't a good thing. I know that I'm looking at forty-eight hours of nothing…which means I need to leave.

Now.

I roll myself out of bed with a look back to the pillow. A part of me wants to yank off the pillowcase and tuck it into my purse. But I don't—I pull on some sweatpants and a hooded sweatshirt and move my ass.

Angus's food bowl is still full, so I pause only to grab my keys before running out the door. I run downstairs and into my car. I rev the engine with unnecessary vigor and hightail the hell out of the parking lot.

I drive on instinct, and it takes me only a few minutes to realize that I'm heading toward my parents' place. Another safe place. A safe place without the danger.

I repeatedly glance at my phone, which is lying on the passenger's seat. Fleeting glances that achieve nothing but confirmation that there are no messages or missed calls.

That achieves nothing but irritating me. Making me want something. Some kind of connection to him.

My chest tightens and I take a deep breath, forcing myself to concentrate on the road. *Fuck, fuck, fuck.* This is worse than I thought.

I'm more addicted than I thought I was.

This goes beyond any comprehensible feeling.

This is a wild addiction, one that will never be tamed.

And I love it as much as I hate it.

I can feel it flooding my veins, filling every part of me with a searing need that can only be soothed by his touch. Even his voice—that would take the edge of needing him so completely off.

Because I do. I need him so fucking entirely I almost miss the turn-off to my parents' place.

I catch it in time and swerve down the old road. It takes me just two minutes to travel down it, and as I slow, I realize that I was doing way over the limit. Shit. I'm lucky a cop didn't drive past me.

I tug my keys from the ignition and rest my forehead against the top of the steering wheel. Air fills my lungs with my deep breaths designed to calm and sooth.

When my heart has resumed its usual rhythm, I push open my car door and step onto the drive.

The wet drive.

How the fuck did I forget my shoes?

Yet another deep breath happens. Instead of mulling over and reading into this stupid oversight of mine, I run on tiptoes toward the house and ring the bell.

"The door!"

"Who is it? We're not expecting anyone!"

"I don't know, dear. Just get it!"

"Just get it, like I'm a flamin' slave," I hear my mother mutter as she opens the door. "Liv!" Her eyes light up when she sees me.

"Hi, Mom." I try a smile.

"Where are your shoes?"

I look at my wet feet and shrug lamely. "At home. I kind of forgot to put them on."

Her eyes rise up my body slowly. "Forgot? How does one forget their shoes?"

"When one's mind is otherwise occupied," I reply. "Can I come in or not?"

She opens the door wide. "Liv's here!" she calls then leans in. "You know Marchant is here. You know, your father's therapist friend."

I swallow my groan. Of course he'd be here, and of course she'd shout my arrival before she told me about him. She's obviously—correctly—figured out that my forgetting my shoes has to do with my little issue.

"Liv!" Marchant stands, looking much different than he did the last time I saw him. He's not old—maybe late thirties—but there's a light hint of silver at his crown and lines around his eyes. "How lovely to see you. You look wonderful."

Apart from no shoes.

"It's great to see you, too." I smile. I like the guy. I do. I'd just like him a whole lot more if he weren't a brain analyzer.

"What about me?" Dad asks. "Isn't it nice to see me?"

"Always." I kiss his cheek and hug him.

His arms around my body are warm and comforting. It's a grounding feeling I need right now. My heart is skipping several beats each minute from being in Marchant's presence. And not because he's fairly good-looking, but because I can feel him studying me and looking right through me.

I take a tentative seat next to Dad and listen in as they continue their conversation. Salmon fishing plans, bingo at the local hall, the farmer's market this weekend… They glaze over topic after topic, even mentioning the NFL draft before Mom whisks Dad away for his medication.

Now, alone, Marchant's focus is solely on me. "How are you, Liv?"

"I'm good," I reply.

"So good you forgot your shoes?"

"It happens to the best of us. You should ask my grandmother."

A smile curves his lips. "Your mom mentioned you're seeing someone."

"That's right."

"And how's that going?"

I sit up straight and stare into his eyes. "I'm not here for an impromptu therapy session, March. I'm not eighteen anymore. I have a handle on my addiction."

Silence buzzes between us.

"Do you?" he asks honestly, genuinely.

I suck on the inside of my bottom lip. "Mostly. Sometimes."

"Want to talk about it?"

I raise my eyebrows, and he holds his hands up.

"I won't charge you." He winks. "No, I'm genuinely interested in how you're coping, Liv. And to let you know that, if you need an impartial *friend* to discuss it with, I'm here."

I study him for a minute. His eyes are soft and compassionate. He's leaning back in his chair, his hands resting on his legs. He means it. Just to talk.

And I feel the burning desire to talk to someone who doesn't know but understands. Someone who truly can make sense of everything for me.

The words tumble from me softly. From how we met, to our constant run-ins, to our 'safe' agreement. From the dangerous feelings to where we are now. How all of it makes me feel.

"And he's gone until tomorrow night?"

I nod. "I won't see him until Monday, but I'll be busy working to open the new bar, so I don't even know when." I run my fingers through my hair.

"Is this the first time you've been apart since you accepted how you're feeling?"

Another nod. "Yes."

"And that feels…"

I meet his eyes. "Being apart from him is like someone's torn my soul out and is shredding it right in front of my eyes."

He blinks, my words throwing him off. Hell, they throw me off. No matter how true they are, I'm constantly surprised by the strength of my feelings for Tyler. I'm constantly surprised by how they consume me.

I take a deep breath and stand. "I have to go. I'm sorry."

"Wait." Marchant stands and hands me a card from his pocket. "You ever feel the need for a coffee, call me."

You ever feel the need for a free therapy session over coffee, call me.

I curl my fingers around the card and take it. "I will."

"And, Liv?" He steps closer to me and presses two fingers to my temple. "Addiction is all in the mind. So is willpower. You don't have to succumb to anything you don't want to."

I give him a sad smile and gently lower his hand. I put two of my own fingers to my heart. "But my feelings are in here, and no amount of willpower will make those go away."

"You would be surprised at the power of the mind."

"The power of my mind is why I am where I am and feel what I do. Nothing about that can surprise me any longer." I grab my phone from the table next to my chair and sigh. "I understand what you're saying, March, but it simply isn't that easy. It's not a matter of box A and box B. There's no compartmentalizing when this situation arises. When emotion and addiction collide, you need a whole lot more than willpower."

"Perhaps you should believe in your ability to conquer your addiction. We all have our vices, Liv. Yours are just stronger and more destructive than most." He follows me to the front door and opens it for me. "Perhaps you should use this weekend as a blessing in disguise, time to fight against your addiction. It will make you stronger."

"I'm strong, March. I'm strong enough to recognize and accept this for what it is, but that doesn't mean I'm strong enough to fight it." I walk through the door and look at him. "Rome wasn't built in a day."

"Meaning?"

"Meaning recovery won't happen in a day either. You should know that." With that, I walk to my car and get in, leaving him staring after me.

My phone buzzes in my hand and I pull up the message with shaky fingers.

> *Go by the truffle store and pick up my order. I'm stuck with the caterer and a last-minute menu adjustment.*

I smile at Day's text despite my disappointment.

> *I hope you're wearing a hat to hide your horns, Bridezilla. See you later.*

"Last-minute menu adjustment my ass!" Day fumes. "Just under a month to go and they're all, "We can't get this from our supplier. We'll have it take it off the menu."

"What meal was it?" Tessa asks, crossing her legs in front of her.

"The vegetarian one!"

"So you don't have a veggie option?" I stare at her as she puts three wine glasses in front of us.

Day laughs loudly. "Oh, no, I have a vegetarian option. I told them I didn't give a shit what their usual supplier stocked. If they wanted their payment in full, they'd find me a supplier that *did* stock it."

"And?"

"They've found a supplier that will stock it. After I pointed them in the direction of several." She scoffs, pouring the wine. "Bastards fucking up an already shit day."

I share a glance with Tessa.

"What's happened?" she asks softly.

Day sighs and sits down. "I just wish it were the wedding already, you know? I know, I know. I was freaking out like a week ago"—she glances to me—"but the agency signed a new model two days ago."

"Who was it?"

"Naomi's protégé."

"No fucking way!" I snap. "How?"

Day shrugs. "There was no basis not to. Besides, it's not breaching the rules Aaron set out. It just really bugged me. I know they're the best agency and the girl is promising, but with all the shit with flowers and caterers dropping out and now this, it feels like we'll just never be able to get married and just be fucking happy."

"Marriage is overrated," Tessa puts in. "Seriously, love, he's all picking up his socks and putting his dirty bowl in the sink now, but the second that ring is on his finger, you bet your arse you'll be finding those bowls under the sofa and socks stuffed behind the toilet."

I snort. "Your brother is never changing then."

Day laughs quietly. "Keeping a man is like house-training a puppy. You find their shit everywhere."

"Well, now that you put it that way, Angus's hatred of Tyler makes total sense. I'm introducing him to a dog."

Tessa giggles. "You don't have to worry until you start finding blond hairs on the back of the sofa and a used condom behind the bin because he's a rubbish shot."

Day and I both wince. "Ouch," she said. "So you knew before?"

"I thought he was, but I couldn't go to my lawyer without definitive proof. After all, the maid was blond." She shrugs. "I'm not so bothered anymore. Like I said, he's a rubbish shot. He couldn't find the G-spot if you gave him neon signs inside your vagina."

I choke on my mouthful of wine at her words. It goes up my nose and burns like hell, but I pinch my nose and breathe until the sensation leaves.

"Talk of the devil," she sighs, grabbing her ringing phone from the table.

"Wait. Doesn't he know you're here?" I ask.

She grins and lifts the phone to her ear. "Hello, darling. Has Blondie left your sorry, lost arse already?"

I purse my lips and look away to fight my laughter. Tessa winks and walks to the window. Day and I catch each other's eyes and grab a pillow each to laugh into.

"Don't be unreasonable? I'm actually being very reasonable. You're the one who was playing with toys that weren't yours to play with… It was just once? Pull the other one. I'm not a doormat… Oh, good. You got the letter from my lawyer… You don't agree? Now that is unreasonable. You signed the prenup. You knew what would happen if you went elsewhere…" She sighs and puts a hand on her hip.

Day nudges me and whispers, "How you doing?"

"I'm fine." I frown.

"Without Ty."

"Shit," I answer honestly. "I miss him. He hasn't called yet and I'm sitting here like a girl after a first fucking date."

She squeezes my hand. "He'll call soon, I'm sure."

"I don't need my family to fight anything for me. You forget I run the UK business and very successfully. I deal with my lawyer, not my father, so don't bring my family into your fuck-up…" Tessa laughs silently into her hand. "Okay… Oh, darling, I'd love to meet you for lunch, but I'm afraid I'm not in London… I'm in Seattle."

A loud noise comes through the phone before she drops it and laughs loudly.

"Oh boy, that was fun. Surprise, knobhead!" She giggles again and sits on the sofa. "Well, I imagine he won't be calling again for a while."

"Sounded…interesting." Day smirks.

"'It was only once…' 'I promise it'll never happen again…' 'Oh, Tessa, baby, come on. We can make this work.'" Tessa imitates a man's voice. "Once my arse. Never happen again my arse. We can make this work my bloody vagina!"

"I am never getting married." I grin, hiding behind my wine glass. "There's more drama in it than anyone needs."

"Word," Dayton mutters. "Did you get my truffles?"

"Uh, did you miss the huge box on the kitchen table?" I point to it.

She looks over the back of the sofa and groans. "I should have hired someone to do them for me."

"It's not too late," Tessa says. "You could still hire someone so we can just sit here and drink wine all night."

"I'm with her." I point in her direction and pick up a handful of ribbons. "I mean, look at these. How fiddly are they?"

Day studies it for a minute. She opens her mouth to speak, but my phone buzzing interrupts her. I pull it from my pocket and a grin spreads across my face when I see Tyler's name on the screen.

"Be right back," I tell the girls, skipping into Aaron's office. "Hello?" I answer, a deep breath making me sound breathless.

"Hello yourself." His voice wraps around me like a blanket, and I close my eyes to the sound of it.

"What took you so long to call?"

"My models are bitches. They kept the shoot running two hours over the time slot until they had pictures they were happy with. Naturally, every bad picture was my fault and not the fact they were just shit."

"I thought you forgot about me," I say softly.

"Never," he replies firmly. "How can I forget you when I can't stop bloody thinking about you?"

My lips twitch. "Touché."

"I'm sorry, baby girl. I should have texted you earlier."

"No, you shouldn't have. I'm just being stupid." I run my fingers through my hair. "I just… I miss you. That's all."

"I miss you, too." A door shuts on his end.

"No… I mean, I miss you. Really badly." I swallow and squeeze my eyes shut. "Please tell me you'll be home in time to see me tomorrow night."

He says nothing for a long moment. Every second he doesn't speak, my stomach coils a little tighter.

"Tyler."

"They canceled my second shoot today because of those two bitches. I have to do it tomorrow. Aaron's on the phone to Dayton now. We might not make it back until Monday morning."

I take a deep breath. "What? No." I can't wait that long to see him. Not when I need him so badly already.

"I'm sorry. I'm so sorry. I'm missing you, too."

I swallow and bring my knees up. I drop my forehead to them and take a deep breath through my nose. The tears burn my eyes and I hate this. I hate this fucking weakness.

"Okay," I say, my voice thick. "I'll see you Monday, okay?"

"Shit, no, Liv. Don't you dare hang up!" he shouts down the phone.

I bring it back to my ear. "What? Talking to you is making it worse." My voice cracks on the last word.

"Don't cry, baby girl. Please. Shit." He lets out a quieter string of curses. "Don't you dare cry when I'm not there to wipe your tears away."

"I have to go, Ty."

"I'll be home tomorrow night, okay? I promise. I don't care if I'm up all night. I'll be there tomorrow."

"Okay," I whisper. "I'm going."

"Liv!"

I don't respond.

Then I hear, "Aaron, fuck your call. Get Day to see her now!"

I hang up then and drop the phone. My arms go around my legs and squeeze tight, and my whole body coils into a ball of aching need. The office door opens and I feel the softness of my best friend's arms circling me.

She holds me, does nothing but hold me. The tears drop from my eyes onto my sweatpants, dotting the material with salty wetness.

"I hate this," I whisper. "I fucking hate this. It's killing me. I shouldn't be able to need him this badly."

I turn my face into Dayton and she sits on the sofa next to me. She rocks me gently, side to side, her cheek resting on top of my head.

"What did he do?" Tessa asks through my quiet sobs.

"Nothing, for once." Dayton replies, and I feel her sad smile against the top of my head. "Want me to explain?" she whispers to me.

I nod.

"Liv is…addicted to love. Well, people, actually. It's hard to explain, but this is only the second time she's felt this way. She always avoided it, because the first time she was addicted to someone, some bad shit happened." Day exhales slowly. "Tyler being Tyler, he forced his way in, and together, they're insane. Their addictions mesh, Tessa. Him to her body and her to him in general. It's both scary and fascinating to watch. They don't even realize how good they are together."

"Except we're not," I butt in, sitting up. I look at Tessa, my vision blurred. "We're not good—not for each other. We are the very worst thing either of us needs because neither of us are strong enough to walk away. We're stuck in an endless circle of craving and needing. His addiction feeds mine and mine feeds his. We are so fucking dangerous for each other, and every day, it gets worse because feelings get involved."

"I missed something," Day says quietly.

"It's fucked. We are fucked, because if either of us was going to walk away, it was going to be me. But I can't. Not now. I'm more than addicted to him," I whisper. "Talking to him just now made me realize. Addiction hurts, but not this much. Addiction doesn't slice your soul in two if you're apart."

My best friend takes a deep breath. I know. She knows.

I look Tessa in the eye, too afraid to meet my best friend's gaze. "For some awful reason, I am completely in love with the guy. And emotion and addiction don't go well together. It's as painful as it is pleasurable, but I can't stop."

His twin stares at me. Her eyes give nothing away, her impassive face the perfect mask. Slowly, she steps toward me and crouches in front of me.

"If love doesn't hurt, then you're doing it wrong." She reaches up and swipes her thumbs across my cheeks. "He is my brother and he is the biggest fucking arsehole I've ever met in my life, so I'm not just saying this for the sake of it, okay?"

I nod.

"He likes to think he's big man protector where I'm concerned, but the guy couldn't break the wings off a bloody fly." She smiles. "He's not perfect, Liv, and apparently, neither are you, but if anyone is going to love him, I'm glad it's you. Maybe, when you both start living and stop fighting, you'll see what I do."

"What do you see? Because all I see right now is emptiness."

"Put enough imperfections together and, eventually, you will achieve perfection. But even then, perfection is all about perspective. Maybe you and Tyler and your imperfections will make the kind of perfect you both need." She cups my cheeks and kisses the top of my head. "Sit here, drink wine, and I will go and call my pain-in-the-arse twin to make sure he's not taking a hammer to a door or something."

"Um, say what?" Day calls after her as she darts out of the room.

Tessa reappears with our wine, which has been topped up, and has the biggest grin on her face. "When we were eight, he pulled the head off my Barbie and threw it down the toilet. In retaliation, I hid all his BB gun bullets in the pantry. This was around the time Mum decided to put a lock on the pantry door because he kept creeping in in the middle of the night."

"I see where this is going." Amusement hints at my lips.

"He stole the hammer from the shed and knocked the door down to get to them. I ended up with several bruises from all the times he shot me after that, but it wasn't as bad as the grounding he got for breaking the door. Believe me. That boy had—and still has—a temper. As long as you can tame it, you're fine."

Day smiles at me. "Oh, she can tame it. You should have seen him when you called him to tell him about that dickhead."

"I bet he went all caveman psychotic, didn't he?" She winks. "Well, my ex-husband is still alive, so I'll believe you can calm him down. Although, if you don't mind, I don't want the details."

I smile now. "I won't make you hear them."

"Good. I'm gonna call him. I'll be a minute." She closes the door behind her.

I sigh, sip the wine, then set it down. Silence hovers between me and Day before I say, “Day?”

“Liv?”

“It’s okay if I love him, isn’t it?” I finally meet her gaze.

“It’s always okay to love someone.”

“Even if it doesn’t always feel good? Even if it kills you as much as it makes you feel alive? Then is it okay still?”

Her lips turn up sadly. “I don’t know.”

Chapter THIRTEEN

AFTER three hours of putting truffles into tiny little bags, labeling them, and tying them, I was more than ready to crash and not wake up for a very long time. Unfortunately, my mind had another idea—thousands of them, in fact.

I spent the whole night tossing and turning and only got a couple of hours of sleep when I got a cab home at four a.m. The sleep was broken and restless, but it was there at least.

I yawn and scratch Angus's head. "Oh, buddy. What am I going to do?"

He looks at me and walks to his food bowl. For an animal that can catch a dumb amount of birds and mice, he's sure dependent on me for food. I get up and give him some biscuits, muttering about needing to go to the store before it closes.

My eyes fall to the clock on the wall. It's barely ten a.m., but my apartment is already cleaner than it's been in, well, a couple of years. After weighing it up, I grab my car keys and make the drive to the bar.

Or Crimson Lounge, as the sign outside now proclaims.

The 'L' reaches up until a cocktail glass comes out of the top of it, totally eclipsing the word 'crimson.' But it looks incredible.

I unlock the door, push it open, and step into a different bar. All the furniture is now in its rightful place, albeit still covered, but the bar is as good as ready to go. Apart from the bottles I have to install into the optics this week and the glasses to put out, it's done. The lights are all in place, curtain poles are up, and even the upstairs is done.

The place is empty, so I go upstairs, running my hand along the solid-wood banister. Upstairs is different than downstairs. The red is darker, the white brighter, the leather seats smoother. The bar is smaller and curved whereas downstairs it's straight. The solid mahogany of the bar sets off the rest of the place, even the black floors.

I walk to the railings and lean over. Whoever designed this place did a great job. Better than great, actually. An amazing job.

I walk back downstairs and go the bar. A file is sitting on top of it. I missed it a moment ago, but I grab it now and read the note attached to the front.

Liv,
Here are all your applications for the bar. We filtered out the majority. Security is already hired, as is cleaning, so you just need to focus on bar staff, possible wait staff for busier nights, and an assistant manager. I'll do the assistant manager interviews with you, but all the others are yours.

A

I open the file, my interest piqued. Considering they've already taken a bunch and said no, I'm assuming I'm getting the best of the bunch here. I better be, at least.

Although, I could sure use the distraction of a bunch of crap applicants.

I flick through each application, setting some aside whenever I read some good ones. Aaron—or rather his assistant—have sectioned off the applications, so it's easy for me to do. There are plenty for cocktail shakers, and I'm definitely going to need proof of those skills before they're hired.

That and I love watching them do those fancy-ass moves.

I set my number-one applicants to the front of the file and head back toward the storeroom. If the sign is up, chances are all the promotional items and other things are here too.

I'm right—there are boxes upon boxes in the room. I blink at them a few times before I unstack them. I look around for something to tear them open with, and some smart cookie has obviously thought of this because there's a penknife on a shelf.

I grab it and slice through all the tape holding the boxes down. One box holds drinks mats for the tables. Another holds cloths for the bar. Another is full of menus, printed already, and I pick one up.

It's in the club colors—red and white with a hint of black—and the logo is at the top. They're gorgeously designed, with each part sectioned off just like Dayton suggested.

The Classics. Date Night. Girls' Night. Break-Up Night. To Heck With It

Night. Final Night of Freedom.

I see she went all in on the 'night' theme. I smile and put it back down. Amazing. There are all sorts of other little things in here, but right now, all I really want to do is pull all that plastic off the furniture and get this place looking like a real bar.

So I do. I leave the storeroom and pull the plastic off every table, off every chair, and I dump it all in the middle of the dance floor. But the sleek, leather booths and thick-glass tables and stools all look even better now.

I eye the bar and rest my hands on my hips. I want to pull it all off.

Oh, to fucking hell with it. I'm the manager here.

With a loud giggle, I put the file on a stool and whip the plastic off in one go so I can examine the bar properly. Smooth, dark, incredible. Perfectly carved and lit, it's a little slice of heaven, perfectly adapted for cocktail-making.

I do the same with upstairs, not stopping until every bit of furniture is free of the constraints of the plastic. I don't stop until the leather seats are breathing freely and I'm breathing harshly from the exertion.

Then I sit, all the plastic removed, with nothing left to do. And the ache that disappeared in my fleeting hour of excitement is back.

I sigh and lean my head against the wall. Maybe I should call applicants for some of those interviews.

I take the newly installed phone from the wall, sit at the bar, and dial the first number. Within an hour, I've left three messages and set up five interviews.

I sit back, my foot tapping in front of me. It's the middle of the afternoon. I've been here longer than I thought. No wonder my stomach is rumbling and in the early stages of digesting itself. I haven't eaten at all.

I grab my keys from the bar and lock the door behind me. There's a little sandwich place just down the street, so I make my way there. A light, early summer breeze flurries down the street after me, and I step inside gratefully. It's not quite warm enough to appreciate that yet.

I order my sandwich, grab a bottle of Coke, and head back down to the bar. I don't want to go home yet. It's still too empty.

The Lounge is a place relatively untouched by Tyler.

I sit back at the bar once inside and open my sandwich. The optics at the back of the bar are empty, ready for the big bottles to be delivered tomorrow, and I stare at them, wondering how to organize them. I grab my pen and flip over the sheet of paper with Aaron's note on it.

I absently scribble on it, scrawling the spirit names as I stare at the back of the bar.

"You didn't have to get me anything to eat."

I jolt, drop my pen, and turn. Tyler grins at me—a big, boyish grin that makes my breath catch.

"You're back?" I stare at him dumbly.

"I'm back." He holds his arms out and I dive into them, curling mine around his neck.

I hold on tight to him. My face buries into his neck and I breathe him in. Relief and relaxation seep through my body at the feel of his lips against my neck and his hands splaying across my back. At the simple sound of his voice, at the touch of his hands, at just being near him.

"You could tell a guy where you are, you know? I've been up the arsehole of this damn city trying to find you."

I pull back and smile at him. "I didn't think you'd be back until tomorrow."

He grins and runs his thumb across my jaw. "Some things are more important than stuck-up, self-righteous size zeros."

Our lips meet in a soft kiss, one that sends shivers through me with its tenderness.

"It's a good thing I'm not a size zero," I murmur.

"Don't ever be a size zero," he murmurs back, setting me back on my stool and slipping between my legs. "You're far too fucking sexy to lose your curves." He slides his hand down and over my hip and thigh as if to prove his point.

I smile and wrap my arms around his waist, laying my head against his stomach. He hugs my shoulders, understanding instantly that I just need to touch him. Need him to touch me.

His stomach is hard beneath my cheek, rising and falling lightly with every breath he takes. But it's not enough. Still not enough, so I slide one of my hands beneath his shirt and flatten it against his bare skin.

He twitches beneath my touch but doesn't move. "What are you doing?"

"Trying to figure out what order I'm putting the bottles in," I answer, staring at the bar again.

"Really? It looks like you had a party for one in here." He looks at the dance floor and then down at me.

I tilt my head back to meet his gaze and smile innocently. "It was pissing me off. I wanted her to look like a real bar."

"Her? You talk like she's your baby."

"She is. Kind of. And I want her to be perfect." I squeeze him and let my arms drop. I reach for the other half of my sandwich, but a larger hand grabs it. "Hey!"

Tyler takes a big bite. "What? Aaron might be a freakin' billionaire these days, but he needs a decent damn chef on his plane."

I stare at him flatly. "Oh, I feel for you. Imagine having a bad private chef on your private plane." I roll my eyes, and he laughs like he always does when I mock his attitude.

"I know. You'd think he could afford a good one." He takes the seat next to me. "Why do you have the sloe gin with the whisky?"

"Huh?"

He taps my sheet.

"I don't know. You've been distracting me all weekend. It's a wonder I managed to use my vibrator successfully."

He stops with the sandwich halfway to his mouth. "What?"

I scratch my chin. "It's a wonder I was able to use my vibrator successfully."

"Are you joking?"

I shake my head, swallowing my laughter.

"You used your vibrator and I wasn't here to see it?" He drops the sandwich and grabs my wrists, pulling me off the stool and into him. "You better be fucking joking."

I stare at him, my eyebrows raised in challenge. I didn't use it, but it's so fun to see him this wound up about it.

"Liv."

"I used it all right."

He pulls my head toward his and crushes his lips down onto mine. As he pulls me farther into him, his growing erection hardens against my stomach. His fingers dig into me and his tongue sweeps its way through my mouth with a fevered lust. Our lips mesh in a heated battle that ignites every nerve in my body.

"I lied," I breathe when he pulls away. "I didn't touch it. But it was worth lying about for that."

He narrows his eyes and curves his fingers around my neck. "You're going to be the death of me."

I smile against his mouth. "I'm not sorry for that."

"Don't ever be sorry for that." He sweeps his lips across mine. "But you should be sorry for the incredible hard-on you've gone and given me."

I drop a hand to his pants and brush my fingers up his erection. I lean on tiptoes, settling my mouth next to his ear. "There's no CCTV yet."

He turns his face toward me and his eyes immediately darken. "Are you saying what I think you're saying?"

I step back from him and lock the door. I raise my eyebrows and put one hand on a hip. "I'm saying a bar was on your list, and we have one right here."

He watches me as I approach him and pull my shirt over my head. I throw it on the stool and turn to him. I tug at his shirt and he lifts it off, dropping it on top of mine.

He stands in front of me, not touching me, his chest moving at the same rapid pace mine is.

"Are you asking me to fuck you on this bar?" he asks in a deep, ragged tone.

I step forward and hook my fingers over his belt. "That's exactly what I'm asking."

Without replying, he pulls me over to one of the booths, the one closest to the door.

I watch as he pulls down his jeans and pants, letting his cock spring free, and sits back on one of the leather chairs.

"Come here," he says, holding his hand out. I take it and he brings me to him, rolling my jeans down my legs until I step out of them and my shoes. He pulls me on top of him and his cock rubs against my clit, making me clench. "I've got a better idea. Why don't you fuck me and show me how much you missed me?"

I gasp, but his kiss swallows it. His hands, firm on my hips, grind me against him until I can take no more of the slow heat of my body and slide him inside me. I rock against him, winding my fingers into his hair, and rest my nose alongside his.

Being connected to him as one silences all my thoughts. It eases the pain of being apart from him this weekend and sates what needed to be sated. Being this close, as close as we will ever be, eases the ache.

It means I can give him everything—everything we both need. Because this—this touch—is the one thing that makes perfect sense to us both.

This touch is the one thing that could save us from ourselves.

Chapter FOURTEEN

"My parents are in town in two days."

I look up from the glove compartment of his car. "Say what now?"

Tyler glances at me. "They're coming to see Tessa. They mentioned they wanted to meet you. If you're free to do dinner."

I bite my tongue. "Can we talk about this tomorrow? You just got back and I—"

"Don't want to freak out on me already?" His lips quirk on one side. "Okay." He parks the car, grabs his bag, and then takes my hand as we get out.

A cool breeze blows off the water of Elliott Bay as we walk along the waterfront. A few boats bob in the gentle motion of the water, the ferries docked and ready for their next journey.

"I have to go away for another shoot this week," Tyler says, breaking our silence.

"Oh." My heart sinks. "Where to?"

"Down to California. Santa Barbara. Where you shot last time?"

I nod.

"Come with me." He stops and stands in front of me. "You have Day's hen party in L.A. this weekend. My shoot is on Friday. We can stay over until Saturday. Then I'll fly to Vegas and meet Aaron for his stag party."

"Really? You'll let me come with you?"

He nods and brings me in for a kiss. "Just…don't run out mid-shoot again, okay?"

I open my mouth and close it again. "You might have to tie my legs together to guarantee that."

"Can't do that. I like them open too much," he teases.

I bat his chest and walk again. "You're so bad," I sigh.

"I'm sorry," he says, resting an arm over my shoulders. "What would you like to talk about?"

"I don't know. The time you bashed your pantry door in, maybe?" I glance at him.

His jaw ticks, and I smile. I nudge his side with my elbow, and he grumbles his sister's name.

"She's such a cow," he mutters.

"Cow? Are you Brit-talking me again?"

"Would you like me to Brit-talk you?"

"You're changing the subject."

"You mentioned the Brit-talking."

"I asked you if you were. It wasn't an invitation to Brit-talk me."

"Bollocks," he whispers in my ear. "Knob. Trousers. Knickers."

"Say 'knickers' again."

"Knickers," he whispers, his breath seemingly hotter this time.

"That's the sexiest damn word in existence."

"Knickersknickersknickers!" he says louder.

I clap my hand over his mouth and laugh. "Hey, don't go shouting that shit. I don't want every girl here getting excited over your Brit-talk. That's mine. You hear that, Tyler Stone? Your Brit-speak is mine."

"Just my Brit-speak? I'm offended, my little American bitch."

"You and your Brit-speak are mine." I reach up and kiss him. He drops his arm to my waist and pulls me closer.

He drops his arm to my waist and pulls me closer. "Good," he murmurs. "As long as you know that."

"Me? You're the one who needs to know it, shouting 'knickers' all over the place!"

His grin turns playful. "Watch it or I'll have all these girls wanting to drop their knickers for me."

I roll my eyes. "That ego." I step from his arms and walk along the pier.

I rest my forearms against the railing and close my eyes against the gentle breeze. It's noisy from the restaurant just behind us, but the sound of the wind drowns most of it out into a dull buzz.

My lips curve into the light chill, and I tilt my head back slightly. My hair teases around my cheeks, and I sigh happily.

Warmth covers my back, and two elbows rest alongside mine. Tyler's mouth brushes along my cheek.

"You're beautiful." His words are a whisper but seem like a scream to me.

I run my fingers down his arm to where he's holding his camera. Without saying a word, he tilts it so I can see the screen and brings up his last pictures. They're of me leaning here, looking out at the water.

He rests his chin on my shoulder. "See? Beautiful. I could watch you do nothing all day."

My lips twitch. "That would get boring after a while."

"No." His mouth touches my jaw. "Believe me. It's not boring at all. I watch you even when you think I'm not. I can't help myself. I have to know the exact curve of your jaw, the flutter of your eyelashes, the shape of your lips, the shade of your eyes. I have to know and I have to remember it, because when you're not there, the memory is all I have."

I lift my arm and curve my fingers around his neck from the front. "At least the memory can't talk back."

"Baby girl, the memories of you have nothing on the real thing."

My heart pounds with his words. The honesty in them is overwhelming—and too much. Way too much.

"Who knew a sex addict could be so romantic?"

"And who knew a love addict would be the one to break the moment?" he teases right back, his chest vibrating with laughter.

I look back at him with a smile. "Come on, crazy stalker Brit. I need food."

"Worked up an appetite, have you?" He tucks his camera back inside his bag.

"Yeah. Pulling all that plastic off those chairs was hard work, you know?"

He smacks my butt and grabs my hand right after. "Bitch."

I grin.

"This is such a covert mission. I seriously feel like we're back in high school."

"Shut up and just do it, okay?"

"I'm not the one doing anything!" Dayton gives me a firm look and walks into the store.

I slink down in the seat of the car and nibble my thumbnail. My eyes focus on the door like a predator stalking its prey. My foot is tapping repeatedly against the floor.

I mean, hell. She's right. This is so fucking high school.

She walks out of the store, the white, plastic bag swinging from her hand, and gets into my car. She dumps the bag in my lap. "This is irrational, even for you."

"Oh, thanks. I just… I feel odd." I put the bag—and the box inside—into the pocket in my door. "And it's no odder than when you had to get me one because I thought Gary Coombe came when we dry humped."

"You were wearing pants!"

"I was seventeen and they were down by my knees!" I pull away from the store. "But it doesn't matter. Like I said, I feel strange. I shouldn't have broken down like that over the weekend."

"You sent me to buy a pregnancy test on the basis of your breakdown this weekend? One that was caused by your addiction?"

I don't reply. Okay, so it sounds a little crazy when she puts it like that. And, really, who can deal with falling in love and a pregnancy test in, like, three days? Not me, but here I am anyway.

Because being pregnant is a far more rational explanation for my crazy-as-hell emotions. Even if addiction would—for once—be the preferable answer.

"You aren't going to make me sit in McDonald's while you do it, are you?"

I cut my eyes to her. "Lick a dick, Black. Lick a fucking dick."

She laughs loudly.

"No," I answer seriously. "I'm going to do it at home. He isn't there."

"You aren't going to tell him?"

"That I'm pissing on a stick because I'm fucking insane? No."

"But what if you're not insane? What if your breakdown was because you are pregnant and it was your addiction telling you to listen to your body?" she reasons. "Then what do you do?"

"I tell my sex-addict boyfriend that the object of his desire is about to balloon by forty pounds and get a permanent tiger-esque makeover and an enlarged vagina. Oh, and we get an adorable peeing, pooping, screaming, up-all-night baby at the end of it." I pull up outside her apartment block and look at her. "I have no symptoms, okay? None. Just a strange gut feeling I'm not sure I can trust."

"It could be gas."

"Get out the car and I'll go and find out."

She pushes open the door and glances over her shoulder before stepping out. "Wait. Did you pee already today?"

I clench my legs together and give her a tight smile. "No, so move your fucking ass!"

She gets out without another word and waves to me as I pull away. I'm not joking about the pee thing. My bladder hurts like a bitch.

I break the speed limit on almost every street on the way back to my apartment. Again, I thank my lucky stars that I didn't get pulled over. I tuck the bag into my purse as I go upstairs…just in case. You never know who's going to be around here, and both my neighbor and the old bat downstairs are the biggest gossips in the neighborhood.

They see me with a pregnancy test and, by next week, I'm going to be having triplets with a Latino stripper I met during a photo shoot in Zimbabwe.

Luckily, I make it to my apartment without seeing anyone, and I all but run inside. Desperately hoping Tyler will be here so I don't have to pee on this stick.

Silence greets me though, and the door shuts behind me with a thundering click. "Ty, you here?"

Nothing. I check every room, clutching my purse to my chest. Again, nothing. Not even Angus.

I'm one hundred percent alone.

I have to take this test, although I think my gut knows the answer.

I walk into the bathroom thinking how ridiculous this is. Day is right—one breakdown and a random gut feeling five minutes after waking up this morning don't justify the need for a pregnancy test.

I dump the box on top of the toilet seat and stare at it. Long, rectangular… The answer to my question.

Shit. I'm not seventeen anymore.

I tear the plastic off the box and open it. The test is long and thin, and I pull the cap off, showing the absorbent tip. Taking a deep breath, I pull up the toilet seat, pull down my pants, and sit.

And so begins the awkward How To Pee On The Stick dance.

Opening my legs as wide as humanly fucking possible—Tyler would have a field day if he could see this position—and leaning forward, I shove the stick between my legs and pee.

Hit the stick first time. Bingo.

After the obligatory five seconds of peeing, I recap the stick and pee like a normal person. Thank fuck. I think my pelvis almost snapped right then.

I put the stick on the side, ignoring the way the little hourglass is turning in the bottom corner.

Ignoring? Who the fuck am I kidding? I'm stalking that bitch like it's Channing Tatum walking into my apartment.

I finish my business and shove the stick up my sleeve. I'm alone, no one is here, but I'm hiding it anyway.

Then, like a totally rational human being, I shove it in my knicker drawer and slam it shut.

Shit. I'm even saying 'knicker' now.

And I pace. To the front door. To the kitchen. To the sofa. To the bath. To the spare room. To Angus's food bowl.

To my bedroom.

I sit on the bed and stare. At the drawer. Accusingly. Tapping my foot. Sighing. Chewing my nail. Flicking my hair. Rocking my legs.

Has it been three minutes yet?

I don't know.

I'm too afraid to look.

I stay sitting and count to sixty in my mind. I rationalize that it's surely been three minutes by now. Surely.

Deep breath, Liv.

Deep breath.

I open the drawer and pull the test out. My eyes are screwed shut. Aw, hell. Where are my lady balls?

Mind you, if I had balls, I wouldn't be staring at a stick covered in my urine.

Okay. Shit. Time to look.

I open my eyes and look at that motherfucking hourglass, which is flipping itself up and down, up and down.

"You bitch," I hiss.

That had to have been three minutes! If not, it was sure as shit the longest two of my life.

"Change. Change." I chant, over and over, staring at the tiny screen. "Change you fucking—ooooh shit. Oh. Shit."

Pregnant. 3+.

Chapter FIFTEEN

I DROP the stick like it's giving me herpes.

No no no no no no fucking no!

I have the implant. How is this possible? I didn't actually think I would be.

Shit.

There's a person inside me.

A real-life person.

A tiny baby that is part me and part Tyler.

That will cry at me and poop on me and spit up all over my Louboutins.

Fuck. No.

I must have read that wrong.

I grab the stick and look again, but no. I was right. Pregnant, 3+. That's five weeks... Over a month. Which means I got pregnant almost immediately. When we weren't even in a real relationship.

I hold out my left arm and stare at the place where my implant is. All that pain getting it fitted, and for what? For it to give in and get me knocked up six months before it gets taken out?

Shit. I have to call the doctor. I need this thing removed.

I look between my arm and the test. I have to get the implant removed. There is no other option.

Yes, Tyler and I are fucked up. Yes, our relationship isn't the healthiest. Yes, we both have our issues.

But this baby? It didn't ask for that. It doesn't deserve to be punished for what we suffer from. That's for me and him to deal with.

I look down at my stomach. Fifteen minutes ago I was joking about ballooning, putting weight on, getting stretch marks… Now I'm scared.

I'm petrified.

I pull up my top, lie down, and settle my hand over my lower stomach.

I never thought I'd ever be a mom. I never imagined, not even for a second, that I would find someone I would be comfortable enough and safe enough with to contemplate having a family with.

Only I didn't decide this. It was chosen for me. For some bizarre reason, this baby was picked when I didn't want it to be.

Crap. That sounds so bad. Like I don't want this baby.

I do. I don't. Maybe I do. Maybe I don't.

I don't know what to feel right now. All I know is I have to call my doctor and get this bit of metal out of my arm because this baby deserves more than failing hormones being pumped into my body.

Then I can come to terms with it. Then I can accept the hand I've been dealt, deal with my demons, and look forward.

With Tyler.

Because there's no way I can't tell him.

I just need to accept it myself before I do.

I wince as the doctor cuts a small line down my arm despite the fact that I can't feel any pain. When I called and told her about my test results, she got me in during her next appointment to remove it.

The whole time, she's been telling me how unfortunate it is I got pregnant on the implant, and how I'm in the tiny two percent of people who will. She's also been telling me that I should have been using a condom as well as the implant to practice safe sex.

The whole time, I've been sitting here like, "Dude. I had the implant. You think I wasn't practicing safe sex?"

Regardless, she pulls the device from my arm and puts me back together. I leave the office with an appointment for two weeks' time, a prescription for folic acid, and a pregnancy booklet to read.

Fantastic.

I also leave with a heavy secret and a lead weight upon my heart.

The second I walk through the door of my apartment, I dive beneath a blanket on the sofa and turn on The Big Bang Theory.

My head is buzzing, spinning, swirling into outer space. In the last ten hours, I've discovered that I'm pregnant and had my contraception removed, ready to be a human incubator for the next nine months.

And I still have no fucking idea how I'm supposed to feel.

My phone vibrates against the sofa and I answer it without looking. "Hello?"

"Hey, baby girl," Tyler says. "My parents are in town a day early. Are you free for dinner tonight?"

My whole body goes rigid. *Shit. Too soon.* There's no way I can go to dinner with his parents now.

"I'm not feeling too good," I reply, guilt threading through my veins. "I think I ate some bad seafood for lunch. Can we reschedule?"

"Of course," he answers. "Do you want me to come over later?"

"No, it's okay. In case it isn't the food and is a bug or something." I'm the worst liar ever. *Shit. Crap. Ballbags.* "I'll call you in the morning."

"All right, babe. Go to bed, yeah?"

"Got it. Have fun with your parents." I hang up and drop the phone.

I'm awful.

I'm completely fucking awful.

His baby is inside me and I'm too chicken to tell him. What kind of person does that make me, really? If I can't even tell the father of my very unexpected baby that he's going to be a father? That he already *is?* Inside me or not, this baby is alive. A person. From the second this baby was conceived I became a mom, and he became a dad.

And just a few days ago, I was drinking wine like it's going out of fashion.

Guilt riddles me. Unnecessarily. I didn't know. I had no way to know—it's not like my womb held up a neon sign proclaiming "Baby in residence. ETA: 8 months."

Evolution should really get on that.

But still… I knew this morning. A moment of utter clarity came from nowhere, and something, I have no idea what, told me to drop everything and pee.

I stare at the wall. Everything is about to change. Everything.

I'll have to cancel the Balfour shoot. I can't be the face of a swimwear campaign when I'll look like a beached whale in said swimwear by next season.

The bar. How will I be able to I run the bar when my ankles are swollen and I'm walking with a waddle that would put penguins to shame?

How will anything be what I expected? My job, my dream, even my relationship. My reluctant relationship is now as serious as it's ever going to be. Our fun, playful, heated relationship is going to change the most.

Neither of us will be the same. My body will change irreversibly. What if Tyler never looks at me the same? What if the way we feel isn't enough?

There's no way we can base us on our addictions. Not now. I have to let him say the words and I have to say them back, because they're the truth, the reality, and we'll need to hold on to them if we're going to take our whirlwind relationship and make it into something stable enough for a child.

If he even wants to stay.

I cover my mouth with my hand. What if it isn't what he wants? After all, we're not the ones who should be having a family. We're nowhere near close to a forever kind of commitment.

Well, we weren't. A baby is about as forever as it gets. You won't get anything more binding than that.

And really… What do I know about Tyler aside from the menial things I've asked in a fit of hazed addiction? We've never spoken about his life in London. I know nothing about this guy. Not really.

I pull my laptop up from under the coffee table and rest it on my lap. I open it and type his name into the search engine.

I feel like a stalker. Almost like I'm invading his privacy—which is totally fucking ridiculous because any information I'm going to get is public. That and I haven't clicked on a link yet.

Stupidly, I click on the image search first. There are loads of pictures up. With Tessa. With Aaron. With two people I assume to be his parents. And with countless women. Different women, different nights, different events. I scroll down the page with bile rising in my stomach, twisting and turning up my chest until it burns my throat.

I swallow it down and get off that search. I click on the first link, which happens to be his website. The only new thing I gain from this is his portfolio. Family photos, relationships, headshots. There's just about everything, including images from campaigns he's shot. But my favorite part is the store. It's full of landscape shots, from city images to beach sunsets.

I flick through the images, wondering why I never knew that he did so many shoots for fun.

I go back to the search and go down the list of sites. There are charity auctions he's participated in, the prices some of his images sold for—*holymotheroffuckingfuck!*—and his name associated with some big names. Both professionally and personally. Both here and in London.

Do I even know him at all?

The man I know is down to earth. He's relaxed and playful, and he doesn't hesitate to hold anything back. I know he can rock a suit as much as the hottest New York billionaire and wear his jeans as well as the hottest music heartthrob.

I don't know the man standing next to that world-famous model or the up-and-coming actress. I don't know the man smiling with the TV host or the man dining with the country's most famous journalist.

My eyes burn with the realization that I don't know him. For all my questions, all my desires to know who Tyler Stone is, I've never really discovered anything.

He's a mystery to me.

I press the back button and set the laptop on the coffee table. Angus hops up onto the sofa with me and curls up on my thighs. He rests his head and front paws on my stomach, and I smile sadly as I run my fingers across his head.

"What am I gonna do, buddy?"

He rubs his head against my palm and purrs.

My lips twitch again, still sadly, and I rest my head back on the arm of the sofa. I scratch behind his ears and look down at him blindly, embracing the silence of the room.

It's sure quieter than my mind.

The lamp in the corner of the room clicks on, jolting me from my sleep. I sit up sharply, rubbing my eyes. "What the hell?"

"I could ask you the same thing." Tyler's voice drifts across the room. It's quiet, but there's a razor-sharp edge to each word.

"I'm not following." Angus jumps off my legs and runs into the spare bedroom.

Angus jumps off my legs and runs into the spare bedroom. Tyler leans against the wall, his hands in his pockets, his button-down shirt undone halfway. The shadows from the dark side of the apartment mingle with the light from the room, casting an eerie glow across his face.

"Bad seafood," he says simply. "I didn't think anything of it. It's reasonable—until I realized halfway through dinner that the only seafood you eat is salmon."

"So?"

"You can eat salmon uncooked. Plus the fact you eat it at least once a week because it's your favorite food—you'd know instantly if it wasn't right."

I freeze.

"So I spent half my night worrying about how you were when, in reality, you'd lied to me." He looks up and the emotion is his gaze cuts me. "If you didn't want to meet my parents, you just had to say. I wouldn't have forced you into it if you weren't ready."

Guilt. Heavy, heavy guilt wedges into my body and takes up residence in my heart.

"It's not that," I whisper, getting up and walking into the kitchen. My mouth is dry.

"Then what is it?"

I turn on the tap and fill the glass. I take a drink before I reply. "I don't… I don't know if I can talk about it."

My phone buzzes from the sofa and I walk back to it. Then I glance at the screen.

Dayton: Well? You've surely peed by now!

I throw it back down, set the glass on the table, and wrap my arms around my stomach. Like holding it will keep the baby a secret.

"Don't know if you can talk about it?" he asks, repeating my words back to me, anger sneaking in now. "What the hell does that mean? You lie to me and can't even tell me why?"

"Yes," I reply, closing my eyes.

"What the fuck, Liv?"

"I'm going to bed. Maybe you should go back to your place for tonight."

I turn, but the second I walk past him, he grabs my arm and spins me into him. His dark eyes hold mine captive, the anger and frustration mixing with worry and sadness.

"No. I'm not leaving until you tell me the truth."

I shake my head.

"We're in a relationship, Liv. That's how this shit works. We don't lie to each other and we sure as hell don't keep secrets!"

I snatch my arm away and step back. "We do when we're not ready to share."

"What could you possibly know that you're 'not ready' to share with me?" He raises his voice. "'Not ready' is absolute bollocks. Complete shit! Tell me."

"I can't."

"I don't do secrets, baby girl. Tell me right now or that's it."

My chest tightens at his insinuation. "You'll probably leave anyway when you find out," I whisper insecurely.

And there it is. The real reason I can't tell him.

I'm too afraid that, once I say those words, those two tiny words, he'll walk right on out that door and I'll be alone.

"What? I don't…" He runs his fingers through his hair. "Stop fucking around and tell me!"

My chest burns with my hurried breaths. Oh hell. I feel sick.

"Tell me!"

"I'm pregnant!"

Chapter SIXTEEN

MY words ricochet off every surface. They echo, ringing in my ears, until they finally peter out into silence.

I'm still standing here, my arms around my stomach, only now my eyes are on the floor. I can't look at him. He's not talking. He's not moving. He's breathing though, and that's the only noise in the apartment right now.

"Pregnant?"

"I found out this morning," I answer quietly. "I went to my OBGYN and she took out my implant and confirmed it."

"Why the fuck didn't you call me?"

I step back into the wall. "I was in shock. I still am."

"When is the… You… Us… Shit." He exhales loudly. "When is the due date?"

Is it mine? is what he's really asking.

"I don't know for sure, but the test said I'm five weeks. My OBGYN guessed mid to late December. I have an appointment with her in two weeks. She said she'll know better when she's seen the baby."

"Seen the—seen the baby? Like a scan?" His voice trembles.

I finally look up. He looks like he's seen a ghost. I don't blame him.

I feel like I have.

"Yeah." I nod slowly and hug myself tighter. "Like an ultrasound."

"Wow. Shit." His fingers go through his hair again, and he blows out another long breath. "And you didn't know? At all?"

I shake my head. "I feel fine. I just…had a feeling this morning."

"I knew something was wrong with you." He drops his hand. "Why didn't you tell me?"

I raise my eyebrows. "On a gut feeling that could have been nothing but paranoia? Really?"

"Okay, but you should have called me. As soon as you fucking knew, Liv! Fuck. If you feel half as rattled as I do right now, I should have been here for you!"

It clicks.

His anger isn't at me.

It's because he wasn't here with me.

"I'm sorry," I whisper. "I just… I panicked. Then it was positive and I had to get that stupid failing piece of crap out of my body so it didn't hurt our baby and then I panicked some more and then you called and then I panicked a little more and then I panicked myself all out."

His lips twitch. "Still got a little in there, huh?"

I exhale shakily. "A little? A lot. But I figure I have eight months to panic, so why waste all that in one day?"

"You…" He sighs and walks toward me. He wraps his arms around my shoulders and pulls me into him.

His hold is strong and certain. Warm. Steady. I turn my face into his chest.

I turn my face into his chest. "You don't have to stay, you know. If you need to go to…digest it…I get that," I murmur into his shirt.

"Silly woman," he says into my ear. "My silly, panicky bitch."

I crack a small smile at those words.

Tyler pulls back and rests his palms against my cheek. "Look at me."

I do.

"I'm not going anywhere," he says slowly and clearly. "You got that? You'll have to remove me with brute force to get me out of this apartment, and even then, I'd put up one hell of a fuckin' fight."

"Why? How?"

"I'm not saying this again," he breathes, pulling my face closer to his. "You and I, we're in this together. We both made this baby, so we're both going to raise this baby. Every day. Every single day, I will be there. And not because I have to be. Because I want to be. Because, dammit, Liv, you're a pain in my bloody arse, but there isn't a place I'd rather be than right by your side."

I swallow harshly to stop the buildup of emotion.

"I'm not saying this is going to be easy. I'm not saying we'll always get along or that we'll get it right. We won't be perfect. I'm shitting myself. I've never been so afraid of anything in my life."

"But us?" I whisper. "We're fucked up, Ty. We're volatile and we're not good for each other."

"Then we've got eight months to sort our shit out, haven't we?"

"What if I can't do it?"

"You don't have to do anything. *We* will do it all." He lowers his lips to mine. "We're all kinds of fucked up, but that doesn't mean we can't be fixed. It doesn't mean we can't fix it."

He drops his hands to mine and pulls my arms from around me. My arms fall limply to my sides. I'm still afraid.

He rests his hands against my sides and trails his fingertips down to my hips. They linger there as he hesitates. I breathe in slowly as he moves his hands across my stomach and stops them in the center, right above my pants.

He brushes his thumb back and forth across my skin, sending tingles and shivers through me.

"In there?" he says softly. "There's really a baby in there? Our baby?"

"Really, really," I reply just as softly.

Then he drops to his knees and lifts my shirt. I run my fingers through his hair as he gently touches his lips to my stomach. His kiss is light but lingering. It seems to last forever.

And neither of us moves. He stays pressed against my stomach and I stay holding his hair.

Time stands still. All there is is this moment. A moment where silent promises are made and words are left unspoken, because right now is proof that actions speak louder than words.

For one second, his touch has silenced all my fears.

I revel in this second, I hold onto it, and I take the plunge. "I love you, Ty."

His eyes snap to mine. They widen before they smile, lighting up with a happiness that's reflected in the curve of his lips. He stands, cups my head, and tilts my face toward his.

"I love you," he replies, his words buzzing across my lips with his kiss. "You're a pain in my fucking arse, but I do."

"Way to ruin the moment, asshole." I poke his chest.

He laughs and wraps his arms around me. "It was getting a little heavy in here. Thought the mood could do with lightening."

"Pregnancy and declarations of love will do that to an atmosphere, I guess." I smile against his chest. "We'll be okay, won't we?"

He kisses the top of my head. "I promise. And if we're not, we'll keep trying until we are."

Tyler stares at me across my kitchen table. Contemplative, curious.

"What?" I ask. "I can eat cheese spread on toast if that's what you're wondering."

He smirks. "No."

"Then what?" I pick up my juice.

"Can we still have sex?"

I spit out my juice. "What?!"

"You know. With the baby. Is it safe?"

I blink at him in disbelief. "It's a baby, not a fucking vaginal stitch-up! Of course we can still have sex!"

"Can't I hurt it? I mean… I have a beast of a cock."

I put my glass down and rest my head in my hands. *I will not laugh. I will not…* "Oh my god!" I laugh and look up. "No, honey, your 'beast of a cock' will not hurt the baby!"

"Good to know." He goes back to his cereal without another word.

I, however, am still staring like he's grown two heads. This is easily the strangest breakfast conversation I've ever had.

"Where did that come from?"

"I'm an expert on the female anatomy as far as the G-spot. I could navigate to that bitch blindfolded and drunk. Anything past that is like a black hole," he explains. "For all I know, there's, like, a jelly layer and the baby could feel me poking you or something."

I blink at him again. "Um, no. The baby won't feel a thing."

"Like I said, good to know." He grins. "Because I'm still kind of pissed the hell off about the secret thing and we all know what happens when I'm angry."

"Are you threatening to fuck me over breakfast? Because that's underhanded."

"I told you. I don't threaten, I promise. I'm promising to fuck you over breakfast." He drops his spoon into the bowl with a clunk. "I mean, crap. Do you even want sex still? Don't pregnant people go right off of it?"

Now it's my turn to grin. I lean forward into him. "Honey, you have a beast of a cock and the dirtiest mouth this side of the Pacific. You could make a nonexistent libido come back to life with one word."

"Cunt," he says. "Is it back yet?"

I throw a piece of toast at him. "It never left, you dick."

He gets up and walks to me. "Good." He leans in for a kiss. "You. Me. Later."

"Oh, seduce me." I roll my eyes.

He laughs. "What are you doing today?"

"I have an appointment with my agent. It was to get the stuff for the shoot, but…" I shrug a shoulder.

"Hey, you can still do it."

"No, I can't. They're not offering me a contract for maternity swimwear." I push some hair from my face and get up. "It took me long enough to get this far. Maybe this baby is telling me that modeling isn't the thing for me. Maybe she happened at the right time."

"She?"

"He. She. Whatever they are."

Tyler steps up behind me and wraps his arms around my waist. "Maybe they're telling you that you look amazing pregnant and barefoot in the kitchen."

I look down at my bare feet and laugh. "You're such a comedian."

"It's part of being British. We're all naturally fucking hilarious." He kisses my cheek. "Do you want me to come with you to see Sheila?"

I spin. "No! Can you imagine how awkward that would be? 'Hey, I'm going to have to leave modeling because the photographer you hooked me up with hooked up with me and knocked me up!'"

"That sounds badass when you put it like that." He steps back and pats his cock. "Good job, mate. Good job."

I stare at him openmouthed as he walks through to my room. "Did you seriously just pat your cock and tell it, 'Good job'?"

"Hey!" He steps out, shirtless. "Everyone will hug you and tell you well done. My cock needs some recognition for his part in it, too."

"Seriously? Next you'll be rubbing your balls to soothe the sperm that didn't make it out." I grab some jeans and a shirt.

"Should you be wearing jeans? Won't the button cut into your stomach?"

I smack him with the pants before I hear his raucous laughter. "If you're going to piss me off for the next eight months with stupid comments like that, I'm going to go all hormonal on your ass, Tyler Stone!"

He grabs me and hugs me tight. "I can't help it, baby girl. You look so incredulous every time. You should have seen your face."

I shove him away. "Don't forget. This whole thing is your fault. I get to hormone your ass anyway. Giving me a reason will just make it worse."

He acts shocked. "My fault? For all Seattle knows, you trapped me. I'm quite the catch."

I hit him with my shirt this time. "I'll catch your balls with my father's fishing pole if you keep going!"

He laughs loudly, an infectious laugh that makes me giggle along with him, and before I can pull my shirt over my head, he pushes me back on the bed and leans over me. His dark hair flops in front of his forehead, and his dimples show with his ever-growing smile.

"For the record," he says, grabbing my thighs and wrapping my legs around his waist, "I quite like being trapped by you."

"I did not trap you!" I flick his ear.

"I know. It's not a trap if you come willingly." He grazes his teeth over my bottom lip.

"Coming willingly is the issue here."

"I see no issue. We had incredible sex, my magic, beastly cock pulled some strings, and now you're stuck with me. It could be worse."

"Worse than being stuck with an egotistical, cocky, British asshole?"

"Yep." He kisses my nose. "You could be stuck with you."

"Fuck you!" I laugh.

"You will later." He winks and gets up.

I pull my shirt over my head and watch as he gets changed. Into clothes from my drawer. I lick my lips, the tang of my orange juice coming off them. His muscles flex as he pulls a shirt on, and I swallow.

I guess I should get used to sharing drawer space.

"What time will you be done with your agent?"

I drag my gaze away from his lovely butt and look at him. "I won't be long in there. Why?"

"Because we need to talk to my sister."

"Why? What's the rush?"

He grabs my hands and pulls me up. I'm not going to like this. He has that don't-you-fucking-dare-argue glint in his eyes.

"Tyler. Spit it out."

"Put your hackles down, bitch," he murmurs. "She needs to know she's moving into your place and you're moving into mine."

Apparently, drawer space isn't all I should be getting used to.

"Excuse me?"

"You're pregnant. My baby. You're living with me."

"Correct, correct, and we're coming back to this."

"No, we're not. I told you I'd be there every day and I mean it. That means I'll be holding your hair when you're sick and carrying you to bed when you pass out on the sofa because you're tired. It means I'll rub your feet when they're sore and look after you all the time."

"I'm pregnant, not sick." I put my finger over his mouth. "And you need to lay off the sugar, because if you carry on being so fucking sweet, I might actually *get* sick."

"You're moving in with me, Liv. Just like I wouldn't give up on you, I'm not giving up on this."

"I don't doubt it." I brush mascara over my lashes and pull my hair into a ponytail. "And just like I wouldn't stop fighting you on that, I won't stop fighting you on this." I meet his eyes through the mirror. "Twenty-four hours ago, my world was completely fucking rocked. Right now, I'm still hanging between a good rocking and a bad rocking. Let me come to terms with that before you throw another big change at me, okay? Please."

He lays his hands on my hips and kisses the back of my neck. "One week. You have one week to accept it because you're moving after Day's hen party."

"That isn't what I asked."

"But that's my offer, and it's the best you're going to get." He grabs his keys from the dresser and kisses me once more. "Call me when you're done with Sheila."

"Offer? That isn't a damn offer! That's a fucking demand!" The door opens. "Tyler!"

The door shuts.

I scream and throw my hairbrush out the door. *Sweet or demanding, they both piss me off.*

I grab my own keys and head out to meet my agent for the last time.

I leave the building with a heavy feeling in my heart. Shit. That was horrible. She was so nice and didn't even bat an eyelid when I told her that Tyler was the dad. She simply smiled, a knowing glint in her eye.

I get in my car and take a deep breath. It seems like there are a thousand things that need to be done right now—already. Before Tyler even decides to move me out of my home and into his. I look at the clock and note the time. I have to get to the Crimson Lounge for an interview.

I pull away and head in the bar's direction. In one week, it'll open and I'll be on my feet for hours every day. How will I cope when I'm all big and tired? How will I cope when my hormones really kick in *now?* Hell, when my cousin got pregnant a year ago, she spent the first few months in bed sleeping.

Of course, she was having twins, but…

Holy crap. What if this is twins? Tyler's a twin, right?

I dial his number and he answers immediately. "Are you okay?"

"What if it's twins?!" I shriek. "Two of them!"

"Then it's twins," he answers calmly. "I have experience with them, you know."

"Yeah, but two babies? Two? No. I quit."

"Liv? Liv, breathe, babe. It'll be fine."

"I'm pretty sure this is today's panic quota."

"And I can hear that you're driving, so calm the hell down before you kill both of you."

I blink harshly and pull into the parking lot of the Lounge. "There. I parked. Can I freak out now?"

"No. You're not allowed to freak out unless I'm there," he says firmly. "Can you do lunch?"

"I have to interview for the bar. I'll call you then. Okay?"

"Okay. See you later."

I hang up and walk into the bar. The guys stop me to tell me that they signed for a big delivery from the supplier earlier, and glee makes me clap my hands together. I skip off to the stock room and stop dead at all the boxes.

Oh, alcohol. Alcohol everywhere.

Alcohol I can't touch.

Oh, well. I guess I'll have to ply Dayton—and Tessa for as long as she's here—with my cocktail recipes.

I glance at my watch. I don't have time to install all the optic bottles before the interview. I lock the door, pocket the key, and walk back out into the bar. A guy who looks barely ready to graduate college is waiting at the bar, looking around.

"Hi—are you Dylan?" I ask, approaching him.

He turns to me and nods. "Are you Liv?"

"That's me." I hold my hand out, shake his, and motion to the bar. "I'd offer you a drink, but we only just got our delivery in."

"Don't worry."

"So…" I run through the standard interview questions. How old are you? Have you done this before? How flexible are you? Can you do weekdays as well as weekends? Days as well as nights?

I was right in assuming that he's in college, which means he's good for weekends and some evenings, but not much else.

Usually, I wouldn't give him another thought. But Aaron's words about looks and drawing in the college crowd as well as adults filter through my mind. Dylan is kind of cute—cute enough to bring girls in and keep them coming back.

I thank him and tell him that I'll be in touch in a few days.

Rubbing my forehead, I close the notebook and sigh. I'm actually glad no one else could get here today. One interview is mentally exhausting.

I'll ignore the fact that I have three to get through tomorrow.

My phone buzzes. I pick it up and read the message from Tyler telling me where he's having lunch with Tessa. I stare the screen. I don't particularly want to go and have this conversation, despite its inevitability, but since I flaked on him with his parents last night, I probably should.

At least they're in a public place so emotion will be kept to the minimum.

I'm still pissed about the 'Me, Tyler. You, Liv. You pregnant. You live with Tyler' display this morning.

On my way,

I reply to his message and head out to my car. I'm about to get in when I realize that the restaurant they're at is only two blocks over. Since the sun is out, I lock my car again and make the walk there instead.

I feel really awkward about this conversation. I just met his sister a few days ago, and now I have to tell her that I'm carrying her niece or nephew. And I also no longer have no reason to not meet his parents.

And that's going to be even more awkward. *Oh, holy hell.*

Holy hell on a plate of llama balls.

I stop outside the restaurant and take a minute to breathe. *It's okay. This is another one of life's curveballs.*

I'm not kidding anyone. Since the second Tyler walked up to me in that club, my whole life has been the curveball. It's twisted and turned in ways I never saw coming, colliding with both my heart and my mind on its way to this moment.

Now, looking at the restaurant and knowing that my boyfriend and his sister are inside it, I wish I could be left to swing with the curveball and absorb what it's throwing at me.

"Hiding?"

I turn and smack into Tyler's hard chest. "Hesitating," I correct.

He smiles and tucks some hair behind my ear. "Don't worry, baby girl. She's not here. I changed my mind and texted her a minute ago."

"You changed your mind?" I raise an eyebrow.

"I thought about what you said. You're right. Both of us need time for it to sink in before Tweedle Dum and Tweedle Dee start planning baby showers and all that shit."

Tessa and Dayton. "Don't forget decorating the nursery. You know they'll be all over that."

"Oh, shit. Don't. When Tessa was thirteen and redecorated her room, it took her five different shades of pink before she found her favorite."

"Let me guess. It was the first one she tried?"

"Of course it was." He brushes his fingers across my cheek and holds up a paper bag. "I got us lunch. What do you want to do?"

I thread my fingers through his and lean into his arm. "Let's go to Kerry Park and just sit."

"Just sit?"

"Just sit," I confirm, walking with him.

Our feet are perfectly in sync as we take the turn toward the park. Tyler releases my hand and wraps his arm around my back, curving his hand around my hip. I step into his side and inhale slowly, breathing him in, breathing us in, breathing *hope* in.

I can almost convince myself that we don't have issues we need to work through. That we're not still trembling from yesterday's surprise, because that's what this baby is.

A surprise.

"You're thinking," he murmurs. "I don't like it when you think. You tend to fuck shit up."

"I'm thinking good things," I reply with a smile.

"Bloody hell. Five weeks and pregnancy is already messing with your mind."

"It'll mess with my libido if you don't watch it," I say under my breath, sitting down on the grass. It's not warm but it's not cold out. It's that comfortable temperature that rarely happens without a bunch of rain.

Tyler grins, sitting opposite me. "That's not what you were saying this morning."

I narrow my eyes at him and take my sandwich. "I didn't have much of a chance to say anything before I was informed about new living arrangements."

"You were offered new living arrangements."

My eyes narrow even further. "I'm not arguing with you."

"That makes a change."

"Is my vibrator lodged up your ass or something?"

"No, but if you're into that, it could be lodged up yours." His eyes glimmer with amusement.

I glare at him as I bite into my sandwich and shake my head. No ass fun for me, thank you very much. One-way hole.

We eat without speaking any further. The park is relatively quiet, the only sounds coming when people walk past us, deep in conversation.

I finish eating and lie back on the grass. The sun filters through the clouds, its gentle warmth spreading over my face and chest, covering me in soft light. I close my eyes and breathe the spring air in deeply, letting it fill my lungs and relax me.

For once, my mind is silent. No worries, no fears, no hesitations.

At least it's silent until Tyler gently covers my lips with his own. Now, it fills with a buzz. A high, energetic zing of desire that coils throughout my body and sets all my nerve endings on fire. I reach up and curl my fingers around the back of his neck, holding his face down to mine, and just feel his kiss.

His lips move softly over mine, brushing, caressing, probing. I arch into it as his hand slips beneath me and flattens against the small of my back. I push further into him and my breasts rub against his chest. My nipples harden inside my bra and I gasp as an unexpected throb aches my clit.

"Don't do that." He kisses the corner of my mouth, his voice raspy and breathless. "You make that noise whenever I bury my cock inside you and it makes me want to do that too much."

"I like it when you want to fuck me," I murmur, threading my fingers through his hair.

"So do I, but that doesn't mean I should in the middle of the park."

"Never stopped you before."

"I'm leaving you some dignity…"

"And?"

He laughs quietly and drops his forehead to mine. "And myself frustrated so I can fuck you harder tonight."

"Frustrated? Sounds like a challenge." My lips quirk at one side, and he raises his eyebrows.

Before he can ask me what I mean, I reach between us and wrap my fingers around his half-hard cock. I stroke him with my thumb, tiny, teasing movements. He grows in my hand, the change almost instantaneous, and his eyes darken as he stares at me.

"Liv."

I squeeze. He grunts quietly. I fight my smile and push my lips against his. He attacks my mouth harshly, but the second I unbutton his pants and reach inside his boxers to hold him properly, he stills.

"What are you doing?" he rasps, jerking when I rub my thumb over the tip of him.

"Frustrating you." I kiss his bottom lip. "You're not the only one who can take and fulfill a challenge, Tyler Stone."

I wrap my fingers around his shaft, the smooth skin stretched over his hardness hot to my touch. I stroke him slowly, drawing each movement out… Wishing I could get away with moving and lowering my mouth to him as well.

"Shit."

I move my hand faster. "If you can't take it, don't give it."

He tilts my head back so I'm looking dead in his eyes. "I can take it, and you know I can more than give it."

"Ever been denied an orgasm, honey?"

He stills once again—or tries to. His hips still move against my hand, fucking my fist. "Never."

I smile to myself and kiss my way along his neck. His movements become jerkier, his breathing more erratic and broken. He groans my name into my shoulder, a heavy plea.

I release his cock and pull his boxers back up. "First time for everything."

When I move away, he jerks, hurriedly doing up the button on his pants despite the astonished frown on his face. Astonishment quickly turns to pissed the hell off.

I stand, but he's quicker. He flips me round and pushes me into the tree with his body, his hands clasping mine, his chest firm. His cock rubs against my core, the sensation made stronger by the seam of my jeans, and with one clench of my pussy, my panties get wet.

"First and last time," he growls, his mouth right by my ear. "You're going to pay for that stunt later, and you're going to pay fucking hard."

"I'm counting on it."

Chapter SEVENTEEN

MY phone is buzzing incessantly with messages and calls from Dayton. The last message she left involved a lot of shouting about why the hell I haven't called her and surely I've peed on the damn stick by now and another why the hell haven't I called her?

I ignore her, feeling guilty but knowing it's the right thing to do. She's my best friend and I love her for buying the test, but we have to tell our parents first. I understand this much.

I stop stirring the pasta sauce. I think I'm coming to terms with it now. It's hard when there's no visible signs of a baby aside from a word on a little screen. Perhaps I won't truly come to terms with it until I see the baby on a real screen and I can believe and know one hundred percent that there's a tiny person in there.

Until that happens, though, I can't freak out. I can't put shit off because of my obsessive and addictive tendencies.

Tyler's all but made it clear that he and I are it. Done. A forever deal.

Two months ago, that would have freaked me the fuck out. I would have been running for the hills, but now…

Now, I want it. With everything I have, I want it. Sixty-plus years to be addicted to Tyler Stone? Hell yes. I can totally take that. As long as I can step forward right now and manage what needs to be managed.

I give the sauce a quick stir, ignoring the burning tomato at the bottom of the pan, and grab my phone. I dig March's card from beneath a couple of takeout menus on the fridge and dial his number.

I shove pasta around the pan with a wooden spoon while I wait for him to answer. When he doesn't, I leave a message asking him to call me to arrange that coffee.

I don't want to talk about it, but I'm not willing to hide behind my addiction anymore. For years, it's controlled me and held me captive. In an odd kind of way, I'm thankful for it. If it hadn't, I never would have met Tyler. I never would have experienced what it's like to trust someone with your body and your mind and, eventually, your heart.

Because he has it all. I trust that man with every inch of me purely because I have no choice. He all but stole it from me when my back was turned. One by one, mind and heart, body and soul, he stole them and he trapped them somewhere within himself.

In a way, I'm no longer a prisoner of my addiction—I'm a prisoner of Tyler. But this time, there is a massive difference. This time, I want to be a prisoner. I want to be kept by him and I want him to tease my body and control my pleasure.

More than that, I want him to keep my heart somewhere I'll never find it.

I don't want it back.

It's his.

"The sauce is burning."

I snap out of my thoughts. "Shit!" I run to the stove and stir it frantically. I think I saved it… Just…

"That was some deep thoughts running across your face, baby girl." He puts his bag down by the door, shuts it, and walks to me.

"Today must be my annual thinking day," I quip, turning the heat down on that damn sauce.

"Have you hurt yourself yet?"

"Nope. I'd say I'm doing good." I grin over my shoulder at him. "There's beer in the fridge if you want it."

He hesitates. "Are you sure?"

"You're good with beer. Opening a bottle of wine will be the problem here."

"Okay." He kisses my bare shoulder and grabs a bottle from the fridge. The cap comes off with a click and a quiet fizz.

"Good day?"

"My couple were all loved up. Would you believe I didn't want to attack them with my camera stand?" He raises his eyebrows like it's such a surprise.

"I say it once and your balls shrink like you're naked in the Arctic. Really, Ty." I roll my eyes and turn, the pasta pan in my hand. "Move your butt."

Obediently, he steps to the side so I can drain the pasta. "What can I say? I'm a sucker for the L-word."

"Llama?" I tease. "I can see how that would affect you."

He grins. His eyes follow me as I dish dinner up. "Is this safe to eat? I mean,

I've eaten your cooking before."

"I'll spank you with this wooden spoon if you don't watch it," I threaten, holding it up. "My cooking is perfectly fine. Not Michelin-star grade like yours, Mr. I-Can-Do-Anything, but good enough. Besides, pasta isn't hard."

"No," he admits, glancing over my shoulder. "But, uh, Liv? You forgot to cook the chicken."

I pause, my spoon hovering over one of the plates, and I glance at all the pans. *Oh, fuck a duck!* "Oops."

"It's a good thing I like saucy pasta."

"You like anything if it's saucy," I retort, handing him a plate.

He grins again and sits at the table. "Especially my women."

"Wo-*man*," I correct. "Only one of me now, buddy. One bitch for the foreseeable future. Can you cope?"

His eyes sparkle. "Foreseeable future? Try forever, flighty bitch. For-fucking-ever. You're not getting rid of me now."

"Dammit. There I was, concocting one last plan to hook Channing Tatum."

"He's got nothing on me, baby girl." He means it, too. And he's right. "I'm one of a kind, and so are you, and that's why we make total sense together."

"A.K.A., we're both kind of fucked up, but when you put us together, all our broken edges kind of…mesh together."

"Broken edges are that way because they're looking for the piece that can fix them. We fix each other, even if we have to jiggle about a bit until we do." He grabs my hand and kisses my knuckles.

"I'm glad you think that way." I curl my fingers around his cheek. "Because I want to meet your parents tomorrow. And tell them."

He pauses. "You mean that?"

"We're stuck with each other now," I say more softly, rubbing my thumb across his cheek as a sense of peace settles over me. "Don't you think they should know they're going to be grandparents?"

The smile that spreads across his face touches every part of me. "I agree completely. I'll call in the morning. Dinner?"

I nod. "As long as I don't have to cook. I don't want to scare them off entirely."

Tyler jabs some pasta with his fork. "At least it's not hard."

"Well, I figured it wouldn't be fair to have both the pasta and your cock hard tonight."

"That so?"

"Mhmm." I take my hand back and eat, chewing slowly.

His eyes drop to my mouth when I flick my tongue out and over my lips. Then they darken and his jaw ticks at the same time that he stabs his fork into his dinner. Even his biceps flex, although I'm pretty sure that was a conscious movement. His eyes are still fixed on my mouth as I lift a forkful of pasta to it and close my lips around the food.

I slowly draw the fork out of my mouth. I know exactly what he's thinking. He's thinking that he wishes the fork were his cock.

He's thinking about how I left him hanging not six hours ago in the middle of the park right before a shoot.

He's thinking about his promise of making me pay for it.

And I'm thinking that he should hurry the hell up about it.

"Something wrong, honey?" I ask sweetly.

"That depends on what underwear you're wearing," he answers without batting an eyelid.

Now I'm fucked. "Red and black that don't match."

"Get changed. Now."

"I'm eating dinner."

"I don't care. Get. Changed."

I stand and walk around the table, pausing next to him. "Into what? A ball gown?"

His fingers close around my wrist and he tugs me into him. "Are you taking the piss, Liv?"

"You'll have to explain your foreign English to me."

He stands, his body emanating a heat I can feel everywhere. "Are you *sassing* me, Liv?"

"Ohhh," I coo, stepping forward. I run a fingertip down his chest to the top of his pants. "Yes. I am. What are you going to do about it?"

His hand sharply connects with my ass. "You're awfully cocky for someone about to be fucked so hard you'll feel my cock inside you for a week."

"And you're awfully cocky for someone who has yet to get your cock inside me." I skip backward out of his hold with a challenge in my eyes.

I know it's there. I can feel it—it's in my words and the way my hips sway as I leave the room. If it's in every step, it's in my eyes, too.

I run into my room and strip off my clothes. I open the drawer and pull out the pale-pink set—his favorite. My favorite.

The door opens before I can put it on and Tyler snatches it from my hands. He stands between me and the drawer, his breathing heavy and heated, and runs his eyes over me. They peruse my body, leaving no part untouched by his hot gaze.

Goose bumps coat my skin in the wake of his stare and heat sizzles across them. I shiver when his eyes hover at my bare, exposed pussy.

He trails his fingers from my shoulders, over my breasts, down my stomach, and finally to my hips. He grabs me quickly and pushes me back on the bed. Instead of screaming, I gasp, and he covers my body with his.

My legs, my hips, my breasts—he's over them all, flat against me, his fingers in my hair and his mouth working mine.

"Fuck the underwear," he mumbles, running his hands down my sides. They skim over my skin and set off a whole new round of charges.

His skin is like an electric current across mine, ignited only when we touch, sparking sensations in places I didn't know I could feel. My fingertips are humming as they travel up his back, and there's a level of material between us.

Material I want gone.

Material I'm smart enough not to ask about.

I know who's in control here. I know who's holding the strings and who's tugging them. It isn't me—it never is. It's always him, playing and yanking and teasing.

His mouth travels down my neck to my breast and he takes one nipple in my mouth. He pinches my breast from beneath, his thumb massaging the soft flesh, and he hums as he flicks his tongue over the hardened and extra-sensitive nipple.

I cry out, half in pleasure, half in pain. A sweet pain, one that twists my stomach in the best kind of way.

He turns his attention to my other nipple and I swear to fucking everything unholy that, if he keeps this shit up, *I will come.*

I put my fingers in his hair and tug in an effort to get his mouth away from my breasts. He grasps my wrists and holds my arms out wide, his longer arms holding mine steady despite a lame wriggle.

"I told you you would pay for what you did earlier. I don't care how you writhe between me, Liv. I just care that you do. I'll have you writhing all night until you finally come if that's what it takes."

He releases me now and bends down to the floor. He stands, my pair of pink panties in his hands, and a sexy grin takes his mouth.

My own drops open as he grabs my hands and secures them using the lace underwear. *Holy. Shit.* The man is a master of sexual manipulation.

He works the buttons of his shirt until it falls open, exposing his toned abdomen. He shrugs it off his shoulders and lets it fall to the floor with a quiet swish. The sight of him half naked before me is so teasing that I still entirely while he undoes his pants.

The pants follow the shirt until only his underwear remains, and I wish I could sit up and tug them off, too.

He leans over me again and sucks lightly on my pulse point. It's thrumming, pounding, pulsating beneath the gentle caress of his tongue. My body is alive and waiting, anticipating, ready.

He wraps his arms around me and lifts me to standing. "Time to get wet," he whispers, pushing me toward the bathroom.

I ache as he leads me into the room and then the shower. My breath catches when he turns the water on full force and steps out of his boxer briefs.

His erection pings free, standing upright and resting against his stomach. I swallow at the sight of it. God—it's long and hard and I know exactly how that fucking tastes.

My tongue darts across my bottom lip, and I know he catches it because he wraps his hand around himself. He walks back into the shower, his fist stroking his cock and his eyes on me.

"Come here."

I walk into the shower cubicle and he closes the door behind me. The water is hot and sprays down on us forcefully, but that thought is quickly discarded when Tyler's mouth descends onto mine once more.

I'm quickly swept away in the intensity of his kiss.

"Against the wall," he whispers between kisses.

I step back, jolting when my back hits the cold tiles. He steps forward and lifts my arms over his head.

I'm bound, my arms around his neck, holding on for dear life.

He moves his hand between us and runs his fingers along my wet pussy. "So easy," he murmurs. "So quick to get wet and ready for me." He pushes a finger inside me that's quickly followed by another. "You'd take my cock now, wouldn't you? You're ready for me to lift you and fuck you deep, aren't you?"

I breathe out a yes. His thumb finds my clit and flicks.

"Is that what you want? Tell me, Liv. Tell me if you want me to wrap your legs around my waist and force myself inside you."

I can't speak, my body overcome with waves of delight from the movement of his hand. His fingers stroke me quicker than he speaks, his thumb going around and around and around…

He drops his hand. I ache for him, for his touch. "Please," I whisper. "Please, Ty. I need you."

"Need me where? Here?" He touches my breast. "Here?" He runs two fingers along my cunt. "Or here?" He rubs the head of his cock against my clit.

"There," I cry, dropping my forehead onto his chest.

"Just there? Like this?" His cock presses the spot above my clit and he circles, barely brushing the swollen spot begging for attention.

"No, you bastard," I hiss, wishing I could reach down.

"What, Liv?" His breath across my lips eclipses the heat of the water. "Where do you want me, babe? You can't show me so you're going to have to tell me."

"Your cock—inside me." My breath hitches as that teasing rub nudges my clit. "My legs around your waist. You inside me. Please."

"You begging, love?"

"You bet your dirty British ass I'm begging."

He cups my ass, pulls it from the wall, then slaps the wet skin. The sharp noise rings out through the room, but all I know is that his hands are curving my thighs and lifting me, settling my legs around his waist, and his cock is nudging my entrance.

I tilt my hips forward and take him inside me. He fills me with a swift thrust and I moan, his hard cock red hot against my sensitive folds.

"This what you want?" he whispers against my neck.

"Exactly this," I reply, grabbing his hair the best I can and opening myself to him.

His hands are on my ass, holding me steady as he fucks me. And he fucks me harshly, relentlessly, pounding into me until my heartbeat matches the pace of his thrusts. Until I only know the steady beat of our bodies syncing perfectly.

Until our hearts, our breaths, our thrusts match to the ninth degree.

Until we come together for the first time, our releases a mixture of names and cries and sighs. Of clenches and thrusts and grips.

Until he slowly lowers me to the floor, pulling himself out of me, and holds me to his chest.

I rest my cheek against his chest and wave my arms awkwardly. He laughs loudly and tugs the panties from my wrists.

"Thank you," I murmur, wrapping my now-free arms around his waist.

"Any time," he replies, his arms creating a safe and comforting cocoon around my body.

We stand beneath the spray of water until my legs stop trembling. Tyler reaches for the soap and runs his hands over my body, caressing my breasts lovingly and massaging my back. He kneels when his hands curve over my behind so he can do my legs.

I watch him with a smile, amazed at how he can switch his demeanor so quickly. Minutes ago, he was fucking me like our lives depended on it, and now, he's touching my body like I'm a goddess worthy of worship.

I reach up and kiss him when he stands and grab the soap myself. I wash him down, running my fingers over the ridges of his abdomen and the tightness of his backside and thighs. Over the broad shoulders that eclipse me and the arms that hold me so steadily.

When step under the spray together, I scrunch my face up at the onslaught of water. He laughs, grabbing shampoo and attempting to wash my hair beneath the spray. I shake my head repeatedly. I'm not opening my damn eyes with shampoo washing down my face.

He finally gives up, and after a moment longer of standing under the water, presumably to wash all the shampoo off me, he pulls me out.

"Shit! Towels!" he snaps.

I finally open my eyes and laugh. "I think I'm rubbing off on you!"

He comes back into the room, dripping wet and still totally naked, and wraps me in a large, warm towel. "Then we're all fucked."

I smile and snuggle into the towel. Hot. Fluffy. Soft. *Mmmm.*

If he gets you towels straight from the dryer, he's a keeper.

I follow him into my room, my eyes fixated on his butt as he walks. Holy crap, he has a nice butt. Especially when there are water droplets running over it.

Hello.

"You're staring at my bum again, aren't you?"

I look up and grin, unashamed. "It's a nice *bum.*"

His expression matches mine. "Come here." He grabs the towel from me, dries himself, then sits me on the bed. He climbs up behind me and covers my head with the towel.

I laugh as he rubs my head playfully, getting most of the wetness out of my hair. He grabs my brush from the floor and runs it through the wet locks before bringing the towel up again.

He repeats this three or so times and I giggle my way through it. When he's finally satisfied that my hair is dry enough, he yanks the covers from beneath us and throws me back for a second time tonight.

He smiles at me and sweeps me into his arms. I tuck the quilt over us and snuggle into him, the warmth of his skin soothing to me as we entwine our legs and drape our arms around each other.

"Where's Angus?" he says against my forehead.

"Out getting pussy. No pun intended," I add when his body shakes.

"Good lad." He tightens his hold on me, and I smile.

"You wouldn't believe you had me against the shower wall not so long ago."

Tyler laughs softly. "It's what I'm here for, baby girl. I'll fuck you hard and love you gently. That's all that matters."

Too true. I curl into him, savoring the feel of his skin against mine. His breath flutters across the top of my head.

"Love you, dirty Brit boy."

"Love you, sassy American bitch."

Chapter EIGHTEEN

YET again, Tyler Stone is navigating his way around a kitchen with ease. The guy is handsome as hell, fucks like a god, and can cook up a storm—it's really quite unfair.

He's also protective, almost to a fault.

If I have to tell him one more time that he didn't impale the baby with his penis last night, I'm going to take the knife out of his hand and shove the handle up his ass.

Agreeing to dinner with his parents, in hindsight, wasn't my smartest move. The moment I smelled coffee this morning, I had to make a rather swift detour to the bathroom. As it is, my toilet bowl and I are now very well acquainted, and I've broken up with coffee.

It was a sad moment, but considering that my stomach is still a little vile, I'm glad I chose to do it.

My relationship with my phone is also on hold, given Dayton's newfound hobby of calling me every five fucking seconds.

I rest my chin in my hands and watch Tyler flip the chicken in the pan. "Did you tell your parents already?"

He shakes his head. "No. I wanted you to be there when they find out."

"Great." I sigh. I wish he'd told them before now. The introduction is going to be awkward.

Hi. I'm Liv, your son's girlfriend. And also the mother to your future grandbaby! Rock on!

Tyler puts the oven mitt down and turns to me. He leans over the table and cups my face with his hands then sweetly brings his lips down on mine. "Don't panic, okay? They'll love you."

"It's kind of unconventional."

"So add it to our list." He grins. "Really, you sound surprised."

I roll my eyes. "Not surprised. Wary. Nervous." I swallow. "Nauseated."

"Do you want some water?"

"Honestly, I'm too afraid to put anything in my stomach in case is comes back up and I vomit over your mom's Jimmy Choos or something."

There's a knock at the door, and he laughs. "Good choice."

I draw in a long, shaky breath when he walks to the door. I've always loved the open-plan setup of his apartment and how easy it is to move from room to room.

Now, I hate it because the door is right behind me. Give or take a few feet.

"Hi, Mum, Dad."

I think I'm going to vomit.

"Hi, love. Is she here yet?" his mom asks.

I can taste the bile. Is it rude if I run out now?

"Yes, she's in the kitchen. Come on through."

Oh holy shit. I clap my hand over my mouth as the bile burns my throat. I mumble an unintelligible, "Excuse me," and run past Tyler to the bathroom.

I kick the door shut and make it to the toilet just in time. I lean over it and retch. My eyes sting with tears as my stomach empties itself of the water and ginger cookies I've been nibbling all day.

Morning sickness my motherfucking ass.

"Liv? Baby girl, are you okay?" The door opens and closes within seconds, and Tyler's hand rests on my back.

I shake my head. "I'm sorry," I whisper.

He kneels next to me and rubs my back. "Don't be sorry. I'm afraid the cat is well and truly out of the bag though."

I lean my head against his shoulder. "And here I was, worried it would be awkward."

I cough as the urge to vomit hits again. Tyler rubs my back and makes soothing noises in my ear.

"I'm good," I say to myself more than him. "Can I have my toothbrush?"

He gets up and rinses it under the tap. I lean against the bath and take the brush from him. I scrub my teeth and tongue to get rid of the awful vomit taste and push myself up. Or try to. My legs are shaky, so Tyler steps forward and helps me up.

"Thank you," I mumble through a mouthful of toothpaste. I spit it out and sigh, setting the toothbrush back in the holder.

"Okay?" Ty asks, pulling me into him.

I take a deep breath and nod against his chest. "Okay. Let's go."

He holds me back. "I can tell them you're not up to it. They'll understand."

"What?" I look up. "You're going to invite them here, drop the bombshell on them, and then ask them to leave?"

"Bombshell?" He raises his eyebrows.

"Well, it is, isn't it?" My voice dips at the end with insecurity, and I swallow.

His fingers dig into my back as his body tenses. It's easy for him to say it isn't—he's not the one who's looking at spending the next ten weeks hugging a toilet.

"Sure you're okay to spend the evening with Mum and Dad?"

Nice subject change. "I said I'm fine."

He shrugs and lets me go. Just before he opens the door, he grabs my face and kisses my forehead softly. I lay my hands at his waist and close my eyes at the lingering touch.

"Sorry," he whispers. "I'm trying to remember how different this is for you compared to me and I'm not doing a very good job."

"Join me in the bathroom again. It'll soon sink in." I smile up at him. "Come on. Go and introduce me to the people I have to thank for you."

He kisses me again and opens the door. His arm stays firmly around my waist as he leads me toward the front room and to the couple sitting on his sofa.

He looks like his dad. From the dark hair to the strong jaw, Tyler is his dad thirty years ago. And his mom—her light hair isn't what I expected, but she's just as gorgeous as Tessa. For real, this family has some serious genetic luck.

She stands and Tyler steps to the side so she can hug me. "Liv, it's so lovely to meet you. Both of you!" She laughs, stepping back and glancing at my stomach.

I smile, even if it is kind of weak. "It's great to meet you, too. I'm sorry about disappearing just then."

Tyler's dad stands and embraces me the same way his wife just did. "Don't apologize to the woman who had twins. I considered moving the bathroom into the bedroom several times during that pregnancy."

Now that I can believe. Already.

"Anyway, congratulations!" He kisses my cheek. "What a wonderful surprise." He claps Tyler on the shoulder and pulls him in for a hug.

"How are you feeling, love? We can reschedule if you'd like," his mom asks, resting a hand on my arm.

"No, no! You don't have to do that. I feel fine—mostly."

"It started this morning," Tyler explains, sliding a hand down my back soothingly. "We're going to the doctor tomorrow."

I frown at him. "We are?"

"We are now."

I blink a few times and look away so I can roll my eyes.

His mom catches it and throws a wink at me. "Don't worry, Liv. All men go a little caveman-esque when their better half is pregnant."

"It's not caveman," Tyler interjects. "It's caring."

"Precisely," his dad agrees. "But get the bucket down the side of the bed, lad. It's easier at two a.m."

My eyes widen and he chuckles.

"Dad!"

"Todd! Give the girl a chance to adjust before you go throwing horror stories at her!" Tyler's mom swipes his chest with the back of her hand.

"It's okay," I interrupt. "You don't have to sugarcoat shit. I already know it's a load of crap."

"In that case," his mom says, "it fucking hurts."

Yup. Figured that much out for myself from watching Teen Mom.

"Okay. Let's go and sit at the table." Tyler all but pushes me toward the kitchen.

"Why don't I know your mom's name?" I hiss into his ear.

"Shit. Kate. It's Kate," he whispers back. "Mum, would you like some wine?"

"Water, please." She sits next to me at the table and leans over. "I had dinner with some friends when I was pregnant. No one knew yet, so I claimed I was on antibiotics. They were all drinking, and I spent the whole two hours wondering how many years I'd get in prison for hitting them with the bottles." She winks.

"At least drunk people are fun when you're sober," I reason. It's a good reason. One I'm going to have to get used to.

The apartment door opens and I turn to see Tessa walking in.

"Oh, balls!" She exclaims. "I'm sorry. I didn't realize you guys were here."

Tyler shoots her a dirty look.

I, however, feel relieved.

"Come and sit down," I say and turn to Tyler. "There's enough for her now that I'm not eating, right?"

"Why aren't you eating?" Tessa narrows her eyes at me, lowering herself into the free chair next to her dad.

"Because she's pregnant. That's bloody why," Tyler mumbles, clearly pissed at her for interrupting dinner.

"No shit!" she shrieks. "You're pregnant?"

"Ask the toilet," I reply dryly.

"Oh my god! Wait—oh, crap. Now this makes sense." She looks at her parents. "Did you already know?"

"We just found out," Kate replies.

"Ohhh!" Tessa claps her hands excitedly. "Please let it be a baby Liv. I can't deal with a baby Tyler. My nerves won't stand it."

Todd laughs. "Your nerves?"

"My nerves won't flippin' stand it. They barely cope with him," I mutter as Tyler sets the plates down.

He catches it and glances at me, and his lips twitch.

"At least I know why Dayton was freaking out earlier," Tessa muses. "You haven't answered her calls in two days."

"Well I couldn't tell her before Tyler knew," I answer.

He nudges my foot under the table and hooks it round my ankle like a kid holding on to their best friend. It's adorable and fills me with warmth.

I want to lean over, wrap my hands around his arm, and close my eyes, but I can't. In fact, after spending my day either vomiting or wondering if I'm going to, I'm exhausted.

And now this.

No offense to his family, but seven p.m. is crazy late.

Shit. It's only seven?

I sip a glass of water. By sip, I mean I wet my lips. And by wet, I mean dampen.

Listening in to the conversation around me, I rub my socked foot against Tyler's. He reaches beneath the table after a few minutes and leans in.

"Are you okay? You look like shit."

I snort into my hand. "Thanks. I feel it."

"Crap. I didn't mean it like that," he laughs quietly. "I meant you look tired."

"Cut the bullshit and just use shit," I reply, smiling. "I'm tired. Feeling sick all day has tired me out, I think."

"Do you want to go to bed? No one will mind."

Yes. Oh, god, yes. I'd love to go home to my bed.

"No, it's okay. I'll wait until dinner's over at least."

"Don't be a hero, baby girl. That's my job." He kisses my temple and reaches for his water.

"So, when are you planning to get married?"

Tyler chokes on his water at his mom's words. I go completely rigid and I'm almost certain my eyes are bugging out of my head.

Married? What?

"Mum!" Tessa hisses.

Tyler knocks his fist into his chest a couple of times. "We haven't thought about it yet. Or discussed it. Or mentioned it."

He glances at me. My heart is thumping.

Why did I never think about marriage being a possibility?

With a baby comes a binding tie—one most women connect to marriage. It never crossed my mind that Tyler would want to marry me—or that I might want to marry him.

Then again, it's only been two days and I've barely been able to think at all.

"Yep," I murmur. "I'm ready to go to bed now."

Tyler squeezes my thigh as his mom apologizes profusely. I tell her that there's no need to worry. Privately, I think that, to her, marriage and babies are a reflexive action. To me, they're run-like-fucking-hell actions.

"I'm really sorry to have to leave you guys, but I'm exhausted, so I think I'm going to call it a night," I say softly.

"Of course. Sickness takes it out of you." Kate nods. "I hope we can see each other again before we leave at the weekend. Perhaps for lunch."

"I would love that." I smile. As long as she doesn't mention weddings again.

I say goodnight to Tessa and Todd and stand. I grab my purse from the side of the sofa and freeze when Tyler talks.

"What are you doing?"

"I'm going?"

"Where exactly?"

"To bed."

"At your apartment?"

"Um, yes?"

He shakes his head and stands. Then he crosses the apartment in a few long strides and snatches my purse. Before I can ask him what he's doing, he scoops me up, one hand around my back and another beneath my knees. I squeak and grab him, the sudden motion upsetting my stomach a little.

"What are you doing?!"

"Putting you to bed," he answers, carrying me calmly past his family and down the hall to his room.

"Tyler! I can't believe you!"

He laughs. "Be a love and open the door."

I twist the handle and shove the door open. He carries me in and sets me on the bed.

"Lie back."

"Why?"

He puts his hands on my shoulders and slowly pushes me back. "You're not going anywhere tonight. You're ill. I'm going to keep an eye on you."

"I'm sick from hormones and being a human incubator. You can't keep me with you every second to hold my hair and wipe my forehead when I'm vomiting."

He peels my jeans down my legs then sits me up and removes my shirt. "I can try. Into bed."

"Such a fucking hero," I mumble, climbing into bed and scooting over to the middle. I roll over so I'm facing his side, and the scent of him that lingers on his pillow encompasses me.

Tyler walks around the bed and switches the television on. He turns the volume down to a low hum. He sets the controller down on the nightstand next to me and kneels. A cold draft flutters over my bare skin when he whips back the covers.

A chill that's quickly alleviated by his hand on my stomach.

He spreads his fingers wide, covering all of my lower tummy, and leans up to me. "I never wanted to be a hero until I met you. You're mine, Liv, and this is my baby. Do you get that? *Mine*. Both of you. That means you're mine to love, mine to protect, and mine to look after. If I want to do it, I'm going to, no matter what you say. I can't imagine it being any other way and it never will be."

I run my fingers through his hair. "I know," I say quietly. "I'll try to let you."

"No trying. You will let me because I'll make you." He nudges my nose with his. "If I want you to sleep in my bed because you're poorly, then you will. I don't want you away from me."

"Okay."

"Okay?"

"Okay." I smile sleepily.

He smiles back, staring into my eyes for a moment. He pulls away and presses his lips to my stomach. The heat of his mouth lingers on my skin even after he moves his lips to mine.

"I'll let you be my hero," I whisper against him.

He smiles, covering me up with the duvet and tucking me in. "I'll be your hero, baby girl. I'll be your hero so damn well, Superman will be jealous of me."

My smile widens. "Cocky British bastard. Go and spend some time with your family."

He nods, kisses me once more, and heads for the door.

"Ty? I'm sorry."

He stops and looks over his shoulder. "Don't be. Don't ever be."

He closes the door behind him, and I settle my cheek against the pillow. I look at the TV without really seeing it. I stare blindly until my eyelids grow heavy and I give in to the lull of sleep.

The bed creaks next to me. I force my eyes open and roll over to see Tyler crawling into bed. He turns the television off with the remote and lies down, only seeing that I've noticed him when he turns.

"C'mere, baby girl," he says in a low voice, pulling me into him.

My eyelids drop as I snuggle into the warmth of his body. His arms fold me into him fully, and he rubs his hand over my back. His breath scoots across the top of my head, and I smile when he brushes his lips across my forehead.

"I can't believe your mom thought we were getting married," I mumble through a yawn and press into him further.

He laughs softly but doesn't respond. He keeps soothingly rubbing my back, settling me back into the lull of sleep.

But not before I hear him finally reply, "One day, Liv. One day."

Chapter NINETEEN

THERE are two types of freak-outs in the world. Shocked-what-the-effing-hell freak-outs and angry-what-the-effing-hell freak-outs.

I've experienced both in the past sixty minutes. The former from my mom and the latter from my best friend. In fact, Day is still going.

"I can't believe you didn't tell me! I bought the friggin' pee stick. How could you leave me hanging?!"

"Yes," I reply dryly, pouring a glass of water and leaning against the counter. "My new state of mind is nauseated, and in a few months, a person will be passing through my vagina, but let's focus on how I didn't let you know immediately."

"You're lame, you know that?" She narrows her eyes. "How did Tyler take it?"

"Better than I did," I admit, summarizing the events of that night.

"What about his parents?"

"Asked us when we're getting married."

She snorts. "And your parents?"

I sigh and put the glass down. "Asked me when we're getting married."

Her snort switches to a laugh. "Shall I continue it?"

"Try it and I'll tie you to the Space Needle by your baby toe." I glare.

"I know. But seriously…?"

"We're not getting married, okay?" I throw my hands up. "We just got into a relationship, had a baby thrown into the mix, and I have to move in here next week. Let's not add rings and shit into that equation, got it?"

She hides her smile. "Got it. Although the baby kind of came first."

"Fuck you, Black. Fuck you."

I let the last interviewee out of the bar and bang my head against the wall. One of five interviews today has been worth my while. The others were all jacked-up college kids who can barely tell their left from their right.

My stomach growls angrily, reminding me that I haven't eaten today. Thing is, I don't want to eat. I feel sick, but that's an empty stomach kind of sick, not a 'Hi, Mommy, I'm in here' kind of sick. But I'm afraid that, if I do eat, the sick will change.

I poke my stomach lightly. "You're already making my life hard. I know you're only a few weeks into this growing thing, but go easy on me, yeah?"

"Are you talking to your stomach?" Aaron is grinning when I look up.

"More specifically the person inside, but yes, I suppose."

"Tyler called me this morning. Congratulations, Liv." He hugs me and kisses my cheek.

"Thanks. I'm still getting used to the idea."

"Talking to your stomach will probably help with that." He smirks.

"You might technically be my boss, but you're also my best friend's fiancé, and if you keep that up, I'll have a few hormone induced words for you, sir." I flounce over to the bar and separate the résumés .

"I don't doubt it," he responds, joining me there. "Any luck?"

"It's going okay. Two cocktail-shaker guys—I really have to stop calling them that—and two bar girls. One guy for the weekends. I still need another four or five staff members."

"You and Tyler go to California tomorrow, correct?"

I nod, sighing.

"Let me know who you want in and I'll have Dottie set up the interviews. Dayton can do it in your place."

"I can do it when I get back."

"After the bachelorette party?"

"Ah. Yes?"

"Don't. You'll stress yourself out. Dottie will call, Day will interview, and then you two can pick the best ones. Got it?"

I glare at him. "I won't stress myself out."

"The bars need setting up still, the tables need organizing properly, and staff have to be trained. It's one less thing for you to worry about."

"I won't break from running a bar."

"No, but you forget that your baby is my family, too, so I'm going to make it as easy as possible for you."

I sigh and head for the store room. "Fine."

"What are you doing?"

"I'm going to set up the bar. God forbid I should stress myself out." I roll my eyes and open the door. The boxes containing the large spirit bottles are by my feet and I bend to lift one.

"And for your next trick..." Aaron mumbles, taking it from me.

I throw my arms in the air and follow him back to the bar. "Holy hell! Why don't you and your cousin just put me on bed rest for the next eight months?"

"That's not a bad idea." Tyler's voice carries across the bar. "Although I have doubts about its success."

"Fantastic. Both of you now. Here's an idea. Why don't I just sit here at the bar and supervise you?" I drop onto one of the stools.

"That's a brilliant idea." Tyler kisses my cheek as Aaron shrugs off his jacket and rolls up his shirtsleeves. "Tell us where to put them," he instructs.

"There are another three boxes in the storeroom before you start that." I rest my cheek on my hand.

They both disappear and return with all three boxes.

I flip the file to where I have the setup mocked up and tell them where everything needs to go. They do as I say, no questions asked. Although I'm secretly enjoying having both Aaron and Tyler doing exactly as I say, I keep my face blank and my voice down.

I mean, seriously. One hot guy in a suit and another—my hot guy—in a polo shirt that fits his shoulders and arms properly are moving fairly heavy stuff around.

I'm not saying the view is bad. At all.

"There, you see? You're a manager and you just did a great job managing and you didn't have to lift a finger."

I stare at Aaron. "I'll manage your ass out of here if you keep treating me like a china flippin' doll."

He laughs. "Is that everything you'd like done today, boss?"

I click my tongue and he grabs his jacket.

"You two have fun in California. Try not to do too much, Liv."

I flip him the bird behind his back. Damn protective males. Tyler's mom was right last night—cavemen, all of them.

God help Dayton when she gets herself knocked up. That's all I'm sayin'.

"What was that?" Tyler says as a rumbling noise erupts from my stomach.

"Um."

"Have you eaten today?" His gaze flashes with annoyance.

"I'm sensing 'no' is the wrong answer here, so I'm going to plead the Fifth."

"Liv," he growls. "You have to eat!"

"I'm taking my vitamins. I'm okay as long as I drink."

"No, you have to eat," he repeats, walking round the bar. "No wonder you look like you're about to collapse."

"I don't want to be sick again, okay? I just don't want anything."

"A little bit of something, even if you are sick, is better than a whole lot of nothing. Now get up and grab your purse. We're going to get you food."

I drop my head back like a petulant child and get up. "I don't want to go for food. I want to go home, get in my sweatpants, and watch The Big Bang Theory until my ears bleed from Penny's sarcasm," I huff.

Tyler sighs and cups my face. "Then we'll go home, get in sweatpants, and watch The Big Bang Theory. But you're still eating." He kisses me quickly and pulls me to his car before I can argue any further. "Pasta, okay? Just some plain pasta. It'll give you energy and line your stomach."

"Fine. I'll eat some pasta." I get inside the Mercedes. "And when you say home, whose home do you mean?"

"My home is your home," he responds, pulling away. "But your apartment for now, I suppose."

"Good. Sean moved out last week, so Angus is left to his own devices. Fuck knows how many birds and mice are in my apartment right now." My head pounds at the thought.

"And you want that animal to live with us?"

"That animal is my fur-baby."

"Funny. He's always been a pain in your arse."

"True, but you pushed him right out of that spot. It's all yours, honey."

He shoots me a smile and laughs. "It's always good to know our feelings are entirely mutual."

"You know those heels I have, yes? I can be a physical pain the ass as well as a literal one."

"The literal pain is more than enough to cope with, thank you very much." He parks outside my apartment and we get out.

I reach out and take his hand in mine. A calming feeling washes over me as our fingers entwine and his thumb rubs the back of my hand. The elevator doors close in front of us, and I curl my body into his, just needing to be held by him.

It comes fleetingly—the urge to touch him, to have him touch me, to have that connection. It's always strong and irresistible, and as he slides his hands down to my ass and kisses my neck, I'm reminded that we're still very much governed by our addictions.

He still craves my body, and in turn, I still crave his heart.

Our love just has a way of pushing it to the side, smothering it a little. I think more of how I love him than how I'm addicted to him… And maybe that's the key.

Maybe that's how we'll make it work.

Perhaps our love and our addictions are intertwining into an intricate knot that makes total sense.

I reluctantly step from Tyler's hold and put my key in the door. And pause. "I hear flapping."

"Are you serious?" Tyler asks, knocking my hand away and opening the door. "Shit!" he cries, ducking when a bird comes flying clumsily through it. I shriek, thankful that no one has taken Sean's old apartment yet.

Angus comes flying out, hissing at the bird.

"Oh no you don't!" I scoop him up and throw him back into my apartment. I tug Tyler inside and slam the door. "Before the thing gets back in."

"So you're just going to leave it there flying around the hallway?"

"Pretty much." I dump my purse, put a can of food in Angus's bowl, and head into my room to change. Tyler watches me as I go and, the second I turn into my room, laughs at me.

Nice of him to try and hide it.

He's an awful actor.

Cupboards open and close and pans clang from the kitchen. I pull some sweatpants and a tank top on before I pad my way back out. Tyler already has some water boiling on the stove when I turn on the DVD player and lie back on the sofa. Angus finishes his food and strolls across the apartment to jump onto my legs. He circles a few times and I wince at his claws digging into my thighs.

He lies down, his head on my stomach, and I smile.

"So he brings a bird home and is now keeping the baby warm. Is that like an offering to it or something?"

I meet Tyler's eyes, my smile still in place. "The bird is for me. He thinks I'm weak, and given that he had no food, he assumed I needed help to feed him," I explain, scratching my cat's head. "And cats can sense babies. I was watching Teen Mom and one of the girls had a cat—it was always sleeping on her stomach."

He raises an eyebrow. "Is your knowledge of pregnancy all courtesy of Teen Mom?"

"No. It makes you pee a lot, makes you sick, and makes your boobs really tender. I figured those out for myself."

He stares at me for a minute before smiling and turning back to the pasta. *Yeah, you smile, buddy. You fucking smile now. You won't be smiling so much when I'm having the baby.*

I'm pretty sure those hours of labor are reserved purely for Daddy's suffering. I get pain relief. He gets broken fingers.

To be honest, it seems like a fair trade to me.

Tyler brings me over a bowl of pasta with a sprinkling of cheese. I take the fork from him and rest the bowl on my stomach. This isn't appealing to me—not in the slightest. But I'll eat it because it will make him happy. And as sexy as an angry Tyler Stone is, I don't have the energy to deal with him tonight.

He'll have to wank instead.

Wait. When did I start thinking in British?

Bloody hell.

Shit. There it is again.

"Have you packed yet?"

I shake my head, my mouth full of food. "Last time, you did it, so I figured you could just do it again."

"Last time, you were taking your vibrator. This time, you don't need it."

"Why? Did you pack yours?"

He steals a bit of pasta. "No. I reckon I only have a few months before you tell me you're done with sex and I'm not wasting them with a vibrator. So, until after the baby is born, the only thing inside your pussy will be me."

"Well, how does a girl argue with that reasoning?" I jab some pasta and shove it in my mouth.

I look down at the bowl. I've eaten just over a quarter of it. That will do. I set it on the coffee table, ignoring the way Ty's brow furrows, and turn to the television.

He rubs my thigh and gets up. He turns in the direction of my bedroom, presumably to pack for me. My phone buzzes after a few minutes and I awkwardly pull it from my pocket in an attempt not to dislodge Angus.

Marchant's name flashes on screen. I swipe to open the message.

Monday. Starbucks on Pike Place. Noon.

I swallow my groan.

No choice in meeting. He must have spoken to my mom.

Fucking hell. That's the last thing I need—a conversation with a therapist about my pregnancy and my addiction.

I drop my phone on the floor with a thunk.

"Liv? You okay?" Tyler calls.

"Mmph."

He comes back through to the front room and leans against the door. "What is it?"

I look up and can't help but notice that his shirt is off. Yes. The noticing is entirely accidental. Just like the way my eyes flick over his abs and down that V that disappears beneath the waistband of his pants…

"Liv."

I snap my eyes back to his and catch his smirk. "I'm sorry. What was the question?"

His lips curve a little more. "What's up?"

I'm guessing that 'my libido' isn't the right answer. "My mom kind of freaked earlier when I called and told her. Not about the baby, but how I'll cope with it…and you. She's a little overprotective. Anyway, my dad has this friend he fishes with who's a therapist. It's never bothered me before, but he was there when I went over there last week and started asking me questions. I know my mom put him up to it."

"And?"

"And he said if I wanted to talk to call him. I did—a couple days ago, just after I took the test. But I got his voicemail. I was still in panic mode then, but now that I've calmed down, I don't need to talk. But he just texted and said to meet him Monday for coffee."

"You're not going alone."

"He's not going to upset me, Ty."

"I couldn't give a shit, Liv. We're in this together. Besides, he can go back to your mum and tell her I'm a great guy, can't he?"

"Of course he can. He'd be crazy to think you're anything else."

"Do I detect sarcasm there?"

"Probably."

He leans over the sofa and kisses me. "Your sarcasm sucks."

"No, I suck," I mutter, nipping his bottom lip.

"Good thing, too. We have an hour or so in a plane tomorrow. Since you denied me the last time we flew together, you can put your sucking to good use, can't you?"

"A challenge?"

"A demand."

"Far be it from me to deny you your demands."

Chapter TWENTY

I FOLLOW Tyler onto the plane with a swirling in my stomach. I lick my lips several times, as if I can shift my focus from it. It doesn't work. I get the feeling that the half slice of toast I had this morning before we left isn't sitting well and will soon be making its reappearance.

I settle my hand over my stomach as I sit on the plush, leather seats. Tyler eyes me, concerned, and I remember him talking about going to the doctor. Sure, we never made it, but I'm starting to wish I'd called and got an appointment.

If she can give something, anything, to make this awful all-day-long sickness go away, you bet I'm gonna jump on it.

"We can delay a little bit if you need to," Tyler says softly, pushing hair from my face.

I nod, not daring to open my mouth. He gets up and knocks on the door of the cockpit. I hear him ask them to hold for fifteen minutes. Then he'll come back and let them know if we need to delay further.

My stomach cramps as he walks toward me, and I get up, darting around him. One hand on my stomach and the other clamped over my mouth, I run to the bathroom. He follows me and opens the door.

I drop to the floor in front of the toilet, and my suspicions are confirmed.

Tyler holds back my hair as my stomach empties itself into the sparking porcelain. He rubs my back as I choke and splutter, seemingly unaffected by my vomiting.

My eyes burn with hot tears once again, and I reach up to flush the toilet.

"Fucking hell," I mutter to myself.

Tyler releases me, and when I turn, he's holding a packet of face wipes and a toothbrush. I offer him a weak smile, and he crouches next to me.

"I came prepared." He opens the wipes and tenderly cleans around my mouth and chin before handing me some for my eyes.

I wipe my makeup off completely. Right now, I don't give a crap how I look. I grab the toothbrush from him and get up. Bile rises in my throat for a second time and I pause, gripping the side of the sink.

"Are you—"

I shake my head and wave my hand at him. I take a few deep breaths through my nose and the feeling subsides. Thankfully.

"Now." I shove the toothbrush at him and he puts some toothpaste on.

I scrub hard and reason that at least I'll have clean teeth if this keeps up. As long as I don't become one of those pregnant women who hates toothpaste. Then I'm really going to have some problems.

I rinse the brush and leave it on the back of the sink since there's no holder. "I'm okay," I reassure Tyler. "Let's go in case it comes back."

I precede him out of the bathroom. I sit in my chair again, secure my seatbelt, and lean forward on the table. Ty takes the seat next to me after talking to the pilot.

"I guess the blow job is off the cards," he quips.

"Start a tally. I'll make them up to you when the thought of something in my mouth doesn't make me want to gouge out my stomach."

"Well, it's nice to know you're so attracted to me."

I smile, closing my eyes. "Any time you doubt it, all you have to do is ask, honey."

"I think I'll avoid it if I'm honest." He reaches over and rubs my back again.

I hum at the soothing sensation. The pilot speaks over that we're heading for the runway to take off and that the weather in California is sunny, clear skies, and eighty-six degrees.

Well, that's just fantastic. Another fifteen or so degrees is just what my nausea-ridden body wants right now.

I sigh it off and relax into the feeling of Tyler's hand trailing up and down my spine. The warmth from his palm seeps through my skin and eases the tension in my muscles, even as we lift off.

"Water?" he asks softly.

I shake my head.

"You need to try, Liv. It's hotter in California. You'll dehydrate."

"Fine."

This is going to be a long few months.

I climb out of the cushy hotel bed and open the balcony doors. We have an incredible view of the beach from our room. The only thing that interrupts it is a few palm trees, their leaves swaying in the gentle sea breeze.

My stomach has somewhat settled, and although I know it could come back at any moment, I call down for some toast and water.

My stomach might be settled, but it's clawing at me for some kind of food.

I rifle through my suitcase and pull out a light, cotton dress. Today was supposed to be for us, but Tyler got dragged into another shoot almost the second we landed. Naturally, I did what any woman would do and headed straight to bed.

Well, any pregnant woman, that is.

If I'm sleeping, I don't have to think about him being around half-naked models. I don't have to consider him staring at them, even if it is through a camera lens.

It's my number-one insecurity, something that's now increased tenfold. So instead of thinking about him working, I'm going to sit here, aimlessly nibble on toast, and sip water while staring at the waves crashing on the beach.

How fucking romantic of me.

I twist my hair into a knot on top of my head and secure it with a tie. The door knocks, and I answer it. A cart is wheeled into the room for me and left by the table.

The toast is hot, and the scent of melted butter assaults my senses. My stomach growls and I breathe it in. For the first time in three days, I want to eat.

I grab the plate of toast and bottle of water and walk out onto the balcony. There are two chairs and a small table in the corner shaded by a large umbrella. I take a seat in one of the chairs, ensuring that I'm under the shade but leaving my legs in the sun.

I pick at the toast and look out at the beach. I'm not looking at anything in particular. I'm just letting the sounds roll over me and relax me.

Before I know it, I've eaten the whole slice of toast and am reaching for the second. I blink and shake my head. Eating a second slice is just asking for trouble. I reach for the water instead, sipping slowly, letting the coolness of the liquid soothe my throat.

No one ever tells you how raw your throat gets when they talk about morning sickness. Sure, they mention how horrible it is and whatever, but they never tell you the little bits.

My eyes move from the beach to my stomach. It's still flat—aside from some light bloating that probably isn't even visible to anyone else. I wonder when that bloat will become bump—when it'll be obvious to everyone else that there's a tiny baby in there.

I lift my dress up over my hips and run my finger across the skin above the waistband of my bikini briefs. It's smooth, hot, perfectly unmarred.

How long do I have until it changes? Until the beauty of what's inside reflects in permanent markings that will only ever fade?

How long do I have until I'm no longer me?

"It's not every day I get to finish work and come home to my girlfriend showing her knickers off."

I look at Tyler as if to say, *Really?* "They're not knickers. It's a bikini."

"I like it when you say knickers," he murmurs, leaning in to kiss me.

"I like it when *you* say knickers." I let him sweep his lips across mine and pick up my water again.

"How are you feeling?"

I point to the toast. "I ate a slice." I wiggle my bottle. "And I've drunk half of this."

A smile that tugs at my heart in the best kind of way stretches across his face. "Good. I was worried about you."

"I slept the whole time. I woke up maybe half an hour ago."

"Good. That means we can spend the day out."

I chew the inside of my lip. "What if I get sick again?"

"We'll make sure we're within running distance of a loo at all times," he reassures me.

I smile at his use of the word 'loo.' His words are as charming as his accent.

"Have you ever thought about moving back to London?" I ask, standing.

"Why? Have you?"

"No. But you grew up there, right? Don't you miss it?"

He shrugs, pulling his T-shirt off. "Not really. I mean, yeah, I miss some stuff. Like proper fish and chips, and Crunchies, and people talking properly."

I shove his arm properly. "What's a Crunchie?"

"Honeycomb covered in chocolate. You've never heard of a Crunchie?"

"You just told me you miss them, so what makes you think I've heard of them?"

His dark eyes settle on mine, glinting with amusement. "I can tell you're better. Your mouth is back." He steps forward, shirtless, and runs his thumb over my bottom lip.

"You sound disappointed."

"About your mouth being back? No. I happen to find it sexy as fuck when you argue with me."

"It's not arguing. It's replying with attitude."

"Attitude or arguing, whatever. Either way, it's sexy as fuck."

He curls his fingers around the back of my head and pulls my face to his. A whisper of air hovers between our lips where they're not quite touching but not quite apart. I flatten my hands against his stomach and slide one up his chest. It curves around the side of his neck, my fingertips teasing the hair at the top of his neck.

Slowly, he touches his lips to mine, his kiss tender. The softness of his mouth massaging mine makes me giddy, and I lean into him as he deepens the kiss.

His tongue sweeps through my mouth, fighting mine, pulling me deeper and deeper into him. Every movement he makes intoxicates me. I feel his touch everywhere like it's burned into my skin.

"Tonight," he whispers against my mouth. "Tonight, you're mine."

"I'm yours every night," I say back. "But it makes me all kinds of excited when you say that."

His lips curve into mine. "How excited?"

"You'll find out later, won't you?"

He dips his hand between my legs and runs his finger under my bikini briefs. I gasp, my eyes drawn to his when he pulls his finger, glistening with my wetness, to his mouth and licks it off. My pussy clenches, sending red-hot desire ricocheting through my veins.

He releases me with a sexy grin and disappears into the bathroom. I stare through the doorway, getting a brief glimpse of his naked body as he steps into the shower.

Need consumes me—memories of the times we've been together in the shower flash through my mind in quick succession. That first night when we were in our relationship that wasn't really a relationship and a few days ago.

I want to tear off my clothes and walk in there with him. Feel him hold me to him, feel him inside me, stroking me.

My indecision holds me still, and by the time I take one step forward, the shower is off and Tyler is toweling off. My eyes drop his to ass.

Damn.

He has a really nice butt.

"What is it with you and my bum?"

I lift my eyes to his. He's looking at me over his shoulder, his lips quirking upward. I shrug and turn away.

"Come on. I want to go out."

I lie back on the sand and sigh. It's hot against my skin as I grab a handful and let the fine grains run through my fingers, only to fall to the very place where I picked them up. Tyler sits next to me and crosses his legs.

He gazes down at me and puts a fry between my lips. I eat it to pacify him, although I'm still full from the slice of toast earlier. He offers me another and I shake my head. He shoves it into his mouth with way too much vigor—but I'll forgive him since the owners of the restaurant were British.

So, despite his earlier statement, he can get "proper fish and chips" here. This has delighted him to no end, and despite my teasing, I love seeing the satisfied glint in his eye.

"How did your shoot go earlier?"

"Fine. For once," he answers, waving some fish in front of my face.

"Ugh, no." I purse my lips. "Get it away. That smell!"

Tyler laughs and eats it. "I don't think you understand how good this is," he says around the fish.

"Don't talk with your mouth full, you savage!" I thump his thigh.

Another laugh. "That thing about Brits being polite? It's bullshit."

"What, so you don't say sorry ten million times to someone?"

"Do I look like a groveler?"

"No, but you look like someone who pisses people off a lot, so it's a viable question."

He flings a fry at my face and I laugh.

"Only you. But I think that's a boyfriend requirement. Right?"

I raise my eyebrow. "Yes, because there's a book for that shit. Didn't you know? I saw a Barnes and Noble down the road—why don't you ask them if they have a copy?"

Another fry comes my way. This time, I grab it from the sand and throw it back. He catches it in his mouth before he realizes that it's covered in sand. He splutters, putting his box of fish and chips down. I laugh at the way he scrapes his tongue with his fingers.

He launches himself at me and I roll away.

"Liv! You bitch!"

"Living up to my pet name!" I giggle, kicking my legs when he jumps on top of me and grabs my wrists.

He pins them above my head and drops his face. His eyes search mine. His lips, quirked to the side, show his dimple. I yearn to reach up and dip my finger in that soft dent in his cheek, to feel the smoothness of his skin beneath my skin.

I yearn to feel his skin against mine, at my own will, more than anything.

Like he can sense how I feel, he moves his thumbs. They rub across my palms, loosening his grip on me ever so slightly. Still, he gazes down at me.

And there's wonder in his eyes. A glint that wraps around me with warmth and safety. One that gives me everything I never imagined myself having. Happiness. Stability. Love.

I bend my fingers so the tips of my nails brush his hands. He slowly lowers his mouth to mine , every inch a torturous bit of space I'm desperate to fill.

Because I crave him. Even when he's straddling me, his hands securing mine, I crave him. Even when his skin is searing into mine, I crave his touch, because I know nothing else.

When he touches me, nothing else exists.

"I love you," he whispers, his voice thick with emotion. "I love you so bloody much."

I wrestle my hands from his grip and slide them into his hair. "I love you, too." I reach up and brush my lips across his. "And as much as I hate to ruin the moment, I really, really have to pee."

He stops and his eyes meet mine for a brief second. "For fuck sake, Liv." He drops off me and sighs dramatically. "How can you romance a woman when all she wants to do is pee?"

I smack his chest as I climb up. "You don't put a bun in their oven. That's how!"

His laughter follows me across the street as I duck into the nearest restaurant to use their restrooms. I push open the door and step into the cubicle, my bladder screaming at me.

I swear to shit, I almost 'ahh' as I pee.

It feels that damn good.

I finish my business and wash my hands. When I walk back out into the bar area of the restaurant, I hear his name—on the lips of another girl.

Everything in me tells me to keep walking.

Almost everything.

There's that one percent, that tiny niggle in the back of my mind, that tells me to stop. That one percent is made up purely of addiction, of pure need.

I take a seat at the bar and ask for a glass of still water. Bottled so I don't look like a total dick. Who asks for tap water, really?

I sip and listen in on their conversation. Like the complete fucking loser I am.

Because his name is my drug. I hear it and I have to have it. I have to know. Every little thing. It doesn't matter if it hurts. I need to know.

So I listen, blocking out all other sounds. I listen to them say how ridiculously hot he is. "Have you seen his pictures? Amazing. Wow. Have you seen him through that camera? What a babe. Did you see his modeling pics?"

Wait. What? Modeling?

"Have you seen that chick he's with?" I listen to them describing me as his latest weekend fling. Someone he'll throw to the side when he's done. "Because have you seen that model he's shooting tomorrow?"

"Holy shit. It's only Carmen Dallas, the hottest thing this side of America."

My stomach twists because I know her name. Who doesn't? Who remotely connected to the modeling world doesn't know her name? Long, perfectly black hair that curves at her waist. Big baby blues that captivate every man within in a ten-mile radius. Curves that could make a mafia boss cry.

I swallow. The heavy lump in my throat is too much—way too much. If he'd told me if it was her, Carmen Dallas, I would have refused this trip. But would that have made it better? No.

No. It would have made it worse. But can I go to the shoot tomorrow knowing that it's her? Knowing that he's staring at America's sexiest woman for a number of hours through his lens?

No. I can't be here, but I can't not be here.

I feel sick. For once, it's not a baby sick. It's a nervous, heart-wrenching kind of sick. And I need to run somewhere, anywhere. To breathe.

I push my empty glass across the bar and push out of the restaurant. I run across the road to the beach and feel the sand through my bare feet, soft and hot, spilling between my toes. And I keep running. I run until the sand turns wet and hard and cold water crawls over my feet.

I stop at the water's edge, far enough into the sea that my feet are always covered but farther away enough that it can only reach my ankles with a wave. I wrap my arms around my waist and breathe in the salty sea air, taking solace in the silence.

Taking the peace of the beach as insanity reigns inside.

Tyler's hands slide down my arms to rest over mine at my waist. "You okay?"

"I'm fine," I lie. "It was just hot in there. I needed air."

He runs his fingers along my forearms, wrapping his arms around me from behind. "Okay."

He doesn't believe me. I can hear it in his voice. But of course he wouldn't believe me—if I can't convince myself of a lie, I can't expect anyone else to be convinced either.

"When is your shoot tomorrow?" I swallow, hoping he can't hear the gulp.

"Ten a.m. Are you coming?"

I hesitate just long enough.

"You can come later," he says softly. "Or I'll meet you after."

I nod and look down. The white foam capping the waves swirls around my ankles with each push of the water. Each one is certain yet unsteady, their force known but their direction wavering.

I feel like the waves. In this moment, I am a wave, crashing repeatedly. I'm powerful and strong, but I don't know where I'm going. My path is so uncertain with so many choices.

My fingers twitch under Tyler's.

We are the waves. Our love is the force, the crash, and our relationship the slow crawl up the sand, the one with no direction.

Because we have no direction.

Our love is leading us blindly into an ending that might not be all that happy.

My heart twists with that thought. And the doubt—always the doubt. Nudging at the corners of my mind despite fighting it away. I know it's irrational and it's wrong, but I can't hold it at bay.

Now, the doubts are infinitely more. Just…more. More painful. More intense. More potentially devastating. Because I have two hearts to consider.

Two hearts beat inside me. Two hearts love inside me.

Two hearts that can be easily broken.

"Liv? Are you really okay?"

"I'm tired," I reply softly. "I want to go back to the hotel."

Tyler steps to the side and settles his arm around my shoulder, steering me back up the beach. He pauses for a moment to grab our shoes before reaching for me again.

I lean into his embrace, and instantly, I know my lie has driven a wedge between us. A part of me wants to take it back, to be honest with him, but I know it's not that simple.

My addiction is my issue, just like his is his. I won't try to fix him, but I know he'll try to fix me.

As each day goes by and I fall further and further into him, my doubt over being able to be fixed grows.

As I fall further and further into Tyler Stone, I am more certain than ever that I will have to say goodbye.

Chapter TWENTY-ONE

I WISH, more than anything, that I were back in Seattle. I wish I were alone in my apartment with Angus. I wish I could drink coffee and eat pizza and hide the 30 Day Shred DVD behind the sofa.

I wish I could have time to lay out all the thoughts in my mind into something that even remotely makes sense. Right now my brain is a hive of sensations, and none of them are good.

They are fears and doubts and hesitation and anxiety. They are the things I've avoided successfully for so long. They are weakness.

And I'm beginning to feel it. That weakness. Like a bad drug, it's clamping down and taking hold of me, winding its way through my body. It's pulsating through my veins and itching across my skin.

It's in every beat of my heart, in every shuddered breath I take as I fight the panic back down.

It's on the tip of my tongue.

I am weak.

The love I have for Tyler has coupled with my addiction and intertwined with it in the most intricate way just like I feared, and the strings that bind me to my feelings are too strong. They hold me captive within my emotions and my addictions. They expose me to my fears.

I'm looking for things that aren't there. I'm listening for things that haven't happened. I'm thinking of things that aren't in my control.

If you look enough, listen enough, think enough, you'll create your own world. You'll create a warped kind of universe where nothing is right. It's a universe borne entirely of insecurity and anxiety.

Insecurity and anxiety make you weak.

I am weakness.

For the first time, I'm in too deep. This isn't like before with Warren. This isn't a teenage dream. This is a real love, the kind you feel deep in your bones. It's the kind you feel so acutely that it could transcend time and space.

I love Tyler wholly, with every part of me. I love him with who I was and who I will be one day. I love him with who I am right in this second.

Except the person I am right now isn't much of anything.

She is scared. Unsettled. Broken.

She's addicted in the worst kind of way.

The thought of not being with him every day makes my lungs burn with the force of my breath. The thought of not being able to touch his face, kiss his lips, or hold his body physically hurts. It rips through me unrelentingly.

But being with him hurts, too. There isn't a middle ground or a happy medium. It's one extreme or the other. It hurts either way because both ends of my addiction, of my love, are devastating.

Without him, I could be nothing but an empty shell, living desperately for the one thing I'd have left of him.

With him, I'm bursting with life, but it comes with every insecurity a woman has to face.

Addiction hurts.

Nothing can feel good for so long without inevitably crashing and burning.

I scrub my skin with the puff until it's raw. I scrub every part of pain away from my skin before I step out of the shower. If only it were easy to scrub it from beneath my skin.

If I could take every bit of pain out of my body, I would.

I would rather not love him than hurt us.

Because that's all I'm doing. I'm hurting us both. Sure, he'll hold me and wipe my tears, but I see the pain in his eyes.

Last night, I crawled into bed and sobbed into my pillow.

He didn't know why. He didn't ask again.

He just lay there, holding me against him, stroking my hair until I fell asleep.

Even this morning, he kissed my forehead before leaving the hotel for his shoot.

With Carmen Dallas. Model extraordinaire.

And I'm just Liv. The model who never was.

I stop in front of the ceiling-high mirror and drop my towel. I look down at my body—my slightly swollen breasts, my tender, enlarged nipples, and my barely bloated stomach.

I turn to the side and look in the mirror. My chest heaves as I brush my fingertips over my lower stomach. I know it's bloat. I'm not seeing things that aren't there, but my stomach isn't flat.

Gas, water, whatever.

I curve my hand below it, holding it, and rest my other just over my belly button.

Beneath it all is a baby.

In this second, I'm not Liv, the model who never was.

I'm Liv, the mom who will be. And that's more important.

I don't care if this baby defines me. I don't care if he or she becomes the reason I am who I am. I just care that they matter to me.

And they matter enough to know that the way I feel isn't healthy. To know that the way I feel will eventually destroy them, too.

With one more look in the mirror, I turn to my suitcase and get dressed. I tie my wet hair on top of my head and take the elevator downstairs.

Tyler is shooting at the beach directly across from us, and when I look out of the lobby, I can see the people everywhere. They're never quiet, the shoots. They're always busy and bustling with life.

I don't know why I'm coming down here. Perhaps it's because the torture of watching him watch another woman will be less than the torture of imagining him watching another woman.

I cross the street and turn onto the beach path. The sand slips between my toes, spilling over my flip-flops, and I look around for Tyler.

My eyes find his dark head leaning next to an even darker one. My gaze drops—her hand on his bicep, his hand on her back…

I turn before I look any more.

Innocent.

I know that.

But my addiction doesn't.

This is why we're not good. This is why I should have fought it from day one. Why I should have punched him in the dick instead of fucking it.

He's my kryptonite and my trigger.

He's my good and my bad.

But this can't be about him anymore. It can't even be about me. It has to be about our baby. And having parents who are so hopelessly fucked up isn't going to be good for them.

It won't be good for us.

I slam the hotel room door behind me and call the hotel we're staying in for Day's bachelorette party. By some crazy stroke of luck, they have a room spare. Not the one we're staying in, but a room is a room.

I shove all my things into my case and set it on the bed.

Is running worth it? But am I running if it's right? If being apart from him, no matter how it hurts, for a short time is right for us?

Not even for us. For me.

Because me? I'm the one with the addiction that could destroy us. We both have to face up to them, but I'm the one of the edge of breaking.

His is physical. Mine is emotional.

I'm not a fucking princess and he's not a Disney prince. We can't overcome the villain by one of us suddenly performing a miracle. He can't save me, and I won't let him.

I am my own to save because I am weak.

I am my own to save because I am strong.

Because, in weakness, there is strength.

I believe that, to make this work, to let my love truly overcome my addiction, I have to walk away. I have to be strong no matter how it will kill me.

I don't know how long I've been standing here, staring at my bag on the bed. It feels like an eternity of seconds passing by needlessly.

But the hotel room door opens and time stands still. It hovers in the air around me in its own sense of purgatory.

"Liv? Where are you?"

"In here," I say, my voice cracking.

"One of the guys said a blonde girl came onto the beach earlier but left. Was that you?"

I can almost feel his footsteps as he walks into the room. I nod. "Yep."

"Why is your bag packed?"

I grip the handles. "I'm sorry," I whisper. "But I can't do this. I can't pretend I'm okay with what you do. I can't fake the smiles or act like it doesn't matter when it does."

"What—Liv?"

I turn, slowly lifting my gaze to his. Tears fill my eyes and I can feel my heart crumbling despite how right I know this is. In a few steps, I cross the room to him and rest my hand against his cheek.

His stubble is rough and familiar against my skin, and his dark eyes are filled with the inevitability of this moment. He knows. I know.

Two hearts will be broken today, but one can be saved.

"I love you, Ty. I love you so fucking much that it hurts me. You have to know that. But that's why I have to go." A tear falls as I swallow the sob building. "But I'm too selfish to ask you not to wait. I want to know you'll be there when I come back, even if it's a lie. I have to go for me. I have to go for all of us."

"I don't understand." His hand covers mine. "Why? Why the fuck do you have to go?"

"Because I can destroy you, but I can't destroy our baby." I stroke my thumb across his cheek. "I can't hurt our baby. Even if, in the end, she is all I have, I can't hurt her. Nothing matters more than she does. Let me go and let me deal with what I have to."

"You aren't making sense!" He takes my face in his hands the way I have his.

I can barely look at him. I can see his heart fucking breaking in his eyes. I can see it cracking and falling away as the tiny pieces shatter with my words.

"I love you, but you hurt me and you don't even know," I whisper. My voice is thick and I can't breathe. My throat is tight, so tight, my vision so blurred, and I don't know anything anymore. "You don't mean to, except I think I hurt myself. And you don't deserve that. You deserve perfect, and until I can give you something more than broken, I have to go."

I kiss him one last time. It's bittersweet, and my heart breaks all over again when I pull away.

He stands, staring at me, his eyes burning a heartbroken hole into my back. I walk to the door, every part of me hurting, my soul being ripped to shreds by my own words, and open it.

"I don't want fucking perfect. I want you. Just you."

"I'm sorry," I whisper one last time before stepping through the doorway.

Walking away from pain into pain.

Because that's addiction.

A never-ending circle of pain and devastation.

If you have the object you crave, you hurt.

If you don't, you hurt.

No—if you don't, you shatter.

The pain is crippling.

I barely have time to climb into a taxi waiting outside before the tears stream down my cheeks. It feels like a cruel sense of déjà vu—except the memory of this moment isn't mine. It's my best friend's.

She got in a taxi and drove away from the only man she ever loved.

I'm doing the same thing. Except this is my choice. I made the decision to walk away from the person I love more than I ever knew was possible.

Chapter TWENTY-TWO

THE hotel is no different than the one I was in six hours ago, except this one has no Tyler. It just has me. It's quiet. Too quiet. It doesn't matter that I've slept since I got here. It just matters that it's quiet. If you don't count my tiny sniffles.

It seems like ages since I arrived at the airport, ready to jump on the next flight here, and was directed through first class to Tyler's parents' jet. It hasn't been long, not at all, but that's the funny thing about time. It never feels like a true representation of the seconds that tick by. It's either slow or fast… Or standing still.

I cried the whole fucking way here. From the second I got on the plane, I let my broken heart consume me until I climbed into bed with nothing left but the bare shell of me.

Only from a shell can I grow, can I become the person I can need to be.

I get out to bed to grab my phone and climb back in. The picture on the screen stares at me. Me and him, happy and smiling in a goofy-as-hell selfie. I want to smile, but the image only invokes a fresh flood of tears.

Thank you.

I send the text to him, something so simple. I don't know why he had the plane there ready for me. If I were him, I would have made me fucking walk.

Hell, I should have walked.

When minutes pass with no reply from him, I rest my phone on the nightstand and pull the covers up to my chin. I'm aching everywhere. It's dull but heavy, my heartbreak weighing on me everywhere.

Except my heart isn't broken. Not entirely. It's breaking slowly, every piece that chips off shattering and pulsing through my bloodstream.

My hotel door opens, and something in me tells me that I should be looking for who it is. But I don't. I lie here, staring at the wall.

"Oh, baby."

I drag my eyes away and they collide with Dayton's. "What are you doing here?"

She walks over to the bed and perches next to me. "As soon as the plane arrived back in Santa Barbara, Tyler flew to Seattle."

I swallow.

"Tyler drove straight to our place and told us everything. I was packed and out the door in ten minutes." She pushes hair from my face. "Tessa is here, too. She's getting nonalcoholic wine and ice cream."

I try to smile but it fails. "You didn't need to come."

"Of course we did," she replies as I sit up.

"Your party is tomorrow. I packed my smile especially for it."

Her lips quirk. "Liv, I don't give a shit about that. I care that you're okay. You're more important to me than some stupid wedding."

"Some stupid wedding, huh?" I raise my eyebrows.

"Well, as long as no one is pissing me off, we're good." Her eyes crinkle as she grins. "Wanna talk about it?"

I open my mouth to speak as Tessa walks in. She appears in the doorway of the bedroom and my eyes find hers. The eyes that are so similar to Tyler's. The same long, curly eyelashes.

I lean forward as tears fill my eyes again. Dayton's arms circle me and she pulls me into her. I cry into her shoulder, the warmth of her embrace exactly what I need right now. Tessa climbs onto the bed and sits next to me. She lays her hand on my back and rubs slowly, resting her cheek against my shoulder.

Neither of them speaks. What is there to say?

Nothing can possibly ease the pain of being away from him.

I remind myself that it was my decision. I chose to walk away and I chose to do it for good reasons. And I can't regret that I did it—only that I had to.

When my eyes are so puffy that I can feel the swelling around them and my lips are chapped from crying, I take a deep breath and the words tumble from my lips. I'm barely whispering, my voice coated in thickness, cracking every other sentence.

I tell them everything that led me up to making that decision. As I do, my hand creeps around to my stomach and flattens against it. Like I can protect the baby from this situation.

Neither Tessa nor Day speaks until I've been quiet for a few minutes.

"You did the right thing. You know that?" Tessa says softly.

I nod. "Yeah. But it hurts." I sit up and meet Dayton's eyes.

In them, I see pain and worry. Shadows of the past darken her normally bright eyes, and it hurts me even more.

"Don't," I plead. "Don't look at me that way. I'm hurting, but I'm okay. I have something to live for this time. I haven't even thought about it."

She takes a deep breath. "I know. I'm just afraid for you. And him. Shit, Liv. I wish I could just reach inside you both and take away all your pain."

I squeeze her hand. "I'll just avoid him…somehow…until I'm ready."

"Liv," Tessa breathes. "You can't. You see the doctor this week. You really think he won't be there?"

"I know," I whisper. "And I would never stop him. So other than baby things, I'll avoid him. Totally. I'll run away at the end of the appointment if I have to."

"Bloody hell!" She snorts. "Good luck with that."

I shrug a shoulder. For the first time in hours, my lips curve at the corners.

Tessa grabs a bottle of nonalcoholic wine from the grocery bag at the foot of the bed. "I've never seen my brother heartbroken. Hell, I've never seen him in love. Right now, he's both. And Tyler? He's the biggest fucking fixer I've ever met, and it's a right pain in the arse, I tell you." She hands me the bottle. "He won't give up or leave you alone until he's fixed you both. He will keep at you and pursue you relentlessly until your hearts are so fixed they're one."

"He's a fixer and I'm a breaker. Just another reason why we're bad for each other."

Dayton smacks me on the side of the head and I squeal.

"What the fuck?!" I stare accusingly at her.

"Shut up! Shut the hell up!" She narrows her eyes at me. "You think love is good? No. Love is the biggest load of bullshit I've ever dealt with in my life. It will make you and break you in the blink of an eye. But if you keep thinking about why it's bad, it'll never be good. Stop focusing on your flaws and start thinking of the good stuff, because you two are so perfect for each other that it makes me sick."

"But this isn't about love." I look down. "This is about addiction. This is about how much it fucking hurts to love him. Until I have my shit sorted out, I can't let myself love him. I can't hurt him that way."

"But you're hurting him anyway," she replies. "You're hurting both of you, Liv."

"You don't get it. I love him so much and I am so addicted to him that I hate the fact that other people can even look at him. I wish I could drive us away to where no one could find us and hide us forever. I wish he didn't have to look at other girls for his job or talk to them or touch them!" I run my fingers through my hair, grabbing at the loose strands and tugging in a desperate bid to make that pain overrule the ache inside. "I wish he could be mine. Just mine. Just. Mine."

"But he is," Tessa implores. "You don't see it. None of you do. But I see it all, Liv. I see how he looks at you, and he is completely and utterly yours. There isn't a part of him that you don't have the power to crush. And although I hate seeing him so hurt, I respect your choice. I understand why you made it. Now, if you aren't doing something about it first thing on Monday morning, I'm tacking your pregnant self with an IOU arse-kicking."

She reaches over and unscrews the cap of my fake wine. I swig from the bottle and sigh as the taste of wine fills my mouth.

So it helps. Sue me. A girl can pretend.

My phone vibrates on the nightstand, cutting off whatever Day was about to say, and I reach for it. Tyler's name flashes on the screen, stopping my heart.

I'll look after you 'til Hell freezes over. You're mine.

I'm beginning to get very acquainted with the inside of toilets.

I wonder how long it'll take for it to get old. I mean, how many times can one person vomit before they get sick of it? No pun intended, of course...

I spend an hour in the bathroom vomiting up a big, fat fucking nothing. That's right. My throat burns and my mouth tastes like sterility for no reason whatsoever.

Thank you, baby Stone. I appreciate it.

I sit on the floor and lean against the bath while I wait for the next wave of nausea to pass. When it does, I crawl into the bedroom, grab my glass from the nightstand, then crawl back to the bathroom to fill it. No sudden movements. All easy, flowing moves.

I sit back down and sip very slowly from the glass. It's more to wet my lips and mouth than for a drink—I feel as though I've been swirling sand around my mouth for the past few hours.

The glass smashes as I drop it and grab the toilet. Whatever water I just drank comes back up violently and I punch the toilet seat. Fucking hell. I pull the flush and take a deep breath. My stomach hurts ridiculously. It's cramping relentlessly, sending hot flushes through me.

And I'm sitting next to a pile of smashed glass.

Fantastic. Fanmotherfuckingtastic.

I have no idea how long it take for the nauseated feeling to go. All I know is that, by the time it does, my ass is numb and my back hurts from leaning against the bathtub.

I tug myself up using the side of the tub for leverage and walk out of the bathroom on shaky legs. The next person to talk about that pregnant woman glow is getting punched.

I change from my pajamas and pull a dress over my head. A series of loud knocks echo through the hotel room, and I walk to the door, resisting the urge to check my phone.

I know there won't be anything there. What can we really say to each other? 'I'm sorry I broke your heart'? 'I'm sorry I'm so effed up I can't have a relationship with you although I'm having your baby'?

'I'm sorry I expect you to wait for me when I don't know what I'm asking for?'

"Are you ready to go down to the spa?" Day asks. "Ack. Or maybe a hospital?"

I give her my best 'shut the hell up' look and grab my phone and room key. "Spa. It's just morning sickness. It'll ease up soon."

Said no sick, knowledgeable pregnant woman ever.

"Are you sure?"

"Yes. Now let's go before you turn into the mom and me the baby." I slam the door behind me and follow her into the elevator.

Tessa darts into it just before the doors shut with a chirpy, "Morning!" and a rosy smile I'd love to wipe off.

Wow. Hello, hormones.

Seriously, these things come out of nowhere. Give a girl a positive pregnancy test and she's suddenly the symptom page of that flippin' booklet they give out.

I follow them into the spa, where we're greeted it a smile and handed robes. Fluffy, fluffy robes. I sigh as we're shown into private rooms to change into them. *Oh, soft, fluffy robe.*

Drinks, breakfast orders, then questions about massages.

"Oh, wait. Do you have a masseuse trained to do pregnancy massages?" Dayton interrupts, pointing at me. "Liv is pregnant."

The girl in front of us widens her eyes. "Oh, of course, but she won't be in until this afternoon."

"It's fine," I say. "I'll do something else."

"We can rearrange the plan to accommodate that for you, Miss Black," the girl says, ignoring me completely. "It's not a problem."

"That would be great. Thank you." Day turns to me. "See? Not a problem. Now let's get our feet done."

The girl leads us over to the pedicure area and I hold in my sigh. And there I was, hoping I'd get another hour in bed.

Chapter
TWENTY-THREE

ICE cream. Chocolate sauce. Strawberries. Banana. Sprinkles. And a whole lot of other so-bad-it's-good-for-you crap.

I haven't vomited for four and a half hours, which, in my meager opinion, gives me free range to devour this calorie-laden beauty in front of me.

And if it comes back up later, then at least I got to enjoy it.

I fill my mouth full of the goodness and close my eyes. I hum low, licking the sauce off the spoon appreciatively.

Dayton laughs. "Do you need a room, Liv?"

I half-groan, half-moan, and look at her. "You have no idea how good this tastes after two days of plain pasta and toast!"

And heartbreak. And crying. And despondent staring into space.

Oh, shit. Someone build me a bridge so I can get over it already.

This is Day's weekend. It's about her. And my ice cream. Oh, crap. The ice cream.

"Seriously. If there were such a thing as snogging ice cream, you'd be doing that right now," Tessa muses. "It's both intriguing and horrifying at the same time."

"No." I shake my head. "Horrifying was you getting the wax earlier. No, I take it back. Your scream while getting the wax earlier was horrifying."

"So I'm a Brazilian virgin. Shoot me."

"How did you…you know." Day waves her hand.

"Seriously. The ex-call girl can't say 'shave your pubic hair'?" I raise my eyebrows.

She shoots me a look. "Fine. Tessa, tell me. How did you keep your vajayjay pretty before today?"

I grin when Tessa spits out her drink.

"I shaved," she answers.

"Oh, effort." I muse. "Not to mention time consuming. Plus, those little cuts? Why are they always on the inside?"

We all contemplate this for a moment. No, seriously. We do.

"Well, it doesn't hurt as much as waxing," she reasons. "So I guess it's worth it."

"Ahh," Day interrupts, waving her own spoon around. "But you won't have to get it done again for around six weeks. If you'd shaved, you'd be in the bathroom with your leg on the side of the bath in an awkward sex position with your fingers pulling your lady parts in ways that only a man should."

"For someone who swears by wax, that was an awfully accurate description."

Day shrugs. "We were all wax virgins once. Except my aunt pinned me down while we stood by and kind of laughed at you."

I snort, licking my spoon again. "Kind of? If I were at the other end of this pregnancy, I would have given birth I laughed so freakin' hard."

Tessa flicks some sprinkles at me. "It's always nice to know the mother of your future niece or nephew has your back."

"Don't anger the hormones. They're evil."

"So I hear," a smooth male voice says behind us.

I stand and spin. "The hell do you think you're doing here, Stone?"

Aaron grins playfully. "Our plane got…lost."

"Lost? Despite the fact we're farther south than your destination, hmm?"

"Air traffic control messed up the coordinates," he tries again. "We ended up in L.A. What were we supposed to do?" He holds his arms out to the sides, but his words are what have caught me.

He holds his arms out to the sides, but his words are what have caught me.

"We? You mean—oh shit. No." I drop my spoon in my sundae glass. "I'm done. Someone take me to the airport."

"Liv," Day says, standing.

"Easy." Aaron gently grabs my arm. "He doesn't know what room you're in and every member of staff has been told if they tell him, they're fired."

I narrow my eyes and look up at him. "Why would you do that?"

"Because this weekend is about me and Day, not you two. Besides," he adds, "you're impulsive but not irrational. You wouldn't have broken up with him if you didn't feel like it was the right thing to do."

"We're not…broken up. We're on a temporary break." The words sound flat even to me. Like I'm trying to convince myself more than him.

"Yeah?" He leans in. "Then you should probably tell my cousin that, because today was the first time I ever saw him cry."

My mouth feels like it got in a fight with a desert and lost.

"He did what?" I whisper scratchily.

"He protested an allergy for a while before finally disappearing into the bedroom for the remainder of the flight. When he came out, no one but me would have been able to tell."

I swallow, the lump in my throat suddenly too big, too painful. "Why are you telling me this? Why are you making a weekend for you about me?"

"Because he's integral to my happiness the way you are to Day's. He's in room 1583. If you wanted to continue the conversation you began yesterday."

I take my arm away from him and look him in the eye. "I don't. And *you* shouldn't even be here to give me the opportunity."

"Touché. I'll still make sure he doesn't find out your room number."

"Considerate of you. Perhaps you should have extended the same courtesy to the hotel." I grab my phone from the side. "Are you guys ready to head back into the spa? I don't want to be responsible for murdering the groom on the party weekend."

"Wow," I hear Aaron mutter as I walk away. "They really are evil."

I stop by the door of the restaurant. "This isn't evil. This is normal. You should be very afraid, Aaron Stone. Very fucking afraid."

I catch Day's shrug before I turn away again. "She's right," she says. "And to think this is a good day. Now, I'm going for a massage, and when I get back, I want you and Tyler out of my frickin' sight, Mr. Stone. Got it?"

I lean against my hotel room door and breathe out a long sigh. Every corner I turned, I expected him to walk around. Every time the elevator doors opened, I expected him to be there, waiting. Hell, when I got to the room, I expected him to be here.

This weekend, not that it ever got off to a good start, has been ruined. Just by him being here, the heavy cloud that lifted somewhat in the presence of Dayton and Tessa has descended once more.

I feel the pain so strongly, wrapping around me and squeezing, like its only goal is to draw all the life out of me. Knowing that he's here, close, two floors up and three doors down, is like an echoing plea. A beg to take me there, to drag me to him.

A desperate plea for my heart to rejoin with my body.

For everything to balance out.

If only it had been balanced to begin with. It wasn't. Away from him, I can see it more clearly. I can see how the needs of his addiction outweighed mine. Fuck now, talk later—it's all good until the talking doesn't happen.

When it doesn't happen repeatedly, questions have to be asked. 'We'll get through it together.' 'We'll do this.' 'We can cope as long as we're together.' They're all good. They're all ambitious, realistic statements.

Until there's nothing to back them up with.

How?

How are we going to cope with our addictions and the way they hurt us? Are we going to continue down this path, clinging desperately to the other person while we battle our way through, only to inevitably hurt the other? Are we going to wake up each morning to the sun filtering through the windows and decide that this is the day we separate the emotion from the addiction and live like that?

Or are we going to call, talk to people, lay it out? Are we going to deal with therapy and the highs and lows? Are we even going to try?

Are we going to look past the idealistic thoughts we have, or are we just going to sit around like a couple of teens waiting for the answer to fall into our laps?

I know Tyler's answer. Believe. Try. Wait. Hope that some little fairy will come along and wave their damn wand and make it better.

That's not how it works. Maybe we have to be apart to make it work.

We might not have anything to lose when we're apart, but we sure as hell have everything to fight for.

And the fact that you might not win the fight is a far scarier thought than losing something you never thought would go.

Maybe the key is to be together but not. Maybe seeing each other, talking, but not really having one another, is the key. Because then we'll remember, every day, what we're fighting for. We'll have something to work toward.

Maybe it's a coffee date, breakfast, or dinner. Maybe it's a movie or a doctor's appointment. Maybe it's even a sleepover.

Just something small, mostly insignificant—the little things that change everything.

I don't believe for a second that Tyler will haul his ass willingly into therapy. For him, I would. I hated every second, but if therapy means managing this and if managing this means having him, I'll go through hours of hell and hurt.

All of it. For him. For me. For the baby.

Without a second thought. Because we're more than addiction. It's hard to remember sometimes; we're stronger than the ties that bound us in the beginning.

We're not addiction. We're love in its strongest, purest form, no matter how wrinkly or rough it is. We're indestructible, and I truly believe that, one day, we'll be able to weather any storm.

Right now, we're the eye of the storm. We're the tornado touching down on the ground, and our relationship is in a whirlwind, destructive spin above us. If we try hard enough, we can slow the spin and the devastation.

If we try hard enough, we can erase the storm and pave the way for the mess to be fixed.

My bed dips as I roll over, yawning. I snuggle back into the covers and reach for the quilt. It feels like something hard, something warm, though. And then fingers link through mine and lips close over mine.

Soft, wet lips. Lips I know.

Lips I know. They're tender, and I tilt my head back to take more of the kiss, because warmth spreads through me at it.

They're salty, like endless tears are streaming onto them.

I take my hand and reach up, my palm resting against familiar stubble, and wipe at the wet cheeks. I don't want to open my eyes, because if I do that, it's not a dream any more. I'm awake but asleep right now.

As soon as my eyes open, I can't pretend. So I fight it, fight to keep them closed. Because if I'm dreaming, I'm not contradicting everything I said to myself earlier.

The addict in me wants to destroy itself. Just a little more. One last time.

Tyler sweeps me against him fully and takes my mouth once more. Each touch is like drizzly raindrops falling on dry ground. Slow, easy, light. Every sweep of his tongue is explorative, leaving no part of my mouth not touched, and mine does the same, drinking in him like he's my life elixir.

His hands, as tender and sweet as his tongue, caress my curves one by one. They stroke and they slide, and his fingers splay, brushing my skin. Every touch is slow and easy, filled with more than anything before.

I want to hold on, because tomorrow, this more will be broken again.

Tyler sweeps his hand down to my thigh and eases my leg up and over his body. Our hips come together at his urging, his hardening cock between us. I ache, too. I ache to feel him once more because I don't know when the next time will be.

I ache for him to fuck me as softly as he's kissing me.

I ache for him.

I sink my fingers into his hair and push myself against him. *It won't hurt,* I tell myself. It won't make a difference when the sun rises.

Because this is a dream, and dreams aren't real, and they don't come true.

He sweeps two fingers along me, easing my underwear out of the way, and settles his cock against me. I push down as he pushes up, our bodies coming together in perfect sync.

The power shifts.

It's not about him or me. It's not about tying up or positions or fantasies.

It's about us. It's about the emotion that lies beneath it and expressing that the only true way we know how to.

And it is, because he moves slowly and torturously inside me. My hips grind slowly, in time with him. But our kiss never breaks. Our grip never wavers and our tears don't stop falling.

Because pain and love are one and the same. To love, you must feel pain. To feel pain, you must love. They go hand in hand.

It's endless, these movements. They go on forever, neither wanting to let go because we know that, when we do, it's over. It's back to the pain and loneliness of the past twenty-four hours.

Finally, it builds inside. The heat prickling across my skin and the tension clenching my muscles erupts, shuddering through my body. But I don't cry out, I don't scream, I don't shout his name.

I whimper. Just a tiny whimper, one that mingles with the salty taste of tears on my lips.

He's quiet, too, as his release hits. Almost silent. I know though. I know because he grips me tight, his kiss turning desperate as he holds himself still and empties inside me.

I don't want to cry anymore, I realize. I can't. It hurts more than the pain.

So I keep my grip on him, kissing the tears on his cheeks, and he kisses mine, and I bury my face into his neck.

I know that, when I wake, he will be gone.

But when I fall asleep, he'll be here.

For one last time, I want us to fall together. To spin dizzily although it's only into sleep. I want to remember this moment for the pureness and the love flowing through my veins. Not for tears and heartache.

Because sometimes, pain can be just as beautiful as love.

No matter how ugly it really is.

Chapter TWENTY-FOUR

I PUSH the door to Starbucks open, and immediately, my eyes find Marchant in the corner. I push my way through the coffee shop, instantly regretting to meet him here. Regretting meeting him at all, even if it has been a week since I got back from L.A. and this is the fourth rearranged date.

Because, ugh, this smell.

My stomach churns and I swallow desperately, begging the three sips of water I chanced before leaving my apartment to stay down. They do, for now, and I slide into the chair opposite Marchant.

"Hi," I mutter.

"You don't look like you're doing too well" he says in greeting.

I look at him flatly. "I've been on a first-name basis with the inside of my toilet for the last damn week. Should I look good?"

"I'm sorry to hear that. Have you seen your doctor for any anti-nausea medication?"

I sigh. "I'm going to call her in the morning."

"You should rest. If I knew you were sick, I would have come to you. Would you like to go home?"

"No," I shake my head. "It's too suffocating in there."

He looks at me knowingly. "Without Tyler?"

I fidget. "Yes."

"What made you leave him?"

"I haven't left him. Entirely. I'm…taking a break from him."

Marchant's lips twitch. "Okay, so what made you need to take a break from him?"

"Everything," I reply. "I feel like I'm so addicted to him that that's all I am. I'm not Liv anymore. I'm just…addicted. I obsess over him literally all the time. I can't do it anymore—I have to be me, too. It hurts."

"So don't let yourself be that bad."

"Really? Years of studying to understand the human mind and all you've got is, 'Don't let yourself be that bad'? I figured that out without the degree." I roll my eyes and set my hand on my stomach.

March laughs. "I didn't mean it so simply. I mean that, once a day, take thirty minutes for yourself and do something that's you. It's all about perspective, Liv. If you allow yourself to make everything about him, it will be."

"It's not about allowing myself. I can't help it. He's the center of my world. Hell, he's the center of my whole damn universe, and all I can do is hold on to his gravitational pull while I spin out of control."

"You can help it. Of course you can. It's your decision, and you have control because you're aware of it. You're in the position where you can grab your addiction by the balls and deal with it."

"Is that professional lingo, Doctor? Grabbing addiction by the balls?"

He half-grins. "If it's not, it should be. It's a very clear instruction, don't you agree?"

"I do agree. And technically, that's what I want to do. I just wish it were easier to separate the addiction from the love. Sometimes, they feel like they're the same thing."

"They are in some aspects. They both make you feel good and they both hurt."

"Too much," I say softly. "So much that it's impossible to differentiate the good and bad feelings."

March sits back and rubs his chin. His eyes study me intently for a moment. "Have you considered that the way you're feeling is less about addiction and more about love? You just admitted that they feel the same, and for someone addicted and without the thing they crave, you're incredibly calm."

"I have to be calm. I have to keep okay for the baby."

He leans forward again and rests his forearms on the table. "The thing about addiction, Liv, is that it knows no bounds. It will destroy everything in its path if you let it—including a baby. The power of it is stronger than anything. If it had a total hold over you, you'd be powerless to stop it. Think about that."

I shake my head. "The baby needs me."

"It does. That's correct. But maybe you need you, too. Maybe your addiction isn't as strong as you think and your hormones have only served to heighten your emotions."

"This isn't about my insecurities."

"On the contrary, I think it's very much about them. Think about it, Liv. You haven't known each other long. You'd barely touched on a relationship before you found out you were going to be parents. That's a huge upheaval on people who have been together for years and planned a baby, let alone a brand-new couple who were surprised by one. Now, I'm not saying call Tyler and live happily ever after. You both have issues you have to work through, and perhaps some time apart is for the best. I'm saying stop and think about what's really affecting you, and for your own sanity, look past what you perceive as your addiction. You can't hide behind it for long."

"Thanks for the ride," I say, getting out of March's car.

"Any time, Liv. Remember what I said, and call me, okay?"

I nod and wave as he drives away. I step into the lobby and hold my cramping stomach. Agonizing hunger pains are assaulting my stomach, but the sharp cramps say that I'm not eating any time soon. They say that I'm about to hug my friggin' toilet yet again.

I've kept water down for an hour.

Go me.

I run into my apartment and go straight to the bathroom. I dry heave into the toilet, gripping the sides. I stay still, letting it run its course, and wipe the beads of sweat from my forehead. Then I flush the bile down and walk back out into the front room.

I don't expect Tyler to be sitting on my sofa.

But he is.

All six foot two of him. Complete with messy hair, a stubble-covered jaw, and eyes that pierce my heart.

Four days since I canceled my doctor's appointment to avoid him and he turned up with ginger cookies. Four days since I looked into those dark eyes I adore, brushed his fingers with mine as I took the package of cookies, breathed the same air as him.

"What are you doing here?" I manage, feeling my stomach twist in a very different way. Can my stomach get a break? Anyone?

"You look bloody awful."

"Yeah, vomiting will do that to a girl," I snap, turning away from him and getting a glass of water.

"The biscuits don't work?"

I swallow and shake my head. "Nothing works." I bring the glass to my lips to wet them, making sure I don't swallow any.

"You didn't drink any of that," he says quietly, standing next to me.

I set the glass down, ignoring the warmth flooding my body at the sound of his voice. "I don't feel like vomiting it up yet."

He brushes his fingers down my pale cheek and I step back, the movement killing me.

"What are you doing here?" I repeat, not meeting his eyes. "I didn't call you. I don't need anything."

Way to be a bitch, Liv, you fucking bitch.

"I miss you. It's fucking killing me, Liv. I just need to see you."

"Well, now you've seen me, so you can go again." I swallow and hug myself. "Please. I don't have the energy to argue with you."

I don't have the energy to fight when the gentle touches of that Saturday night in the hotel are burned into my memory. When they're all I feel—ghostly fingertips caressing my skin, imagined lips pressing against mine. When every touch and kiss and tear is all I see every time I close my eyes, despite the fact that I never saw any of it to begin with.

"So don't. Let me stay and look after you. Shit, you need it, baby girl." Tyler steps forward and grabs my face. "Let me look after you. I'm not fucking leaving when you're this ill."

"I'm fine!" I shout, once again moving away from his touch. It burns me sweetly, intensely, painfully. "I just need to sleep. Okay? I'm just really tired. I'm fine, honestly."

He stares at me, helpless, but I can see the annoyance growing in his eyes. "Really? You call this fine? I'd hate to see your bloody awful!"

"This is pregnancy," I reply lamely. "It's not exactly a frolic in the park on a summer's day."

"And it's my job to look after you. Now let me!"

"I don't want you to!" Tears burn my eyes. "I need space, Ty. I still need time. I can't have you hovering over me while I sort my feelings out. Just let me be sick and sleep and think."

"How the hell do you expect me to leave you? Look at you! I can't walk out of here after seeing you like this! It goes against bloody everything in me to do that."

"But I told you I'd call if I needed you." My head pounds and I close my eyes. "You shouldn't have been here in the first place, so just forget you ever came." I push past him and pull two Tylenol out of the drawer.

And stare at the glass dumbly because I can't fucking keep anything down.

I throw the glass in the sink and it drops with a smash. I rest my forehead against the fridge, the tears spilling over my eyes.

"Liv," he whispers.

"I've never been in so much fucking pain in my life. My head is thumping and my stomach hurts so bad, but there's nothing I can do, because I can't keep a single fucking thing down!" I turn to face him. "I haven't eaten in four days and I'm lucky to keep water down. That's how fucking sick I am! I am so weak and exhausted and I really need you to just go, please."

"What the fuck? Why didn't you call me?"

"Because I don't need you." I push off the fridge, blinking to clear my vision. "Because you make it worse. You just make it worse."

I sway and grab the table to steady myself. Spots float in front of my eyes and I blink again, harder, faster, swallowing.

"Liv?"

"Go!" I beg, my head spinning.

"No."

I open my mouth to argue but no sound comes out, and my legs buckle.

"Shit, Liv!"

And—

Beep. Beep. Beep.

I squeeze my eyes shut before dragging them open. White ceiling. I blink slowly, getting my bearings, and roll my head to the side. I look straight into the face of a sleeping Tyler.

He looks peaceful. The frown from earlier isn't marring his forehead anymore, and his lips aren't turned down anymore. And he's gorgeous. Even if there is still pain etched on his face and his fingers are gripping my sheet. He's so handsome that it breaks my heart a little.

I lift a heavy arm to touch his face, but a big clip on the end of my finger cancels that plan.

I look at it and run my eyes up my arm to the point where an IV is in me.

Shit. Am I in the hospital?

"Liv? You're awake?" Tyler says gruffly, sitting up and rubbing his eyes.

"Where am I?" I whisper, my voice scratchy.

He leans onto the bed and rests his hand on my cheek. "You're in hospital, in a private room. Don't you remember what happened?"

I shake my head.

Worry fills his eyes and he sighs heavily. "You passed out trying to get me to leave. Good thing I didn't."

I passed out?

"You're dehydrated," he explains softly. "They put the IV in and pumped you full of water, vitamins, and anti-sickness. You've been asleep for hours. It's one in the morning."

I swallow. "Can I have some water?"

He stands and pours a cup from the jug on the table. "Here." He presses a button next to the bed and it sits me up.

He feeds me a few sips of water, and it feels like heaven. It slides down my throat in a cool wash. I nod when I'm done and rest my head back against the pillow.

"The nurse told me to get her when you woke up. I'll be right back." He leans over and tenderly presses his lips to my forehead.

I watch him go, still sleepy despite apparently being out for around ten hours. At least my headache is gone and my stomach isn't hurting anymore.

"Well, hello, honey!" the nurse chirps happily. "Good to see you awake. How are you feeling?"

"Like crap," I whisper as she grabs my notes and checks the monitor.

"I expect so. I promise they're worth it in the end!" She gives me a bright grin and checks the IV bag. "Do you feel sick?"

I shake my head. "No. Just thirsty."

"Little sips every few minutes, okay? Take it easy. If you'd prefer, I can get you some ice chips to suck on."

"Yes, please."

"Okay. This all looks good. I'll page the doctor and she'll come and talk to you quickly." She smiles again and glides out of the room.

"Shit. How can anyone be so happy at one in the morning?" I ask Tyler, meeting his eyes.

He sits on the side of the bed and smiles. It soon drops though, and he doesn't reply.

"What?"

"Shit." He leans forward and hugs me. His hand slides up my neck into my hair, and his other arm is firmly around my waist. He buries his face into my neck and inhales deeply. "Don't ever faint on me like that again. You scared the crap out of me," he says in a thick voice.

"It wasn't intentional," I mumble into his chest.

He laughs lamely and sighs. "Never a dull second with you around." He pulls back and looks at me. Tears I never want to see hint at his eyes.

"I like to change things up. What can I say?" I shrug and offer a small smile.

He runs his thumb across my cheek. "Don't. I'm starting to like it better all the same."

He dips his head and lightly touches his lips to mine. They're soft and warm and taste like tea. I lean into his gentle kiss, only pulling away when the door opens.

I look around him and into the face of my OBGYN. "Hi."

"Hello, Liv," Dr. Peters smiles. "How are you feeling?"

"Like crap," I say, answering the same as I did to the nurse.

"I'd imagine you do." She perches on the end of the bed and flicks through my notes. "Now I'm not in the practice of working with private patients, but since it's you and I'm angry at you, here I am."

I cringe.

"Now, why did you cancel our appointment and not call me after four days of not being able to stomach water?"

Both she and Tyler stare at me. Tyler's gaze is scarier. I fidget.

"I…thought it was normal," I admit quietly. "I figured I could sleep tonight then call you in the morning for an appointment and it would be okay."

"And it would have, but you still would have been incredibly dehydrated and I would have had you admitted immediately." She closes the file. "But no, Liv. Sickness this bad isn't normal. What you have is an illness called Hyperemesis

Gravidarum. You are much sicker than most pregnant women who suffer with nausea. This probably won't be the only time throughout your pregnancy you'll find yourself unable to keep any liquids down, and if this happens, you must call immediately so I can provide you with meds to stop it."

I nod. "Will it hurt the baby?"

"No, the illness itself won't, but the dehydration can. Normally, I would listen in to baby's heartbeat now, but since you're so early, I probably won't be able to pick it up."

I curl my fingers around Tyler's and squeeze. Hard. "So what? How can you check?"

"We'll take you for an ultrasound at nine a.m. We took blood when you came in and I rushed the HCG results. The numbers put you at around nine weeks, so we'll get a clear view of baby on the screen." She stands. "The best thing you can do is get some sleep."

"I'll try."

"And, Liv?" She opens the door and stops. "Don't worry. Sickness is usually a good sign. It means you have high hormone levels and a healthy baby in there."

I nod and watch as she closes the door. I turn to Tyler. "Nine weeks?" I whisper. "That means…"

"You got pregnant straight away," he finishes.

"But we used condoms at first."

"Then one split. I'm not in the habit of checking them, so I wouldn't have noticed."

"But it wouldn't have mattered then because I had the implant. Obviously it didn't work, but…yeah." I look at our hands and tickle the inside of his palm with my fingertips.

He jerks at the sensation and snatches my hand, linking our fingers. "It doesn't matter. We'll never know how it happened, just that it did."

I swallow and nod. "It's definitely yours, you know? I didn't sleep with anyone for a few weeks until you."

He lifts my hand to his mouth and kisses the back of it. "I never doubted it, baby girl. Now get some sleep, okay?"

"Because I haven't already had enough," I mutter as he gets up.

He sits in the chair next to the bed and rests his feet on the bars at the side. He clasps his hands on his stomach and closes his eyes.

"Ty?"

He opens his eyes, and I wriggle across the bed.

"Sleep with me?"

"I won't make you ask twice." He gets up and slides into bed next to me.

"Snuggle," I whisper, nudging his arm.

He smiles and curls it around me. Careful not to dislodge my IV or the pulse thing on my finger, I rest my cheek against his chest. I slide my hand beneath his shirt and splay my fingers out on his stomach. The warmth of his skin is comforting, and his arm around my body and his lips against my forehead feel an awful lot like home.

"I want to be your addiction," he whispers into my hair. "Okay? I want you to want me all the time. I want you to need to be around me all the time, because it's how I feel about you. I swear this last week has been hell, baby girl. You just about ripped my goddamn heart out."

"I'm sorry." I slide my hand around to his waist. "But I had to. I had to do it."

"I know you did—for you. But it's over now. You're not being away from me anymore. You clearly can't look after yourself."

I jab his side and he laughs quietly. "You're a twat, Tyler Stone."

"But I'm yours, so I'm a special kind of twat."

I smile and close my eyes. *Too true.*

Chapter TWENTY-FIVE

"READY?"

I nod at the sonographer and hold my breath. My IV pole is standing awkwardly next to me on the bed and Tyler's on the other side. He's gripping my hand so tight that I think he's cut off all circulation to my fingers.

"This will be cold," the sonographer says right before spreading the gel over my stomach.

Cold my ass. It's fucking freezing!

She smiles at my hiss of breath and presses a button on the machine. She grabs the ultrasound probe and wiggles it over my pubic bone, coating it in gel. Then she pushes down firmly and the screen in front of us fills with fuzziness.

"There's the placenta," she says, showing a big blob. "And baby is… Ah, right here."

Tiny.

It's so tiny.

And I can't look away.

"Baby has a good, strong heartbeat," she says, zooming in. "Right there."

Beat. Beat. Beat. Beat. A tiny, dark hole in the chest of my baby is its heart beating away. Inside me.

A small leg kicks out gently and I take a deep breath. The sonographer says something about measurements, but all I can focus on is that tiny little flutter going on inside me.

The baby jerks, a whole-body movement, and a tear rolls out of my eye.

Holy hell. That's my baby.

A real baby.

Tyler's grip on my hand tightens even more as he lifts it and kisses my knuckles. "Wow," he breathes, his voice thick.

I don't even think I can talk right now. I've never been so amazed by anything in my whole life. It's incredible that the most mesmerizing thing I've ever seen is a tiny baby on a screen.

"You're nine weeks and four days," she says. "Your due date is… Ah. Christmas day."

I chew the inside of my cheek. Of course it would be. Tyler doesn't do anything by half.

She takes the probe away from my stomach and instructs me to wipe the gel off my stomach. Tyler does it for me, drying it with a clean piece of tissue. I roll my hospital gown back down, thankful I put on my big panties yesterday.

"Here," the sonographer says, handing me three squares.

I look down at the still photos of the baby and smile. "Thank you."

"You're welcome." She smiles.

Tyler helps me into the wheelchair and I grab my IV pole. He wheels me out of the room and into an elevator after thanking the woman himself.

"Baby," he says, brushing the photo with his finger.

"Your baby."

"Our baby." He looks at me firmly then straight back at the image. He looks at it even as he pushes me out of the elevator and back to my room.

A nurse holds the door open for him, a knowing smile on her face. I sit on the bed, still clasping the pictures, and he puts the wheelchair to the side of the room.

"You look like you're in love already," I tease.

His lips tug up into a half grin. "How could I not be? The baby is a part of you."

I turn my cheek into his palm when he strokes the side of my face. "We'll be okay, won't we? You, me, and the baby? We'll make it work?"

"We don't need to make it do anything. It already works." He perches next to me. "I promise you, baby girl. We'll all be okay, because for once in your life, you're going to do what I want without arguing with me."

I raise my eyebrows. "For once? So all the times I did what you wanted in bed don't count?"

His grin turns sexy. "You had to do that. We had an agreement."

"But they still count!"

"When you're better, you'll have to remind me of how they count." He curves his fingers around the back of my neck and kisses me. "Until then, though, you're moving in with me."

"You already decided that."

"I know. But now I'm deciding again. And while you're resting in bed, growing that beautiful baby and not vomiting all over my shiny toilet"—I punch his leg—"you can house hunt."

"House hunt?"

"Yes. For us."

I blink at him. "Um."

"Somewhere close to Day's place."

"Um." I blink again. "Those are expensive houses, but I'm still stuck on 'um.'"

He grins. "And I have a lot of money."

"Yeah, *still* there with 'um.'"

"For fuck sake, Olivia." He taps my nose. "How much more obvious can a man be? You're going to find a house and I'm going to buy it. Then we—you, me, baby Stone—will move into the house and live there."

"Just like that?"

"Just like that. And you're not going to fight me on it either. I know what you're bloody like. This is for us. We'll raise our baby in a proper family house, with a big kitchen, a playroom, a nursery, and a giant garden."

"Garden." I grin. "And what exactly are you going to do with this *garden?*"

He pulls me close again. "I'm going to buy a summerhouse and put a bed in it so I can fuck you outside in the summer," he murmurs low. "So you should consider finding a house where there are no people."

I smile into his kiss. "You bet. Now how about getting me out of this place so I can start?"

He frowns at me. "Nice try. You're still rehydrating."

"Ugh." I drop back on the bed. "I hate hospitals. The mattresses are like oversized bricks and the pillows are never, ever hard enough. It's one extreme to the other. Plus all the 'coming in in the middle of the night' crap and the checking every time I pee? Not cool. Not cool."

"They won't let you go home until you can eat a couple meals and keep them down, and they check your pee to make sure you're rehydrating. Now get back into bed and stop complaining."

He lifts me up, pulls the covers back, and puts me into bed like I'm a child.

"You're an awful nurse. I want to swap you."

He laughs. "I have my own ways to get you better, baby girl, none of which can be applied here."

"Does it involve a tongue?"

"You are the horniest dehydrated woman ever."

I sigh and drop my head back. "I think it's hormones. One minute, I'm sick. The next, I'm dying for an orgasm. If it carries on, I might have to tie *you* next to me in bed so I can jump you whenever I feel the urge."

"So I look after you when you're sick and you'll reward me with sex?" Tyler raises his eyebrows. "Well. I can live with that."

"That's exactly it. You did a really good job yesterday, so lock the door and come here."

He laughs loudly and I grin.

"Liv, you're sick. As much as I'd love to rip off those knickers and bury myself inside you, it's highly inappropriate."

"So is fingering me in a nightclub and eating my pussy on a boat on the Seine, but that never stopped you before."

He opens his mouth then closes it again. "But you're sick. You weren't then."

"I'm not sick now. But I am being kept here against my will and I can't even get an orgasm out of it."

Tyler laughs again and covers my mouth with his. "Behave yourself, Liv. You're tempting me, and it's bad."

I groan and reach for my water. I sip it several times before I put it back down. Seriously, it's not my fault if I'm suddenly horny. It's not like I can turn it off. And now that I'm not vomiting anymore, I can notice the fact that I do want sex.

Not that I don't ever not want sex with Tyler. It's just incredibly tempting right now.

For real. What does a girl have to do to get an orgasm around here?

"She has to eat and keep it down and not have an IV coming out of her arm," Tyler answers.

Well, obviously I said that out loud.

"This is so unfair."

"If you eat and keep it down, I'll see what I can do when they take the IV out later." He flicks my bottom lip with his thumb.

I nip it. "See what you can do? You either finger me, lick me, or fuck me. There really aren't a whole lot of options, and if you can't do any of those, I'm trading you in."

He smirks. "I'll see what food I can get you."

"I want ice cream. And Jell-O. And sour candy."

He stops in front of the door and looks at me. "You are not having those things."

"Why not? I'm sick. That's what sick people have."

I smile triumphantly when he realizes that he's backed himself into a corner.

"Fine," he relents. "You're not sick. I'll get you food and I'll give you an orgasm later. Okay?"

"At home. I want an orgasm at home."

"Don't push it."

Three hours.

It's been three hours since I ate a chicken sandwich and I haven't vomited.

It's a fucking miracle.

"Did you get me any chips?"

Tyler frowns. "What—oh. Those chips. No."

"Oh. I want some." I exhale. "I'm hungry. And I really need to pee."

I swing my legs out of the bed and grab my IV. I wheel it into the bathroom, do my business, and go back into the room. Tyler watches me with amusement.

"I don't want to get into bed."

He laughs. "You're a bloody awful patient, Liv."

"Well!" I huff. "I'm not being sick. I'm peeing like a goddamn racehorse, and I'm eating. Why can't I go home? Why do I have to stay in bed? My legs work."

He stands and walks to me. "Would you like me to see if you're allowed to get dressed and come to the shop with me?"

"Without this bitch?" I shove the IV forward.

"No, you're not taking it out. They only just changed the bag. You know they said they'll take it out when it's empty. Now sit down and wait a minute."

I sit in the chair he was just in and grumble something I don't even understand. I don't actually think I said any words, just a bunch of awkward, annoyed sounds put together.

Truth is, I know I have to keep the IV line in. I know I have to stay here until they say otherwise, but the problem with hospitals is that they're not exactly relaxing. They're too clinical and sterile. And boring. Completely boring.

"Okay," Tyler says, coming back in. "You can get dressed and come down to the shop with me."

"And how hard did you have to charm her for that?" I grunt, getting up.

He throws my leggings and shirt at me. "I'm neither confirming nor denying any charming happened."

"Oh, please." I snort. "She probably took one look at you, then you smiled and her panties were soaked."

"Do your panties get soaked when I smile at you?"

"With the force of a tsunami. Obviously." I tug my leggings over my butt and take the bag off the hook. "Put this through the holes."

"Sorry. All I got from that was 'put, this, hole.'" He grabs the bag and threads it through the armhole of the gown then my shirt.

I quirk an eyebrow. "Someone needs to get him some."

"Someone's waiting for someone else to get her ass better so he can."

"Your powers of seduction know no bounds, Tyler Stone. Do I have time to change my panties?"

"Just leave them off. Forever. My life would be so much easier."

"Oh, yes. You suffer so much trying to get inside them! How do you do it?"

"It's a hard job, love, but persistence pays off."

"Your persistence is why I'm knocked up and attached to a rolling bottle of water."

He grins devilishly. "I'm a man, babe. I can't help needing sex. It's in my DNA."

"Of course! I forgot the DNA strand that means you must have sex at your earliest convenience. And frequently, too."

"Shame on you. You've come into contact with it plenty."

"Please refer yourself to my earlier comment regarding your persistence." I poke my tongue out and open the door.

He laughs. "Do you want the—"

"If you say wheelchair, I'm slicing off your balls with a butter knife."

He laughs again and slides his hand around my waist. "Note to self: remove all sharp objects from apartment, lest those pesky hormones inadvertently put me in harm's way."

I giggle into my free hand. He grabs it and looks at my nails.

"Maybe we'll clamp down on these talons too."

I flick my hand against his chest. "You never complained about them before."

He pokes my tummy. "Apparently."

I bat his hand away and step into the elevator. Walking around feels so good after having been confined to the bed for basically twenty-four hours. The wheelchair outing to the ultrasound this morning doesn't count.

The hospital is crazy. Noise is everywhere, and the amount of people walking through the hallways is almost panic inducing. Despite Ty's arm firmly around me, it's hard to get through them—especially with the IV. There's nowhere to go, nowhere to move, people in front of me, behind me, closing in on me.

"Outside," I breathe, gripping his shirt.

He steers me off to the side and out the front doors. I take a deep breath and lean against the wall.

"Are you okay?"

"Too many people," I reply, exhaling slowly.

"What the hell are you doing out of bed?!"

Oh, shit. Hide me.

I look up at my best friend. "Getting some fresh air. Am I allowed?"

She narrows her eyes at Tyler. "You're supposed to be keeping her under control!"

My dirty British boy snorts. "Yeah, like anyone could control Liv. She's wild and that's just how I like it." He winks at me and kisses the side of my head.

I smile triumphantly. "Did you bring me chips? I want chips."

Dayton blinks. "I wasn't asked to bring you chips."

I huff.

Aaron laughs. "Cravings."

"You'd be craving food if you hadn't eaten for days!" I grumble, grabbing Day's arm. "Get me chips."

With her at my side, Tyler guides us through the lobby and into the hospital store. I grab a six-pack of salted Lays and shove them at him with a charming smile.

"Please." I bat my eyelashes at him.

He sighs, but the despondent feel to it is destroyed by the sparkle in his eyes and the twitch to his lips. "What's in it for me?"

"I'll stop talking about chips if I'm eating them."

Dayton laughs as he turns to the register, his sigh real this time.

"Oh, you are one fun pregnant woman," she snickers.

"I'm growing a person. I get to be *fun,* and for once, I can blame it on everyone else, because no one argues with a pregnant woman." I grin.

Tyler hands me one of the bags and I tear it open. I dive my hand into the bag and stuff my mouth full of salted chips.

Oh my god.

So. Good.

Chapter TWENTY-SIX

THE past three weeks of searching for a house have been completely ridiculous.

This isn't big enough. That isn't in the right neighborhood. It's too far from Day's place. You call that a kitchen? That bathroom tiling is awful. That's not big enough for a nursery! Are you kidding? We're supposed to share *that* as an office? I wouldn't pee in that tiny room.

And it's all me. Because when your boyfriend gives you a ridiculous amount of money to spend on a house, it has to be downright perfect.

Perfection or bust.

"How did your appointment go?" I ask without looking up from the laptop.

"It was delightful, same as the last few. But if she asks me to dissect my sexual urges one more time, I'm going to take my handcuffs and attach her to the fucking Space Needle." Tyler walks into the apartment and dumps his bag.

"But it's helping, right?"

"Helping me get a bloody hard-on! Do you know how hard it is to explain to these people that my addiction isn't because my parents abandoned me as a child or didn't love me enough?" He raises his eyebrows. "I just like sex. A lot. A lot of the time. Why don't they get that?"

"Because they like to fuck with you." I smile sweetly. "What did they talk about today?"

His face darkens. "When I slept with my student."

My curiosity piques. I've never actually asked about it—why he did it. No matter how much I wanted to, it never seemed like the right time. Besides, it's not dinner conversation, is it?

"And?" I ask, trying not to show my interest.

I fail, because he smirks and joins me at the table. "Liv, if you want to know, just ask me. It's fresh in my mind, funnily enough."

"Uhh. Okay. Why did you do it?" I look at him now.

"Honestly, it was a mistake. I'd met her sister a couple of times, and there was only a couple of years between them. They looked very alike. I arranged to meet her sister for a few drinks one night, but it was actually my student who turned up. I didn't realize at the time." He rubs his hand through his hair. "It's the worst excuse, I know, but it's the truth. I didn't know until she admitted it to me the next morning."

Well, shit.

"Ouch," I wince. "What did you do?"

"Handed in my resignation with immediate effect."

"Really?"

He nods. "I wasn't in the job to abuse the power I had. She was my student, and although, in the end, it turns out she took advantage of my attraction to her sister, I couldn't stay there any longer. It was a year or so after that I took more and more jobs out here."

"So…that…incident…is fairly recent?"

"Three years, maybe?" He shrugs. "I don't know, baby girl. I don't like to think of it much because of my own stupidity. The last time I thought about it was when I told you. Then not again until today."

"Really? Not at all?"

"You kind of took up most of my thinking capacity." He smiles. "Not much else mattered other than you. It's in the past and I can't change it. But you're right, I guess. Talking through our past is the only way we're going to get through this."

I smile because he finally gets it. And despite his protestations about going to therapy, he agreed because it's what I wanted.

"Did you see March today?"

I exhale slowly. "Yeah. He came over. Something about avoiding coffee. I can't imagine why." I roll my eyes to the sound of Ty's laugh. "We talked over how I came to be addicted to Warren then applied it to our relationship. He thinks I was able to stagger how quickly I became addicted to you because I was aware of it. Like a slow trickle or something." I shrug. "He said he's waiting until my hormones calm down before we dive into the whole suicide thing. But he thinks we can be done by the time the baby arrives, and that's what's important, right?"

"Absolutely. We'll get there. Just like I told you." Tyler nudges my foot under the table and taps the laptop. "Any luck today?"

I shake my head. "No. I found one that was really good, but the kitchen was shitty."

"We can rip it out for a new one, you know."

"But that defies the point of spending a dumb amount of money on a house."

"So spend less and we'll remodel."

"It's not a freaking Lego house, honey. You can't just waltz in and change shit up."

He grins and closes the laptop. "I'm a Stone. Of course I can."

I roll my eyes when he leans forward over the table. "You can't just go throwing your name around. That's absolutely doing an Aaron."

"Except I do it with finesse and stunning British charm, so I beat Aaron hands down."

I eye him curiously. "British charm. That's what you call it."

"Are you doubting my charm, Olivia?"

"Doubting, questioning, disbelieving…"

He walks around the table and rests one hand on the back of my chair. My stomach flutters with excitement when he leans over me, his face hovering inches above mine.

"Do you need reminding?"

I run my thumb down his jaw. "Charm is for pussies. I prefer the alpha thing you had going on before."

"Before?" His eyebrows shoot up and he leans down a little farther.

"Yes. Before you went all whipped on me."

No sooner are the words out of my mouth than he has me against the wall, my hands pinned above my head and his hips holding mine.

"What was that?" he murmurs huskily.

"Smooth." I laugh, staring into his dark eyes. "Looks like you've still got it in you somewhere."

His lips twitch on one side. "Are you asking to be reminded, baby girl?"

"Asking… Begging… Is there a difference?"

He lowers his mouth to mine, his kiss testing and gentle, similar to the way it was when he kissed me for the first time. "How are you feeling?" he whispers against me.

I flex my hips against him in answer and he growls low. He kisses me again, this time more forceful and intense, his tongue forcing its way into my mouth.

I melt against him, submitting to the way he takes control instantly. He grips my wrists in one hand and slides the other up beneath my shirt. His fingers travel up my back, hot and rough, and circle around to my front.

He cups my braless breast and flicks my nipple with his thumb. I gasp into his mouth, my back arching into him. He does the same to the other and another sound leaves my mouth, one slightly pained, and he pauses.

"You won't break me," I say, kissing him. "Besides…"

"You like it," he whispers huskily. "I know. C'mere."

He drops my hands and cups my ass roughly. He lifts me and I wrap my legs around his waist, my fingers in his hair. Then I kiss him as he carries me into our room.

He literally drops me on the bed and leans over me. His dark eyes swirl, heated and needing. My chest heaves as he stares down at me this way.

He tugs at my shirt. "Off. Now. Let me see those gorgeous tits."

I whip the shirt over my head and throw it to the floor.

He opens the drawer and pulls out the handcuffs. He dangles them in front of my face and smirks. "It's been too long."

I draw in a long breath when he cuffs my hands together. He kneels on the bed and slowly kisses my neck, the hot, openmouthed kisses trailing across my skin. My pulse thrums beneath my skin when he travels down, taking my nipples in his mouth one by one.

His tongue swirls and skims across my body, tasting every inch of my skin. Each lick is like a blazing swipe of fire, searing into me, branding me to him.

As Tyler travels down across my stomach, he hooks his fingers in the sides of my shorts and pulls. "No knickers. Good girl," he hums against my hips.

"Surprise." My voice hitches as he presses his lips to the top of my thigh.

He smiles against my skin and removes my shorts completely. After discarding his own shirt, he bends down and bends my legs up. My chest rises and falls frantically, my breathing harsh. His fingers tease the inside of my closed thighs, working their way between them.

But more than that, his breath on my pussy. *Oh, god.* I close my eyes as he parts my legs fully and blows on me. I clench everywhere, anticipation trembling in my legs.

"This," he murmurs, kissing my clit. "I love this. You, ready and wet, waiting for me. I'm addicted to this sight."

He rolls his tongue along me slowly, tasting me deeply, and I shudder.

"I'm addicted to this taste. You on my tongue."

He rubs my clit with his thumb and slips his tongue inside me. The feeling of both is intense and pushes me close to the edge, my body trembling.

"I'm addicted to this feeling. You clenching around me." He dives his tongue back inside me and pinches my clit and I let it go.

I let the orgasm shudder through me, and Tyler climbs up my body. He discards his pants and underwear and lifts my legs, sinking into me slowly.

I sigh, still high from my quick orgasm, and hook my handcuffed wrists around the back of his neck. He taps my butt lightly and slips his hands up my back to my shoulders. One goes farther, cupping the back of my head, and he rocks his hips against me.

He fucks me deep and slow, hard and easy. He fucks me with passion and love mixed into both his thrusts and his kiss. He fucks me until there isn't a part of me not crying out for the release, until there isn't a part of my skin that doesn't want to be against his.

Until we're slicked with sweat. Until our breaths mingle so closely that they become one. Until my cries drown out his own low groans.

My pussy tightens around his cock and he changes his pace, going from slow to fast in seconds. The relentless final pounds are all it takes, and I come apart, his name a sobbed cry on my lips.

Because it's too much.

The force of his love washes over me with more of a hit than the orgasm. I feel it wholly, and I feel mine. I feel it over addiction, over cravings, over everything else I feared at the start.

But I feared the wrong thing. I feared addiction when I should have feared love, because it won't be addiction that breaks me.

It wasn't addiction that hurt when we were apart. It wasn't a craving for his touch or his skin that scarred me.

It was love.

It was my heart that was broken, my soul that needed healing.

My love for him runs deeper than my addiction. Addiction can be cured. It can be eased. It can even be erased entirely. You can't do that with love. It's incurable. Nothing but the power of another love can rid your heart of it.

And that's the be-all, end-all.

I'm addicted to Tyler, yes. I'm addicted to the way his voice sounds and the way my skin buzzes when he touches me. But I'm in love with his smile and the way he looks at me. I'm in love with the way he forgets to put the toilet seat down and the way he thinks I won't notice his dirty socks stuffed behind the laundry hamper.

I'm in love with him, completely and utterly, entirely and wholly.

Chapter TWENTY-SEVEN

I WRAP my arms around myself as I watch my now-married best friend glide across the dance floor with her new husband. Eight years coming. Seven years of pain. One year of happiness.

I'm struck with how much she deserved it. Coincidence—or fate, if you believe in that—brought them together after so long. And the smile on her face as she looks into his eyes tugs at my heart.

Love.

Quite simply, love. Nothing more and nothing less.

Tyler steps up behind me and slides his arm around my waist. His fingers tickle across the side of the tiny bump growing. "About time, don't you think?"

I smile. "It took them long enough. Personally, I'm glad I don't have to deal with Bridezilla anymore."

He laughs quietly. "Aren't we all?"

"Aaron especially," I respond, my own laughter bubbling up.

Tyler leans in closer, his mouth hovering above my ear. "I have something to show you."

"What did you break?" I jerk my face round.

"Nothing!" He laughs. "Just follow me, okay?"

I frown but let him take my hand and sneak us out of the ballroom. The evening summer breeze blows my hair, the warmth nice across my bare shoulders.

"Where are we going?"

We stop by a giant water fountain. He pushes some wayward hair from my face and tries a smile.

"Do you trust me?"

I frown again. "You know I do."

He cups my face. "You're the most impulsive woman I've ever met. If you want to know what I'm doing, jump on that impulse and come and find me."

He kisses me quickly and runs around the corner.

"The fuck?" I shriek, running after him. Which is no easy feat in this mermaid-style dress.

Holy shit, this is a maze.

"Ohhh, shit. Tyler, you jerk! You prize butthead!" I call into the waning light. "What in the hell are you playing at, you little British bastard?"

I take a deep breath and rein my hormones in. I hear his laughter from somewhere in front of me.

"I'm in the middle."

"Oh, helpful!" *Fuckshitarsewanktwatbollocks.*

I'm mentally cursing in British. By the time this baby arrives, I'll have the accent perfect.

I run my hand along the wall of the maze as I follow its twists and turns. Dead end. Dead end. Dead end.

I'm really, really not good at this.

Left. Right. Straight on. Back up.

It slowly gets darker as I try to navigate my way through the endless paths offered to me. I groan when I find another dead end and turn back.

Tyler stands, grinning at me, and crooks his finger for me to follow him. "Left, right, left, left, right."

Then he goes again.

I shout another curse after him. What the hell kind of fucked-up shit is this? I stomp after him, following his directions.

Wait. Was the third right or left? Shit. I take a chance and go right…into a dead end. Left it is, then. One more left and the right and *ohmyfuckinghell.*

"What… What is this?" I swallow, looking at Tyler.

He's grinning, but it's nervous. And I don't blame him. I want to know why he's standing next to an officiant and Aaron and Dayton.

"How did you two—what? I don't understand. Tyler, what the hell are you doing?"

He laughs silently and steps up to me. Then he takes my hands in his and slowly links our fingers.

"Marry me," he whispers. "Right now."

My lips part and I shudder out a breath. "For real? This isn't a joke?"

He shakes his head. "Forever, Liv. It's only ever going to be you for me."

I look over his shoulder at my best friend and her new husband. "But—they—"

"Told me to," he replies. "I like surprises, remember?"

I open my mouth, but how do you respond to the truth? I told him that once. "This is your best surprise," I whisper, squeezing his fingers. "Yes. Right now."

His eyes widen. "Really?"

"Turn around before I change my mind."

He laughs and pulls me forward. He nods to the officiant, who starts the traditional lingo, but Tyler shakes his head.

"Skip it all, mate," he says, looking into my eyes. "She's flighty as hell and I'm afraid she'll change her mind any second."

I grin, my eyes filling with tears. "It's true. I'm contemplating running."

"Well, I can't have that," the officiant replies with laughter. "In that case. Tyler Daniel Stone, do you take Olivia Jade Warren to be your lawfully wedded wife?"

"I bloody well do."

He takes a ring from Aaron and slides it onto my finger. I sniff as I look at the diamond-embedded band.

"Olivia Jade Warren, do you take Tyler Daniel Stone to be your lawfully wedded husband?"

He wipes a tear from my cheek, and I take the ring from Dayton. I slowly slide it onto his finger, pausing when it reaches the base.

"No doubt about it. I do."

"Then I pronounce you—"

I don't hear the rest of it because Tyler cups my face, pulls me into him, and kisses me like it's the last time he ever will.

Epilogue

TINY.

I think that's her nickname. Never mind that her real name is Callie or that, at just under seven pounds born, she wasn't tiny-tiny. Tiny has stuck since the moment we first saw her on the screen, and as she lies on her back, her blue eyes wide and staring at the Christmas tree, Tiny fits.

Tyler runs a fingertip along her tiny foot, making her toes curl. "She's so pretty."

I smile, gazing down at her. "You sound surprised."

"I know. I shouldn't be. I mean, look who her dad is."

I roll my eyes. "It's a shame the therapist couldn't talk that ego out of you."

He grins. "We had the ego chat, and if you weren't still recovering, I'd tell you to put her to sleep so I can remind you why my ego is necessary."

I roll my eyes again. "Shut up, you." I look back at our baby, kicking her legs. "I can't believe she's been here for a month already and she's not even due until tomorrow."

Early labor wasn't something I'd imagined I'd have to deal with. I figured that, after the hellish pregnancy, she'd give me an easy time for labor. I was wrong—very wrong. Naturally, panic ensued in the Stone households—yes, all of them—and Tyler rushed me to the hospital. One ultrasound, two steroid injections, and three hours later, she was here.

Tiny, perfect, and utterly gorgeous.

"She just wanted to meet her amazing daddy. I mean, did you get a load of those stories I was telling her? She obviously wanted to meet the man behind the tiger coming for tea."

I smile at him. "Yes, that's it. It was all about the stories."

Tyler grins, still stroking Callie's foot. Slowly her eyes drift closed and she makes tiny sucking noises as she sucks on the pink pacifier in her mouth.

"She's our perfection," he whispers, moving to sit next to me. "She's the beauty borne from our ugly."

I rest my head on his shoulder, my finger still encased in her tight grip. "Yeah, she is. Absolutely."

forever call

A CALL SERIES SHORT STORY

Dayton

MY hands are shaking.

The last time I felt this unsettled was the moment my eyes met Aaron's in the Southfall Hotel. I can't stop the churning in my stomach, the complete and utter disbelief that it's here, about to happen—the thing I dreamed of for so damn long.

I look back now and realize that dreaming was all that kept me going. Seven years, and every night I thought of him. He was always the one my heart cried out for. He was my forever.

And now, I'm here, standing in front of the mirror, a white lace dress hugging my figure. My hair is pinned to the side, tiny diamonds glittering through the curls, a subtle tiara atop my head.

Waiting. Waiting for the moment I'm finally told that I can turn and walk out of the door.

I rub my hands together in front of me and take a deep breath.

"Jesus, someone needs to get you wine."

My lips twitch and I turn to face my best friend. "This is definitely a tequila kind of situation."

Liv laughs and steps up next to me. She curls her hand around my elbow, turning into me.

I gasp. "Look at your bump!"

"Sure, you're the bride, but let's fuss over my bump." She rolls her eyes. "Yes, there's a bump and it's very visible in this dress. But no one will even notice it next to you."

I shrug a shoulder. "I don't care, you know? I thought this was what I wanted—a big, fun wedding. But now, I couldn't care if it were only me, Aaron, you, and Tyler. As long as I get to walk down that aisle and say I do, I don't care."

"Good, because you have, like, two minutes." She laughs. "And can I just say, confidentially, he looks hot in that tux."

I grin slowly. "I can't even imagine. Oh god, Liv." I place my palms against my cheeks. "The man is a walking orgasm in a regular suit. What happens if I set eyes on him and collapse from pure pleasure?"

"I have those paramedics on standby, you know," she teases. Her eyes flick up to the clock. "You ready, Miss Black?"

I open my mouth then inhale deeply. Knowing that it's the last time I'll hear those words shakes me. For so long, I believed I'd never get this moment.

Now that it's here, I'm not sure I do believe it.

Liv squeezes my hand and smiles. Then she bends forward to pick up her bouquet and winks.

Aunt Leigh walks in, kisses Liv on the cheek, and approaches me. "You ready, Dayton?"

Another deep breath. Good God, I'm taking more than my fair share of oxygen this morning.

"Yep." I take my own bouquet, the pale-pink flowers spilling over the front in a trail.

Aunt Leigh smiles, her eyes watering. "God, honey. You don't know how glad I am that you picked this path."

"I never had a choice," I tell her, hooking my arm in hers and looking to the door. "I always loved him too much for anything else."

She places her hand over mine and leads me toward the door. For all my deep breaths, I can't breathe. I'm terrified but I'm excited. Elated but scared. All at the same time.

One squeeze of my fingers and we turn the corner to the aisle. The music is playing—Westlife, Unbreakable. I'd never heard of them until Aaron suggested it, but now, listening to the words, it's perfect.

"Look up," Aunt Leigh whispers.

I do, and I see him. Standing at the end of aisle, seemingly a lifetime away from me, he's staring at me. His black suit is sharp, perfectly tailored, the pink buttonhole in his jacket standing out starkly even against the matching tie.

And I can't help but smile. My heart is pounding; it's pounding so hard. I can barely hear the music over the rush of my blood, but it doesn't matter because he's there. He's there and he's waiting.

He's mine. He's really mine. After everything, we're here. Somehow, someway. We made it.

Almost.

I stop in front of him and swallow hard. I can feel the tears building, and they aren't helped by the look in his eyes. He looks like he's never seen anything more beautiful in his life.

Aunt Leigh places my hand in his. His warm fingers curl around mine, and I hand my bouquet back to Liv.

The beginning of the ceremony skips over me. I can't see anything but the stark blue of Aaron's eyes gazing into mine.

But he speaks, and everything changes, and all of me tenses.

"I, Aaron John Stone, take thee, Dayton Lauren Black, to be my wedded wife," he says in that low voice that hums right through me, "to have and to hold from this day forward, for better for worse, for richer or for poorer, in sickness and in health, to love and to cherish, till death us do part, according to God's holy law, and this is my solemn vow."

I smile and somehow manage to keep my tears at bay to speak for myself. "I, Dayton Lauren Black, take thee, Aaron John Stone, to be my wedded husband, to have and to hold from this day forward, for better for worse, for richer or for poorer, in sickness and in health, to love, cherish, and obey, till death us do part, according to God's holy law, and this is my solemn vow."

He half-grins, somehow exuding sexiness that makes me want to laugh in the middle of all this emotion.

He speaks again, the ring vow echoing around the church but seeming so quiet to me. Like every word spoken so many times before was made just for us. Aaron slides the ring onto my finger, his eyes shining, and then I take his from Tyler.

I repeat the words, his platinum band cold beneath my fingertips, and I ease it up his finger.

His half grin changes to a full one, and a single tear drips from my eye. I never expected it to be this emotional. I never expected to feel so much, to be so overwhelmed with this.

And as we're pronounced husband and wife, Aaron takes me in his arms and I clasp his face. Our lips meet in a promise.

A promise of forever. A promise that this is it for both of us. That there will only ever be the other.

And I know. I know that late call was supposed to happen. I know I was supposed to walk into that booth and see his face. And I know that final call was supposed to happen, too. I know he was supposed to make sure I was his, even if my mind told me otherwise.

And I sure as hell know that this—this moment right here, with his lips still brushing mine—is the forever call we were waiting for.

Aaron

I step up behind Dayton and curl my arms around her waist. She lays her hands on top of mine and turns her face into mine.

"Hey," she says softly, looking out at everyone talking.

"Hey, Mrs. Stone," I whisper into her ear, kissing her lobe.

She smiles, and I link my fingers through hers.

I feel like the luckiest son of a bitch in the country. There were times when I thought this day wouldn't happen—that I wouldn't get to stand here behind her and say those words. There were times when I thought that she'd never truly, wholly be mine.

But she is. And unlike before, there isn't a part of me holding back from this marriage. My mind, my heart—my whole fucking soul—are so embedded into this moment and the rest of our lives.

Every call I ever made was worth it for the few simple seconds I got to press my lips against hers knowing that she's my wife.

"I love you," I say against her skin, my lips easily gliding across the easiness of her jaw.

"I love you," she replies, turning in my arms.

Those dark eyes gaze up at me, that very love shining through intensely. I clasp my hands at the bottom of her back, letting them sit above her ass.

"Have I told you how devastatingly beautiful you look today?"

"No"—she strokes her thumb across my cheek—"but feel free to."

My lips twitch to one side. "In that case, you look so incredible I'm surprised there's a man still alive today."

"I know." She smiles widely, leaning up to kiss me.

I curl my fingers around the back of her neck and hold her mouth against mine. Like it always does, her kiss wraps around me and warms me down to my bones. Every part of me feels her.

"Do you think your aunt and uncle will have a fit when they find out Tyler and Liv got married without telling anyone?"

I grin. "Yes, and I'll be directing them to you when they do, sweetheart. You cooked up the plan with him."

She doesn't even look ashamed. "He wanted her. I know her. You think I'm going to leave a member of my family completely abandoned in such a situation?"

"Your family, huh?" My hand slips down to cup her tight ass and pulls her into me even further.

"Yes. There's a ring that says so." She waggles her left hand in front of my face. "At least now, anyway. And I'll totally plead ignorance."

"No one will believe you."

"I'll tell them you set me up." Her dark eyes sparkle with playfulness. "Then I'll pout a little and everyone will believe me."

"Dayton, believe me." I dip my face toward hers. "If I'm setting you up, it'll be in private."

"Private how?" she asks, her breath catching.

"Private like that huge bed in the hotel suite upstairs."

She hums, the low sound heading straight to my cock. *I know that sound.*

"That depends." Her voice is quiet and the sultry tone takes hold of me. "Are you asking?"

"You should know the answer to that."

"Are you demanding?" She raises her eyebrows and steps away.

I let her. I let my hands fall from her gorgeous body and watch as her eyes flash with a teasing challenge…and a plea.

"What do you think?"

"I think you're not being clear enough."

My lips twitch into a smirk. I snatch her wrist and pull her against my body. She inhales sharply at the force her chest hits mine with, and slowly, she drags her eyes from my chest and up my face.

"Is that so, Mrs. Stone?" I murmur. "In that case…I require you to take your sexy little ass up to our room so I can get you out of this dress. I believe we need to begin this marriage as we intend to continue it."

"And how would that be?"

"You… Me…" I ghost my lips along her jaw to her ear and lower my voice to barely a whisper. "Your nails in my back, my hands in your hair, and my cock fucking your gorgeous pussy until you scream my name."

"Is that a requirement, too?" she asks breathlessly.

"Abso-fucking-lutely."

Dayton pulls back slightly. Her eyes stay steady on mine as she brings up her free hand and trails her fingertips up my chest, curving along the lapels of my suit jacket, brushing the knot of my tie. They finally come to rest just below my chin, and her lips curve upward the tiniest amount.

"I vowed to obey."

Dayton

MY heart pounds furiously as I slip out of the ballroom. I don't know how I've managed it unnoticed.

I step into the elevator and press my hands against my stomach. I smile, spreading my fingers across my belly. The butterflies won't calm. They're swirling, fluttering insanely. It's incredible how he can still make me feel like a seventeen-year-old girl with her first crush.

The elevator doors ping open. I walk out on almost shaky legs. A mixture of excitement and anticipation is hurtling through my body at lightning speed, winding me so tight.

I flatten my hands against the door. I don't have the room key. *Ah, shit.*

"Move." Aaron's smooth, husky voice whispers into my ear.

I do. One step to the side and he's free to slide the keycard in the door. The lock clicks and he shoves it open before resting his hands on my hips.

He pushes me forward, guiding me into the suite, and turns me in the direction of the bedroom. “In there.”

My breaths are all short and sharp, intense, but I do it. I walk toward the bedroom, adding some extra sway to my hips. I didn’t buy this gown just because it was pretty.

I bought it because it gives me a really, really good ass.

His hiss of breath follows me, and I smile to myself. *Require all you like, Mr. Stone.* Until he requires me to stop teasing him, something he’ll never do, I plan to push it to the limit.

“You’re an awful tease, Dayton Stone.” His lips travel down the side of my neck, his fingers toying with the bow at the base of my back. He tugs one arm back, unraveling it, and gently works his way up the corset-back of the gown.

“And you love every second of it.” I turn my face into his, casting my eyes downward.

He smirks. “I do.”

When Aaron reaches the top of the corset, he pulls the material apart wide enough to slide down my body. His fingers brush against my skin, just above my strapless bra, and he lowers his lips to my shoulder. One kiss, one gentle touch, and my whole body erupts in a blast of heat.

“Red,” he whispers against me. “I’m impressed. How did you keep that secret?”

“Extra material,” I reply equally as quietly, my lips quirking. “Like I would marry you in anything less than red lace, Mr. Stone.”

“I approve.” He slides the dress down my body and over my hips, letting it fall in a pool at my feet. “I don’t approve of the fact that you didn’t tell me.”

“You didn’t ask.”

He spins me. His hands clasp my waist and he lifts me over the dress. I squeal, grabbing his shoulders.

“It’s not my job to ask my bride what she’s wearing beneath her dress. It’s her job to show me.”

“When you put it that way…” I peel his hands from my waist and step back a few times.

His eyes burn into me, hot and heavy. His fingers twitch as I turn slowly, and his gaze runs over my body so many times that he might as well be ripping the lingerie off with his eyes.

“Happy?” I step forward and grab his tie.

“Partially.”

“You’re a hard man to please.”

“On the contrary, I’m incredibly easy to please.” He undoes the button on his jacket and shrugs it off. Throwing it to the floor, he smirks.

I undo his tie, leaving it hanging loosely around his neck, and work the buttons on his shirt. I slide it over his shoulders, reveling in his smooth skin, and drop my eyes to his body.

Damn. He told me he had a surprise for me, and I think his abs are it.

Aaron hooks his fingers under my chin and forces my face upward. A sexy smirk is shaping his lips, and I barely have time to say anything before he pulls me forward and silences me.

He forcefully moves his lips across mine, his desire obvious in every brush. And I'm helpless, completely helpless, against every brush, every sweep, every nibble. I'm wholly under his control.

His touch sears into my skin each time he runs his hands over my body. I'm a mass of sensation, of anticipation. As always, whenever we're alone, he's all there is.

Consuming me. Devouring me.

He pushes me toward the bed and I fall backward onto it. He wastes no time running his hands down my thighs and parting them, stepping between them, lowering himself against me.

Through his pants, his cock presses against my pussy. The fleeting pleasure from it rubbing against my clit is almost teasing, something I crave more of. I push my hips up, into him, pleading, begging.

"Are you wet?" he murmurs against me, trailing his fingers along the inside of my thigh.

I gasp because his fingers are right fucking there, slipping beneath my thong, brushing against my wetness.

"Of course you are." He kisses down my neck, slipping two fingers inside my pussy. "You get wet so easily, don't you?"

"Only for you," I whisper on a sharp inhale, tangling my fingers in his hair.

"Damn fucking right." He pushes his fingers farther into me, curving them, pressing his thumb against my clit.

I arch my back, giving in to the waves of pleasure flooding my body.

Aaron pulls his fingers from me and undoes his pants. They fall to the floor along with his boxers. He drops onto the bed on his side, his hands snaking around me and tugging me onto mine.

I look into his eyes, practically fucking panting, and hook my leg over his hip. He touches his mouth to mine once more and rests the end of his cock at my pussy. I tilt my hips toward him and he slides into me smoothly.

He fills me so completely. Like I was made for him, he fills me, no part of me left untouched by him. His movements are swift and easy. Sweat breaks out across his skin and mine, beading, dripping, blending together the way our bodies are.

Because this is hotter and sweeter and more meaningful than any fuck we've ever had.

This is a goodbye to the past and a welcome to the future.

"Jesus, Dayton," he rasps against my skin, burying his face into my neck.

I grasp his hair tighter and move into him more as he thrusts into me. My muscles hug his cock so tight, clenching and releasing, clenching and releasing. Heat swamps me. I can't see; I can't breathe.

I can barely feel anything but the man I've waited eight years to call my husband.

Aaron grabs my ass and holds me against him. His thrusts become relentless pounds, slamming into me unapologetically. The tautness of his body screams for the release mine does, and I let go of all control and put it in the palm of his hand.

"Come," he breathes, nipping my earlobe. "Come hard around my cock, Mrs. Stone, and show me exactly why you married me."

A moan escapes me, because goddammit, this man can dirty-talk his way through just about anything.

His hand slips inside my bra and he pinches my nipple just hard enough that it's painful and pleasurable. And suddenly, instantaneously, my body is on fire, every nerve ending sizzling with the inevitable.

The orgasm hums across my skin and it's not even here yet.

I clench every muscle, clamping down on his cock. Aaron growls loudly, the sound reverberating through my body.

"Dayton." His voice is a pleasurable warning buzzing through me, hinting at the explosion of need yet to come.

Hard and fast, he slams into me, unforgiving. I hold myself still against him, my muscles burning with the pressure of being clenched.

It hits hard. Like a damned sin, the orgasm completely floods me, and I fly high with the pleasure pulsating through my veins. It doesn't stop, taking me and filling me until I'm ready to burst from the sheer pressure of it.

"Dayton… Dayton… Hell, Day…" Aaron whispers into my neck, panting heavily. His fingers are clasping the back of my head and he's buried inside me still, his hips rocking gently, sending final tremors of delight through me.

"Jesus, Mr. Stone," I say against his shoulder. "You couldn't be bad at anything if you tried, could you?"

He laughs, huskily and breathlessly. "Sweetheart, if I could be good at anything, you bet that tight, gorgeous ass it'd be fucking you senseless."

"Lucky for me, you're good at a multitude of things." I smile at him and roll onto my back.

He comes with me, his body hard and hot on top of mine. His lips brush mine endlessly, warm but not, soft but hard, sexual but loving.

"I never thought we'd get here," he admits against my mouth. "But, fuck, Dayton. I can't tell you how glad I am that I get to love you unashamedly for the rest of my life."

I swallow and hold him tight. "Ditto, Mr. Stone. There's nothing I'd rather do than love you forever."

He presses his lips to mine one last time. Then he pulls out of me slowly, both of us reluctant for the contact to end. But it does, and I'm alone on the bed.

I sit up as Aaron heads toward the bathroom. He throws a roll of toilet paper through to the bedroom. I laugh. Shit, he's something else.

Most guys would come and pass a wad of tissue to their new wife.

But no, not Aaron. He'd rather throw the roll fucking blindly.

I pull some off and wipe, throwing it in the trashcan hidden beneath the vanity in the corner. Then I spread my fingers across my stomach again and shout, "Hey, honey?"

Aaron

"WHAT do you want?"

She only ever says honey when she's taking the mickey or wants something.

Her laugh rings out across the hotel room. "I want to ask you something."

"Oh, shit. Where's the room key?" I tease, exiting the bathroom still stark naked.

Dayton, my incredibly beautiful wife, stands from the bed. Her dark eyes are shining, and her hands are pressed against her stomach. "Fuck yourself," she says softly with a smile.

"I'm all fucked out from you, sweetheart." I bend and kiss her quickly. "What's up?"

She takes my hands and pulls me over to the large mirror. It stretches across a lot of the wall in the bedroom, and I can only think of the ways I can position her so I can watch as I fuck her. Or as she fucks me. Either one fucking works.

"I have a secret," she says softly, a gentle smile gracing her lips.

She turns without looking at me and stares at the mirror. Her eyes meet mine there. She grabs my wrists and places my hands over her stomach. Her lower stomach to be precise.

And just about every function in my body stops. My heart, it pauses. My lungs, they freeze.

"What if I told you I was pregnant?"

Her words crawl over me and wrap around me like a warm blanket. "Are you?" I choke out, the words catching in my throat.

She slides her fingers through mine, her eyes still on mine in our reflection. "What if I said yes?"

I swallow. Fuck. My child could be—probably is—inside her right now. A beautiful, flawless product of a love that's stood the test of time and given it a great big 'fuck you.'

"You've already made me the happiest man in the world," I admit honestly, feeling my fingers twitch against her stomach. "It might just tip me over the edge."

"A month. Roughly." Her voice is soft and rough, full of emotion and held-back tears. "I found out yesterday. I wanted to tell you, but…"

"You were afraid?"

"No." Day shakes her head. "Not anymore." She spins in my arms and presses her hand against my cheek. "Not of your baby, Aaron. Not of our forever. See, I had this huge problem buying you a wedding present. What do you buy the guy who has it all, huh?" Her lips twitch. "Then my gut screamed at me to test, and I did. And I thought that he…or she…would be the perfect wedding present for you."

I close my eyes, because fuck. They sting with unshed tears. In twelve hours, I've married the woman I've loved for years and now found out that she's carrying my baby.

I sink my fingers into her hair and rest my forehead against hers. "Thank you," I whisper. "Thank you for making me the happiest, smuggest, most righteous son of a bitch Seattle has ever seen."

She smiles. "I love you, Mr. Stone. So very, very much."

One brush of my mouth against hers and I say, "And I love you, Mrs. Stone. More than you could ever imagine."

To My Readers

Dear readers,

I know what you're expecting.

I do. I know you were hoping to turn the page after FOREVER CALL and have an epic extended epilogue that will tell you everything you didn't want to know about these characters five years from now.

And I'm sorry. I can't give you that. Not here.

If you are reading this, you're as invested in these characters as I am. You've laughed with them, you've swooned with them, you've got hot under the collar with them, and you've sure as hell cried with them. You've seen them grow from unsure individuals to confident, certain couples. You've been there with them throughout their transformation and their growth, just as I have.

So why can't I give you what you want?

It's easy.

I can't say goodbye.

The CALL books and the WILD books are the first series I've ever written that don't resolve in one book. Especially in the case of Aaron and Dayton, this is four books—four books—of story. That's so long. It took me four and a half months to write these stories.

I laughed with them. I sighed with them. I got angry, sad, happy, excited with them. I felt every emotion they felt from the very second I wrote "Chapter One" on LATE CALL.

And that is why I can't say goodbye.

Aaron, Dayton, Liv, and Tyler consumed me. As their stories unfurled, I became one with them. Every heartbeat was for them. Every breath was theirs. Every second I was away from their stories was quite painful. Somewhere along the way, I became wholly addicted to these characters. I fell in love with them, and I never want to fall back out.

I know how their stories end. For me. And that's important—their ending in my mind is mine.

Mine.

Not yours.

That's important. I hate epilogues. Do you know that? I write them, but they're immediate. I can't write years in the future. My view and my ideals are different to yours.

To me, maybe Liv and Tyler had another baby. Maybe Aaron and Dayton had a big family.

To you, maybe Liv and Tyler didn't have another baby—to you, Callie may have been enough.

To you, maybe Aaron and Dayton only had one baby, just like their cousins.

That's for you to decide. And I want that. I want you to choose your happy ending, because I chose mine.

It's the wimp's way out. Yes, I am a wimp. Yes, despite the strength of my heroines, I don't have their balls. I can't write their goodbye.

It hurts me to do it. I don't want to forget these guys. In the grand scheme of life, they've taken up such a small part of mine. But it's not the time that matters.

These people might be imaginary. They may live in my mind. But they impact me in crazy ways, and in the time they've done that, they consumed every part of me until I only lived for them.

I wouldn't change that. I won't. I never will.

That being said, I have written my forever. I have put fingers to keys and typed out my perfect ending. You can find it on my website. If you wish to enter it, the password is Aaron's age-old nickname for Dayton. You know, the Disney one you all loved.

If you don't know it, please message on Facebook. I will be happy to share it with you so you can see my ending.

You can find it here:

I'm not asking you to view it. I'm not asking you not to.

I'm asking you to take this ending and imagine their forever how you want it to be. That way I can't disappoint you.

That's the beauty of fiction. You can take someone else's story and make it your own with your imagination.

Take Aaron and Dayton's story. Take Liv and Tyler's story. And make them everything you want them to be. That's all I ask.

So for now, dear readers, some of my favorite people in the world, I ask you to be the dreamers I know you are.

And brace yourselves, because a goodbye to these characters means a hello to a new bunch. I promise they will rock your world.

Until the next one,

Xoxo,

Emma.

Acknowledgements

First, as always, to Darryl. Your never-ending belief in me outstands me every day. I love you.

Danielle Sanchez, for all your wonderful work marketing my words. You are a true diamond, and I would be lost without you. And all the girls at InkSlinger PR! Thank you for everything.

Michelle Kampmeier, my ever-fabulous editor, for all the laughs and the cries and the gifs. I heart your arse, lady!

Emma Mack, for running your eyes over and catching those pesky things that I always miss. Thank you!

E.M. Tippets, for making my books pretty. Thank you for your genius!

My agent, Dan Mandel, for always being there when I need you. I would be pretty lost without you also.

And to you, readers, for making this story possible. You make all my words possible, and I am forever grateful for you. All of you.

About the Author

By day, *New York Times* and *USA Today* bestselling New Adult author Emma Hart dons a cape and calls herself Super Mum to two beautiful little monsters. By night, she drops the cape, pours a glass of whatever she fancies – usually wine – and writes books.

Emma is working on Top Secret projects she will share with her followers and fans at every available opportunity. Naturally, all Top Secret projects involve a dashingly hot guy who likes to forget to wear a shirt, a sprinkling (or several) of hold-onto-your-panties hot scenes, and a whole lotta love.

She likes to be busy - unless busy involves doing the dishes, but that seems to be when all the ideas come to life.

Website: www.emmahart.org
Facebook: www.facebook.com/emmahartbooks
Twitter: www.twitter.com/emmahartauthor @EmmaHartAuthor

Get ready for my new series, THE BURKE BROTHERS! A sexy NA contemporary that crosses country-rocker with small-town love, it's not to be missed. The first two books in the series, *DIRTY SECRET*, and *DIRTY PAST*, are available to pre-order now.

DIRTY SECRET, coming December 1st:

Conner Burke never expected Sofie Callahan to come back.

Where she's been for the last two and half years is a mystery, and so is the reason she left in the first place. Now, though, she's back in their hometown of Shelton Bay, South Carolina, at the same time Conner's band Dirty B is home on a tour break.

Sofie Callahan has spent the months since her father's death avoiding anything to do with her home town. But with her brother in Afghanistan, she has no choice but to return and sort out her father's house, even if it means facing the boy she fell in love with and revealing the reason she left.

Conner has questions, and when his broken heart and her guilty one collide, Sofie has to start answering them. Their present is rocky, their future unknown. Only one thing is certain:

Sofie's daughter will change everything.

DIRTY PAST, coming May 4th, 2015

Books by Emma Hart

The CALL series:
Late Call
Final Call
His Call

The WILD series:
Wild Attraction
Wild Temptation
Wild Addiction

The GAME series:
The Love Game
Playing for Keeps
The Right Moves
Worth the Risk

The MEMORIES series:
Never Forget
Always Remember

The BURKE BROTHERS Series:
Dirty Secret
Dirty Past

4737809R00130

Printed in Germany
by Amazon Distribution
GmbH, Leipzig